When Love Finds You

Also by the author

Just Married, Please Excuse
Sorting Out Sid
There's Something About You
How I Became a Farmer's Wife
Those Days in Delhi

When Love Finds You

YASHODHARA LAL

HarperCollins *Publishers* India

First published in India by Harlequin
An imprint of HarperCollins *Publishers* 2016
4th Floor, Tower A, Building No. 10, Phase II, DLF Cyber City,
Gurugram, Haryana – 122002
www.harpercollins.co.in

This edition published by HarperCollins India in 2022

2 4 6 8 10 9 7 5 3 1

P-ISBN: 978-93-5264-084-3
E-ISBN: 978-93-5264-085-0

Typeset in 11/14 Bembot Std by
R. Ajith Kumar

Printed and bound at
Thomson Press (India) Ltd

MIX
Paper
FSC FSC® C010615

This book is produced from independently certified FSC® paper
to ensure responsible forest management.

To Peanut, Pickle & Papad. Don't worry, one day you'll be grown-up enough to read this book and hate me for the nicknames—but I'll always love you.

CONTENTS

PART ONE

PART TWO

PART ONE

ONE

CAPPUCCINO

Natasha stared at her cup of coffee in growing annoyance. The chubby new server at Costa had placed it on the table, flashing his teeth in an over-friendly grin. The cappuccino was a tempting light brown with a faint whiff of nutmeg and foam mushrooming neatly on the top. It would have been perfect.

If some idiot hadn't gone and ruined it.

She wrinkled her long nose in distaste and scanned the place for Muthu, the only staff member responsible enough to remember a loyal customer's preferences. This was supposed to be a place for true coffee lovers, not a bloody chain store for yuppies.

There he was, over at the back, standing with his hands behind him, watching to make sure no server was idle. Muthu was now the café manager. He had confided this to her shyly the last time she was here, a couple of weeks ago, and she had politely congratulated him. He'd been serving her here for years. The promise of this promotion to a supervisory post was why he had stuck around. But from the way he was rocking back and forth on his heels, he looked like he was itching to get back into the action. She caught his eye and her raised left eyebrow compelled him to abandon his station immediately. He hurried over to her, head bowed in deference.

'Yes, madam?'

She waited for him to figure it out for himself. He looked carefully at the table – it was spotless, as was the tray in which she had been served. The coffee looked fine too. She gave him a few more seconds.

'Oh.' He looked ashamed.

'Sorry, madam.' He picked up the tray hastily. 'New boy. Silly young fellow from Ludhiana. Always trying to make an impression. I had already told him … Sorry.'

He went to the back of the café with the tray and leaned in to whisper instructions to the tall boy behind the counter – presumably telling him to make Natasha a fresh coffee. He then beckoned to the young server, who approached him with a swagger. After a few words, the server didn't seem as confident. He turned slowly to look at Natasha, who made it a point to gaze out the window at random passers-by. Where was Priya anyway? She hated to be kept waiting.

After a few minutes, Muthu served Natasha himself. She glanced at her freshly brewed cappuccino. *Good.*

This time, no stupid cocoa heart.

She threw Muthu a glance of approval with a brief hint of a smile. Gratified, he backed away from her and marched back to his station. The young boy from Ludhiana looked on with tremulous curiosity, and when he finally caught Natasha's eye, he gave her a bewildered, sheepish smile with a slight scrunching of the shoulders – as if he was apologizing, but wasn't sure why.

She pretended not to see and turned her attention back to her coffee. She hissed, barely loud enough for herself to hear, 'Idiot.'

Where the hell was she?

Natasha was already halfway through her coffee and Priya *still* hadn't shown up. Another impatient glance at her slim, silver Espirit watch – her friend was now a full twenty minutes late. Well, I'm not waiting more than five minutes longer, Natasha resolved. It had been Priya's idea to catch up because it had been 'so many months' since they last met. She knew how Natasha felt about punctuality and respect for time – it was one of the most important indicators of professionalism in her book, and she didn't see why it shouldn't apply to other areas of life too.

Natasha brooded, tapping her foot under the table. She didn't really see the point of this. Priya and she had been growing apart for a while now. And now Priya had gone and had a baby – just like all of their other married friends. Naturally, she had been busy and couldn't catch up with Natasha for their girls' nights out as before. Natasha thought she'd done her bit – she had shown up at the little fellow's fortieth-day ceremony only to endure the fussing and cooing over the baby and Priya's mother's probing into why Natasha still wasn't married. So after handing over her gift – some stupid infant-clothing set – Natasha made her escape, citing an important work meeting.

Well, she had no reason to cling on to anyone, not even someone who had once been a close friend. Natasha knew from experience that people changed and, eventually, one had to look out for oneself. Maybe Priya wasn't going to show up today and maybe that was for the best. Coffee finished, she put down her cup and was craning her neck to find Muthu and signal for the bill when Priya burst into the café with several bags and bundles.

'Nattu!' Her friend's voice rang across the café, and Natasha cringed. Why did Priya insist on calling her that and that too in public – in *here*, a place she frequented? She managed a smile. Might as well get it over with, she thought, half the afternoon was already wasted. 'Hey, Priya.'

She moved over to make room for her friend on the orange sofa. That overenthusiastic man from Ludhiana reappeared, as if anxious to make amends for sullying her coffee experience with cheesy heart motifs, and helped Priya settle down, relieving her of one of the larger bags. Only when Priya finally sat down, rather clumsily, did Natasha realize that one of the bundles was, in fact, the baby.

She had brought her *baby* for a catch-up date? Natasha should have known. She tried to muster up some enthusiasm as she gazed at the chubby-cheeked creature nestled in his bassinet on the sofa next to Priya. Faking things had never been her strength. The only thing she could manage was a faintly surprised 'He's grown'.

It sounded inane to her own ears. Priya looked at her face and then burst into laughter. Natasha winced. Was it just how quiet this place was, or had Priya's laugh always been this loud?

'Of course he's grown, Nattu! It's been five months since you last saw him. Five months and eight days, to be exact.'

That sounded exact, all right. Natasha wondered if Priya counted every day of her life now. If so, she could understand why. It was no easy job, this motherhood thing. Well, so she'd heard.

Priya continued cheerily, 'He was being cranky and didn't want to be left with his dadi, so I thought I might as well bring him to meet his Nattu Maasi.'

'Ah. Nice,' Natasha murmured. *Nattu Maasi?* That sounded like a fat, jolly Punjabi aunty who would dole out gulab jamuns to anyone walking by. Natasha decided she would bring up this Nattu business later.

'So how are things, Priya? Oh, sorry, what will you have?'

'I'm actually really hungry,' said Priya, picking up the menu. Her eyes scanned the pages. 'What are you having?'

'Nothing – I eat salad for lunch. And I had it in office,' Natasha said. She was feeling listless. If Priya was going to stuff herself now, it would only prolong their rendezvous. While she didn't have any client meetings today, she wanted to get back to the office and see if she could squeeze in an unscheduled review for her team – those were the best if you wanted a true picture of the state of the accounts. Could she excuse herself early? Not if Priya was in the middle of a meal. And what if the baby woke up? She would probably be expected to hold him or something. She stared at him, wondering how to make her escape.

Priya caught her looking at her son and said tenderly, 'I know what you're thinking.'

Natasha started guiltily. 'You do?'

'Yes,' said Priya. 'And you're right. Those *are* the clothes you got him. It's a wonderful set. He looks so cute in green, doesn't he?' Thankfully, she didn't wait for Natasha's answer – she was no authority on baby fashion. 'I thought I should make him wear what his Nattu Maasi got him.'

Okay. There it was again. And this was while the baby was asleep. What would happen when he woke up? 'You know,' Natasha began, 'I was thinking we could tell him I'm his cool aunt. So let's forget the maasi thing. Let him call me Natasha.'

Priya laughed, again too loud. 'Nattu, you're being so funny today.' Natasha was, of course, attempting nothing of the sort, but Priya couldn't see past that new-mom glee. Natasha sighed and gave up, and Priya studied the menu again with deep concentration.

Natasha watched her friend, now taking in her appearance. She hadn't lost much of the pregnancy weight. Her erstwhile slimness was hidden under layers of flab and floral maternity wear that only exacerbated her largeness. Natasha felt frumpy just looking at her, quickly glancing down at her own impeccably well-maintained figure for reassurance. She was wearing an elegant grey formal dress with black bellies. Under her stockings, her legs were smooth – she had got herself a pedicure and wax over the weekend. Straightening a crease in her dress, she thought about how Priya should start working out again. Of course, she wasn't going to say it. She knew how hormonal new moms could be.

Priya signalled Ludhiana Boy over. She smiled up at him and said, 'How's the bacon-and-cheese sandwich?'

'Very wonderful and excellent, ma'am,' he said with a big grin. Natasha regarded him coldly, wondering on what basis he was giving it such a superlative review, but all his attention was on her happy and glowing friend. Priya grinned at him. 'Well, then that's what I'm having.' She turned to Natasha and said, 'You'll have some of it, right, Nattu?'

Natasha recoiled in horror. 'Bacon and ... cheese? You must be joking.'

Priya looked puzzled. Natasha cleared her throat and moderated her response. 'I told you, I'm used to having only a salad for lunch. And I already had a large cappuccino while waiting for you.' The edge in her voice seemed lost on Priya. Natasha added quickly, 'You go ahead, have whatever you want.'

She raised her chin at the server and said, 'That's it.' He caught Priya's eye and she nodded her approval. They exchanged what looked like a conspiratorial smile. The jauntiness back in his step, Ludhiana Boy took off towards the back of the café to fetch his newest customer her greasy meal. Natasha shuddered.

Her friend was staring at her. 'So how are you, Nattu?'

Well, at least that was better than the maasi variant. 'Doing very well, Priya. How about you?'

'Me ... You know, it's pretty much all about the baby right now...'

Natasha had gathered as much. 'So when do you think you'll be getting back to work?'

'Work? I'm not thinking about it now. I've taken extended maternity leave – but I think I'll need to take a year or two off.'

Natasha stopped herself just in time. In her view, career progression mattered a great deal and a lot could happen in just 'a year or two'. But who was she to comment on her friend's post-partum choices? She nodded with a noncommittal 'Hmm' and changed her mind about not getting something else – this could take time. She looked around, caught Muthu's eye and signalled for another cappuccino.

'*You* tell me.' Priya looked her up and down and smiled. 'You're looking gorgeous as ever – have you slimmed down further since we last met?'

'Oh.' Natasha looked down at herself again. 'Well, I do yoga three times a week.' She hesitated for just a second – well, Priya had brought it up herself. She said, 'You should try it. It'll help you get back in shape.'

'Maybe I should,' Priya said contemplatively and sighed. 'It's just such a full-time job taking care of a little baby.'

Natasha couldn't help it. 'I *have* a full-time job and I'm still doing it. Maybe it's just about making the time?'

Priya froze. 'I guess,' she murmured. 'You really seem to think I should get some exercise. It's not easy losing this kind of weight, you know.'

'Hey.' Natasha forced herself to sound sincere. She coughed a little. 'Of course. You do it whenever you're ready.'

'What's with the cough?'

'What?'

'You've been coughing – that's the third time.'

'It is not.' She cleared her throat, irritated. Thankfully, her cappuccino arrived and Natasha breathed a sigh of relief, shooting Muthu a grateful glance.

Priya watched her pick it up and said, 'What, no sugar?'

'Cutting down,' Natasha told her, feeling uncomfortable heading into fat-talk again. 'And wheat, too. Just trying it out. It makes me feel bloated.'

'You – bloated?' Priya cried. 'If you're bloated, I'm a bloody blimp.'

'I didn't say I was bloated, I said I've been *feeling* bloated.' Natasha groaned inwardly. Was this whole afternoon to be spent convincing Priya she wasn't really all that fat? Well, it wasn't in her to sugar coat things, and she wasn't about to start now. Luckily, Priya changed the subject.

'So work's good with you?'

'You bet.' Natasha took a sip of her cappuccino and closed

her eyes for a second to savour the taste and feel it warm her chest. 'I'm heading the sales department now. Got a team of fifty people. They weren't too thrilled about a woman boss, but I'm making them toe the line. Anyway – my boss is pretty supportive and that counts for a lot.'

'I'll bet.' Priya looked at her admiringly. 'Well, that's just like in school when you were the head girl, right? You faced resistance from that gang from Section D. But you plodded on and they were your biggest fans by the end of the year.'

Natasha laughed for the first time that afternoon. She hadn't thought about class twelve in years, and besides, it was a silly reference. How could school politics be compared to the challenges of the corporate world?

'School isn't anything like the real world.' She took another sip and looked at her friend.

'Well, maybe but...' Priya was distracted by Ludhiana Boy serving her the cheese-and-bacon sandwich. 'Oh ... Thank god, I was dying of hunger.' She took a bite and Natasha watched her, wondering how she could let those gobs of fat down her gullet.

The food seemed to put Priya back in her cheery mood because after a few moments of steady chewing, she was gazing at Natasha fondly. 'So? Any other news? Like, in the romance department?'

This didn't feel right to Natasha. The last few months seemed to have put a real chasm between Priya and her, and she didn't know where to begin filling her in. Nor did she feel like doing it right now. Priya probably wouldn't understand or appreciate her new dating policy anyway.

'Nothing worth talking about.'

'Oh, come on. Let me live vicariously through you – you've

still got a chance to meet that Prince Charming.' This almost made Natasha gag. If Priya thought she still harboured any hopes of meeting the 'perfect man', there was very little her friend understood about her. Priya continued, oblivious, 'After five years of marriage and one baby, there's absolutely nothing romantic about our life any more.'

'So how is Ramit taking fatherhood?' Natasha realized she hadn't asked about her friend's husband yet. She liked the quiet Ramit and his old-fashioned, courteous ways. He was rather handsome and she recalled thinking he was quite a catch for Priya. Not that Priya wasn't pretty in her own curly-haired, round-cheeked way. Still.

'Oh, he's loving it. Especially since he's still travelling so much on work and doesn't have to stay up most nights with the baby, unlike me.'

Priya said it light-heartedly, but Natasha sensed some underlying tension. She deliberately ignored it and said breezily, 'Well, work goes on, right? You can't expect him to give up his job responsibilities too. At least one person's career should be preserved.'

Priya looked surprised. 'I never said he should compromise on his career.'

Natasha felt both irritated and trapped, and she didn't quite know why. Conversation with her friend had never been this way before. Something had changed irrevocably. She fiddled with her phone, wishing she could find an excuse to get away. The baby was stirring in his basket. She'd be no good fussing and cooing over him, and was wondering what to do when Priya sealed the deal.

'So – speak to Aunty recently?'

That did it. 'You know what, Priya? I really have to get back to work now. Important review with my team. Let's catch up again soon, okay?'

Priya looked bewildered. 'You're leaving already? We barely had twenty minutes…'

'We'd have had more if you'd come on time. But it's okay. I understand.' Natasha had already fished around in her purse and come up with a thousand-rupee note. 'I don't have any change.'

'You don't have to pay,' Priya protested. 'I've got cash.'

'Oh no.' Natasha stood up and put on her blazer. 'You should let me get this.' She didn't give a reason – pointing out that she was the one still earning might not go down too well. She bent to give Priya a quick peck on the cheek and didn't like how awkward it felt.

After getting to the café door, Natasha paused and looked at Priya. 'Sorry to rush off like this.' And then she turned away quickly. She knew she didn't really look sorry. She wasn't.

She opened the door and the Delhi winter hit her like a slap across the face. At least now she could breathe easy. Without looking back, she hurried over to where she had parked her car. If she made it in time, her team was in for it.

TWO

READY, STEADY.

'…*On the right track, baby, I was born this way…*'

Natasha hummed along to the music blaring from the system as she ironed her hair in front of the mirror. The thumping beats calmed her and helped her get through the arduous task of drying and straightening her thick, wavy hair every day. It took twenty whole minutes but the end result was always worth it, leaving her dark-brown hair straight and shiny. It gave her a sense of control. Towards the end of a long day in the office, though, it would go back to its original state and then she would have to tie it up in a ponytail or pin it with a clip.

Why couldn't I have inherited Mom's hair?

It was an uninvited thought and she shoved it away. Maybe she should try that rebonding thing. A couple of women in the office had got it done only to wail on and on about the hair loss it caused them. Natasha wondered if a little hair loss was worth the extra control.

She decided she would book an appointment at Lakmé Salon. The enterprising colony salon, Sonia's Herbal – with the welcoming tagline: men, women and unisex – was okay for stuff like waxing and threading, but she couldn't trust them with rebonding.

Another song started up: '*Tonight, Tonight*' by Hot Chelle Rae. She liked this one – it made her want to dance. She began to swing as she mouthed the words.

It's been a really, really messed-up week...
Seven days of a la la la something something...
And my girlfriend went and cheated on me...
La la la la la something something...

Her towel fell away and she didn't bother picking it up. She was in her bra and panties, proud of her toned body – the narrow shoulders, the slim waist. She had never been big-boobed and had stopped caring a long time ago. Her abs were hard – the planks and reverse crunches were paying off. Too bad for Rishi he wasn't ever going to see her like this; he didn't know what he was missing. Breakups always sent her into a fitness frenzy.

The twinge annoyed her. They all just ended in disappointment. For so many years now, there had been men floating in and out of her life, and getting caught up in emotions distracted her from important things like her career. After Rishi – with whom she had even lived in for a few months, with whom it had even looked like it might get serious – she wasn't going to allow herself another so-called relationship.

Nope. There would only be trysts from now on. Priya may not approve but people have needs. They say a woman sexually peaks at thirty-five and the blow-up with Rishi happened just after her thirty-fifth birthday. So she was at her peak and in control of her life.

Always, always at her place, she had decided. But with whom? Discretion was key for a woman in her position. As a vice president at BizTech, it wouldn't do to have rumours about her floating around, true as they may be.

Married men, maybe? She rolled her eyes at the thought. It was true, though. It definitely wouldn't allow for any emotional attachment and discretion would be a given. She didn't know if she would be able to go through with it though.

She put the straightener down and let her sleek hair sashay around her shoulders. She smiled her most charming smile into the mirror. 'Dance?' she asked and closed her eyes, swaying to the music.

'Didi … Didi…' Only a second too late did Natasha register the squealing near her door. Dammit. She stopped gyrating and picked up her towel as she glared at her maid, Jamuna.

'What is it, what is it?' she said sharply, aiming the remote to lower the volume on her music system. She switched to Hindi. 'How many times have I told you to knock before you enter?'

If Jamuna had been shocked by the sight of her employer dancing alone in her underwear, she hid it well. Her perpetually pained expression intact, she bleated in a voice that grated on Natasha's nerves despite all the years she had been subjected to it, 'Didi … I did, but you must have been too … bijji to hear it.'

Bijji. Bristling, Natasha said, 'Okay, okay, what do you want?'

'What should I make for your breakfast?'

'You already *know*.' Natasha's voice was sharp. 'I only want my green juice and that bowl of Quaker oats.'

'No toast – again?' Jamuna's eyes widened.

'I've told you I'm not having toast any more.' Natasha's

16

irritation was growing. A whole month since she had given up wheat and Jamuna still wasn't reconciled to it.

'And lunch, Didi?'

'The salad. As usual,' she replied through gritted teeth.

'No roti?'

'*No*, Jamuna!'

'Haan, Didi?'

'How long have you been working for me now?'

Jamuna said brightly, 'Four years and three months, Didi.'

'And during this time, how many jobs did you lose as a part-timer?'

Jamuna lowered her eyes and murmured, 'Four.'

'Exactly,' Natasha snapped. 'If you don't want to lose this one, you better stop coming and asking me the same questions again and again. As it is, you don't have any work – you hardly have to cook and clean for the two hours that you are here. So will you stop walking in and disturbing me?'

Jamuna was sullen as she withdrew with a martyr-like 'Sorry *maine aapko phirse dishturb kiya*, Didi.' The emphasis on the word 'dishturb' added to Natasha's irritation and she slipped into her office clothing, her upbeat mood gone.

Dressed in a black, pleated skirt and crisp white top, Natasha sailed out of her room and sat down to breakfast. She and Jamuna didn't exchange a word, which was just how she liked it. She glanced through her copy of *Mint* dutifully to see what was new in the corporate and business world, but found her attention wandering.

She had to admit, she found the garbage in the city supplements more interesting, even if they did involve random factoids about Bollywood celebrities and inane things like their pet peeves and whirlwind romances. Aha – Hrithik and

Sussanne were splitting up. Some seventeen years they had been together. What was the bloody point?

The doorbell rang and Natasha ignored it. It rang twice more in quick succession and she was about to tell Jamuna to ask the idiot milkman to refrain from making so much noise at 8 a.m., but she bit her lip. She wasn't talking to Jamuna. The maid scuttled out of the kitchen, muttering to herself, and disappeared into the hallway. After a moment, she came back and said, 'Didi.'

'What now?' Natasha looked up from her breakfast.

'It is that *aunty*...'

Oh god, it was that Chopra fossil from downstairs. What did she want at this time?

She would have instructed Jamuna to tell the old fogey she wasn't home but her voice would have carried to the door. The Chopra pretended to be hard of hearing but that was difficult to believe given how much she complained about the supposed noise from Natasha's apartment. That was probably what she was here to do. Again.

Natasha sighed and pushed back her chair with a loud grating noise, hoping the Chopra heard it. She walked over in her high heels with deliberately loud click-clacks and swung the door open with a tight smile. 'Yes, Chopra Aunty. Good morning.'

Chopra's face made it clear that the morning was anything but good. 'Hello, Natasha,' she said with a grim smile, which dissolved into her usual sour expression. Chopra Aunty was a tall, spindly woman with grey hair and was always dressed in a bland sari. She might have looked elegant if it weren't for the constant dissatisfaction on her face. She was a widow of many years and one of the oldest residents of Windchimes complex.

She claimed to be one of the very first residents of Gurgaon, from back when it really was a gaon. Everybody was familiar with the sound of constant complaining from her ground-floor flat when she directed her maid and driver and colony guards to clean better, park better, be more diligent. Everybody tried to avoid her. Lucky me, thought Natasha, ending up in the flat right above hers. Just how old was this Chopra? Maybe seventy-five but she looked determined to go on living and cribbing indefinitely.

She continued to stare at Natasha stonily.

'So, anything I can help you with, Aunty?' Natasha glanced at her watch pointedly. 'I was just getting ready to leave for work.'

'I won't take long, of course,' began Mrs Chopra and Natasha groaned inwardly. *Here we go again.* 'I've been thinking about it. You claim that the various sounds I hear from your apartment are a mere figment of my imagination. The sound of high heels, the blaring music at odd hours, the dragging about of furniture that goes on the whole day...'

'Look, Aunty, I've already told you – there's no sound that can possibly go on the whole day. I'm out from 9 a.m. to 7 p.m. every single day and—'

'And then there's the constant thumping noise from your bedroom late every night, although that's the only one that's less these days,' Chopra Aunty continued as if Natasha hadn't spoken, and Natasha thought it best not to comment on that last one.

'...But that early-morning ruckus your maid makes while murdering some ginger or whatever for your morning tea...'

'That's *her* morning tea, I drink coffee.' It was a pointless mention, which was also ignored.

'So I have come up with a solution.'

'What's that?' Natasha said with a resigned sigh, glancing once more at her watch.

'Wall-to-wall carpeting.'

There was a brief silence.

'Excuse me?' Natasha managed to say it politely.

'Since we both agree that the fault here is not really yours or mine, and that it is due to the faulty construction of the building in which both you and I are unfortunate enough to have made our homes, the only real solution is for you to get wall-to-wall carpeting so that there is no longer any of this disturbance, which bothers me in the most important spiritual hours of my declining years.'

Declining years. Natasha had to keep from snorting. Chopra would last forever and even if she didn't, she would find a way to complain from the beyond. She took a deep breath. 'Mrs Chopra, Aunty, it's a wonderful suggestion. However, I invested in expensive Italian marble flooring in the drawing room and vitrified wooden tiling in all three bedrooms. So it won't be possible for me to undertake another expense, which involves covering all of that fine flooring up. However,' she continued brightly, 'you might want to consider some form of soundproofing of your ceiling. These days anything is possible. In fact, your whole house could be soundproofed. It might benefit everyone else too, since they will not have to hear the sound of the early-morning bhajans that you blast or the scoldings you are forced to give your incompetent staff. Do think about it, Aunty. I'm sure you'll find more information – just Google it!'

Chopra Aunty was blustering with indignation. 'What do you mean? "Soundproofing" ... I have never heard of such...'

She recovered and drew herself up to full height, at par with Natasha. 'How do you expect me to tolerate all this noise?'

'Aunty.' Natasha sighed. 'I need to get to the office. I'm sure we'll pick this up another time. In the meanwhile, maybe you could adjust and tell yourself: "This is the sound of the living"?' She added in a hurry, 'I mean, of course, of someone living their life *normally*?' With an exaggeratedly sweet smile, Natasha shut the door on Mrs Chopra's shocked face with just a little more force than necessary.

The two ladies on either side of the door bristled for a moment. Unwittingly mirroring each other, they simultaneously squared their narrow shoulders and stalked off in opposite directions to start their respective days on a worse note than usual.

THREE

NATASHA@THEOFFICE

'Natasha, may I have a word with you?'

Natasha looked up with a frown – why now? She was in the middle of inputting a VLOOKUP formula in her sales-tracking spreadsheet. Her brow cleared when she saw it was Aman.

Aman had been the CEO of BizTech for two years now and Natasha reported to him directly since being promoted to vice president of sales. He was a hands-off boss, just how she liked it. He left her department to her and she ran a tight ship, her razor-sharp mind and frequent reviews leaving no doubt in her team's mind about just who was boss around here.

She stood up and followed him into his office, mentally rehearsing the report she was planning to give him about the slight dip in the previous weeks' sales. It wasn't a big deal, the north branch had already shared their pipeline with her. She felt a twinge of irritation about the west branch head, Shekhar, still not having shared the make-up plan. She thought she had been adequately clear in the review about needing it in her inbox by Thursday, which was today.

She took the chair in front of Aman's desk and crossed her legs, ready to begin. He looked uncharacteristically tense.

'Natasha,' he began, 'I've just had an email from Shekhar.'

'Oh?' she started. That little slime ball. If he had the time to write to Aman, he definitely had time to respond to his immediate boss's orders. What business did he have writing to Aman directly anyway? With an effort, she kept her face impassive and waited for him to continue.

'He says he wants to resign.'

What? Shock and fury flashed on Natasha's face. The guy had just been promoted last year, thanks to her recommendation. She'd pushed it forward at the cost of at least two other team members. How ungrateful of him to even consider quitting so soon. To think he would write an email to Aman before discussing it with her.

She settled her features. 'Aman, I've no idea what's going on with him. We just spoke three days ago in a team review and he indicated nothing of the sort. I'm going to call him, let me—'

'Natasha, I don't think you should. Not right now.' Aman's voice was gentle but firm. 'He wrote me quite a long email. I thought about forwarding it to you but it might be better to give you the gist.' He paused for a moment. 'He says he's been feeling stressed and has been advised to take a break from work. Turns out it's a heart condition. It runs in the family and both his parents have been in and out of the hospital these last few months. It's been taking a toll on him too.'

'Oh.' Natasha breathed. She hadn't known any of this – she didn't like feeling as though she was on a weak footing with her boss. 'He never shared this with me.'

'Well.' Aman leaned back, rubbing his temples, which he did whenever uncomfortable. 'That's the thing. He claims his stress levels have shot through the roof over the last few months because of your management style. He says the monthly targets have been getting harder and harder to meet and your expectations from the sales team have been increasingly unrealistic. He cited the usual product, marketing, competition issues…'

Natasha opened her mouth to contest this but Aman stopped her with a raised hand. 'I'm not saying I *agree* with him, Natasha, I'm just telling you that this is what he said. I think his issue is not having felt *heard*.'

Natasha hated the heat creeping up on her face, likely turning it red. Aman continued, 'He also mentioned the reviews have been getting more and more one-sided and, er, difficult. I believe the one on Monday was particularly … extended?'

This was true. Her afternoon with Priya had left her irritable and she knew she had taken it out on her team. But then again, none of them had met their committed numbers and most of what they said sounded like excuses. She recalled having made some fairly biting comments at the beginning about the west branch's performance. Now that she thought about it, Shekhar had gone quiet after that. In fact, thirty minutes later, she had wondered out loud whether he was still on the line. She had said something like, 'Just a quick check – has Shekhar dropped off or something? Not like him to just listen for so long.' It had only elicited weak laughter from a couple of people before Shekhar's voice said, 'I'm here, Natasha.' She had felt a little abashed but couldn't have done anything as drastic as apologizing, what with everyone else on the line, so she had gone a little easier on him after that.

'It went on till 8 p.m.,' she told Aman, 'but we only managed to start at about 6 that day.' Natasha knew she sounded defensive. 'I don't know why Shekhar is making an issue out of this – these reviews have helped us keep track of our performance on a weekly basis, stay connected and take quick corrective action. In fact, this week's dip, I was just going to tell you—'

Aman cut in, 'Shekhar also indicated, Natasha, that he's not the only one on the team who feels this way.'

'That's not true.' Her face was hot again. 'He doesn't know what he's talking about.' How dare Shekhar speak for anyone else? She made up her mind to call him. Heart problem or not, he had no right to—

'Really, Natasha?' Aman's voice was gentle again. 'Are you sure? Have you checked with the guys? Individually.'

'I talk to almost all of them every day, Aman. I assure you, no one has raised any such issue with me.'

'Yes, but have you been connecting with them *beyond* the numbers?'

'Aman.' Natasha drew herself up. 'When you first took me on for this role, we both knew I would have to earn the team's respect. They were all, to some degree, resistant to the idea of reporting to a woman. And that too, one younger than them. Well, I've got them all to improve their performance consistently over the last two years. I've earned that respect by keeping the focus on work. And we know that nothing succeeds like success.'

'I don't doubt that. The performance has been exemplary, but it's not what I'm talking about. We've been missing it,

Natasha. The team isn't *happy*. They're not performing because they're motivated. They're afraid of the consequences if they do not perform. And that's stressful.'

'That's sales,' Natasha said.

'We haven't had attrition at the leadership level before. We invest heavily in these guys. And Shekhar may only be the first casualty.'

'I'll talk to him, I'll convince him to take back his resignation. There's nothing that can't be sorted out...'

Aman sighed heavily. 'He's expressly stated he doesn't want you to call him. He wrote that just seeing your name on his phone or inbox might result in a nervous breakdown. Now, I'm sure he's exaggerating,' Aman said, holding up a hand to ward off Natasha's indignant protestations, 'but I don't want to take that chance. I'll talk to him myself later in the day. I don't expect it to do any good. He's gone.'

Shekhar: gone. Along with Deepesh and a couple of others, he had been one of her stalwarts. Why? They may have had differences of late, but it didn't have to come to this. Natasha instinctively knew that it would be difficult to get a replacement of his calibre. He had been dedicated to the company. After all, he'd been around since it was a mere start-up creating a stir with its innovative HR process-management tools. How had she not seen this coming? How had she missed the signs?

'Natasha, have you been accessible to your team?' Aman could see she was struggling.

'I'm available to them twenty-four hours for any issue they may face.'

'I asked if you've been accessible, not available.'

Natasha didn't respond. She knew what Aman meant. It

wasn't new feedback – she'd heard from him on a couple of occasions that she needed to listen to and connect with people more, but she had treated them as mere suggestions and assumed she had the right to dismiss them if they didn't suit her modus operandi. After all, she had a serious business function to run and was constantly fighting the notion that a woman boss would get emotional at the drop of a hat.

She stared ahead, stone-faced. Aman leaned back in his chair. He knew her well enough to see that she wouldn't be taking any more feedback in this session. 'Well, there's some other news, Natasha. Slightly more positive, this time.'

Natasha looked at his face and tried to pay attention to what he was saying. She attempted to shut out how insulting it was that Shekhar had done things this way, claiming he couldn't even handle her calling or emailing him again. That little—

'...And you know we're expanding into some new business lines, and that I've left things to you and the others for this core part of the business ... We now need to set up some new strategic innovations...'

No calling or emailing because it might result in a heart attack or something. Bullshit. Well, he hadn't said anything about Whatsapping, and that's one place she could catch him. He was almost always online.

'...So I've decided to create a new position: business head – someone who can handle all the related functions like HR, marketing, product and, of course, sales.'

Natasha finally registered what Aman was saying when she heard 'business head'. She had hinted to him often enough that someone needed to actively lead the business, someone who was ready to be more operationally involved and could bring together all the related units under a common vision.

She had demonstrated, over the last two years, that she was perfect for the role.

She sat up straighter. This made Shekhar's departure pale into insignificance. She would work doubly hard to find his replacement – after all, no one was indispensable. She tried not to let any excitement show. That was what had helped her get this far – the ability to control her emotions.

'And I hope you and Rishabh are able to work closely. I've told him already that you'll be one of the most critical people on his team,' Aman concluded.

'Rishabh?' Natasha said blankly. That last sentence echoed in her head and she finally got the full import of what Aman was telling her.

'Rishabh Sethi,' Aman affirmed. 'Brilliant track record of almost eighteen years. He joins us from an FMCG background, but he's a real technology enthusiast and is known to be a great people person with a huge network of potential A-level clients that he's going to be bringing in from day one.'

'Rishabh Sethi.' She repeated slowly. The blood was pounding in her ears.

Bypassed *again* – this time by her own boss, whom she had trusted and served for two years, working late nights and weekends, sacrificing everything else to ensure the bloody numbers climbed week after week. Aman, whom she had always liked, was calmly telling her that he was bringing in someone *else* for the position she had got him to think through over a period of months. And he didn't seem to have a clue as to how she was feeling right now – he looked perfectly calm and relaxed and so freaking *normal* as he delivered the news about some random jackass who would now, effectively, serve as nothing but a superfluous layer between them. And Aman thought she couldn't read the signs with *her* team? Not that she was giving him any signs. Her clenched fists were hidden away under the table.

Aman leaned forward in full earnest. 'You know, Natasha, I'm hoping you'll be able to pick up more than just the business-handling aspects from Rishabh. I'm hoping he'll be able to coach you in people matters. Maybe you just need closer mentoring than I've been able to give you in this regard. After all, with your impeccable track record, you're next in line as business head. We're all very clear that you'll be groomed for the role under his leadership. Your hard work has not gone unappreciated.'

That was enough. Natasha stood up with a crisp 'Thanks, boss, that means a lot to me. I must get back to work now.'

Aman looked a little taken aback, but said, 'Of course…'

When Natasha reached the door, he called, 'Natasha – are you sure you don't want to discuss this some more? I…'

Natasha turned and said, expressionless, 'No, boss, it's clear – what else is there to discuss?'

'So everything's okay?'

'Certainly. Shekhar's loss is a setback but with Rishabh's, er, mentoring and our very capable HR department, I'm sure we'll be fine and will identify a replacement for him soon. And we'll get someone who's determined to stick it out for the long haul this time.'

Aman looked relieved. 'Sure, Natasha. Will you go ahead and float the job description for the position today?'

'I will. Don't worry, Aman. It'll be a good test to see how we can bring in new leadership talent. We're building our own reputation as a company.'

Aman smiled for the first time in the meeting. 'We are,

aren't we?' She noticed he was getting a call on his cell phone. He waved goodbye and she sailed out of the door and shut it behind her.

She gritted her teeth. He was already busy on the phone now and wouldn't hear her hiss under her breath: 'Oh yes. A reputation for giving people what they deserve.'

She exhaled and squared her shoulders. Without a glance back, she headed to her desk, prepared to focus on that goddamned VLOOKUP formula.

FOUR

WHEN SMOKE SPARKS A FIRE

Natasha sat in her parked red Verna, staring straight ahead with one hand still on the steering wheel. She was home but didn't feel like getting out of the car. It was relatively early, 6 p.m., but with winter setting in, it was already dark. Dreary. Dismal.

It was when she noticed her knuckles turning white that she loosened her grip on the wheel. This was idiotic. She was angry and was beginning to feel the heaviness of depression, a luxury she could not afford. Luckily, she had a little first-aid stash for just such an occasion. She fumbled open the dashboard and retrieved all she needed: one smooth, slim Benson and Hedges and her silver alligator lighter.

Already calmer, she stepped out of the car, leaving her laptop inside. She closed the door and leaned against it as she lit up with unsteady hands. *Oh* ... It had been so long. Even after Rishi had broken up with her, she had refrained from going back to it. She'd been tempted – especially since she had quit because he had asked her to, and her first instinct after the break-up had been to light up again. She had quashed it, deciding it was better to take charge of her health, and had instead doubled her attempts at fitness and dieting. Remembering that her yoga instructor, Ramakant Sir, hadn't shown up for a week, she felt a fresh twinge of irritation. Maybe she should find a new instructor. She hated people who were insincere with their work.

She shivered and took another drag. The taste of nicotine felt familiar, yet new. This wasn't a big deal. She figured as long as she had control over it, it didn't really matter. It had been a really rough day: first, bad news about Shekhar, and then worse about that Bloody Rishabh.

The smoke filled her lungs and she tried to relax with a slow exhale. Her mind raced through the events of the day. Was it a coincidence that Aman had broken the news about Shekhar in almost the same breath as telling her about her new boss? Had he been waiting for her to slip up so he could make a point about how she wasn't mature enough to take over a position as senior as business head? Thirty-five was old enough, dammit. But no, Rishabh and his bloody eighteen years. What the hell did that matter? She had much more experience in technology-related roles and in business-to-business selling. She had looked the guy up on LinkedIn and studied his profile with growing distrust. Sure, it all looked good on paper. The handsome sort, in that slick, corporate way: closely cropped hair, smooth shave, smiling at the camera with his arms crossed, leaning slightly forward in typical I'm-such-a-stud style. Ugh.

Natasha bit her lip thoughtfully. Maybe Aman meant what he had said about grooming her for the role. At least there was a clear line of sight as far as her career progression went. After all, she had to admit, it had only been a year and a half since her last promotion. But the *results*, dammit. She knew she could do the role right now. And she would have loved to be able to officially boss around the others – Dibakar from marketing, Saurabh from product and Renu from HR. Oh, especially Renu from HR. Well, she would get to do that eventually. If she impressed the new guy quickly enough, he would consider her his ally. His right-hand woman. That could work.

Another deep drag and she felt distinctly lighter. She'd pull through as always – she wasn't about to fall apart due to a temporary setback. She couldn't believe that for a moment there, she had actually felt the urge to call Rishi. But no, they weren't on talking terms, even though they had said they would try and be friends. But no, that never worked – best to stay away completely. It had been hard for her, that particular break-up, even though she had shared her feelings with no one. She'd missed so many things about him, but nothing had been worth the arguments that grew to a crescendo of bitterness and pain. Not even the great sex.

She gazed at the grey sky, a twisted smile on her face. Maybe she should go ahead and experiment with the idea that had been playing on her mind: find some nice married man. There would be sex on a regular basis without all the drama of a relationship. She could have a go at being the 'other woman'. It would add a touch of femme fatale to her ball-breaker persona. No, wait – no one from work could know. Her professional image was too important.

Blaring music broke her train of thought. It was from the car that had pulled up next to her – a battered old Accent. She recognized it since he always parked next to her – a muscular young dude called Vicky, who'd started up what he called a fitness boot camp in the colony two months ago. The friendly sort, he often struck up a conversation with her when they met.

He waved cheerily at her now from the car, and she couldn't help but smile back. He was always bursting with energy. And he was surprisingly good-looking, all chiselled, from his high cheekbones to his wide chest and big biceps, down to his narrow waist with the sculpted abs. She remembered him telling her once that he did some modelling on the side. And why not? With his cropped, slightly spiky hair, which gave him the look of a military man with a rebellious streak, he made for an enticing package. She considered this, thoughtfully sucking in some more smoke as she watched him get his equipment bag out of the back seat.

'Natasha ma'am!' He straightened up and grinned at her. 'When are you joining us? You said you might in winter and it's winter now!' He looked her up and down and said, 'Wow, you look really great today – nice dress!'

She allowed herself a short laugh and looked down at herself, glad her legs were so smooth under those sheer stockings.

'Thanks, Vicky,' she said. 'Maybe I'll try your class next week.'

'Not class, it's a boot camp!' Vicky seemed to realize something. 'Arrey! What's this?' He looked totally aghast as he pointed to the cigarette stub in her hand. 'You *smoke*?'

She didn't know why she felt defensive, but something about Vicky's absolute obsession with health and fitness always made her want to impress him. 'It was just one, and after many months.' She tried to look nonchalant and dropped it, crushing it under her heel.

'Just one?' He glared at her accusingly with his clear brown eyes. '*Aise toh nahin hota.*'

'But it *is* like that, Vicky.' She tossed her hair, a little annoyed.

No one had the right to question her like that. She opened her car door and stretched to get out her laptop bag and purse, calling back over her shoulder, 'I don't smoke, really. Gave it up a long time ago. It's very easy for me to control it now.'

She straightened up and faced him again. He was two inches taller than she was in heels. 'Right. See you then. It's cold out here.' She let out a little involuntary cough and started to head towards her building.

Vicky followed her and quickly caught up in a couple of long strides. 'See, it's already starting.'

'What is?'

'The coughing. You just coughed.'

'Nonsense, I was just clearing my throat.' She cleared her throat loudly.

'It's the smoke.'

'No, it's not.' She recalled Priya pointing it out when they last met. 'I've had it for a while. Most people don't even notice. Hell, *I* rarely do.' It was true. Most times, she wasn't conscious of it. Just an irritation in her throat that was to be expected, living in one of the most polluted cities in the world. She decided she would ask her yoga sir about it, maybe he could recommend a breathing exercise. If he ever showed up, of course.

They were at her building now, so she signalled Vicky to carry on to the clubhouse where he conducted his sessions. He waved at her, and then he said the words that made her freeze in her tracks. 'I didn't think you were the type to make excuses!' He walked away, calling back rather innocently, 'If you change your mind, we're starting in twenty minutes.'

Cheeky fellow. She stared after him, annoyed. As if she was going to take the bait.

Who did he think he was, anyway?

—

Natasha wiped a droplet of sweat from her brow. She tried not to let it show - how much every muscle in her body was hurting.

And she'd thought she was fit. The yoga had kept her supple, and she did her own workout every day – crunches, sit-ups, the works. But what Vicky had just put her, and the rest of the students, through wasn't your ordinary workout. It was pure torture.

Planks. Lunges. Something new with the silly name Burpee, incorporating a jump, plank and the hateful, hateful push-up. Jumping jacks, how old-school. And those squats, with the dumbbells – her arms felt ready to fall off.

There were six other women in the class. She barely knew them – they struck her as the variety that had nothing much to do besides fuss over their kids and themselves. In her judgement, the entire class had a massive collective crush on Vicky, and that was probably motivation enough for them.

He was attentive to each student during the hour, and was as professional as he was relentless in his training.

They were on the cool-down stretches now. These she managed pretty well. She paid close attention to his demonstrations – the exact angle of the bend, whether the pressure was on the heel or the toe and so on.

Vicky bent towards the left, hands stretched out, and they all followed him. Natasha had to admit the workout had done her state of mind good, although it had hurt her body in places she hadn't known existed. She felt much better about her day.

'Wow, look at that stretch. Awesome, Natasha ma'am.' She kept her head bent low, almost touching her knees, legs completely straight. He walked over in a couple of quick steps to stand behind Natasha. 'Stretch forward now. Back flat.' He took her hands in his and made her stretch out further than she ever had before, but even the pain it caused couldn't drown out the tingling his touch had kindled. Well now, what was this?

'Ouch, Vicky, that's it,' she couldn't help cry out. He let her go and grinned around the room. A couple of the women were smiling at her reaction, but most kept their faces impassive. One of them, Reema, said, 'Vicky, you said you would bring your wife to meet us one of these days, no? What happened?'

'Oh, yaar, can you believe she still hasn't moved from Lucknow? Now some family wedding has come up. It'll take her another couple of months.' He looked at Natasha to explain. 'She's also a fitness instructor. I was thinking we could do a session together here.'

Reema smiled at him, batting her eyelashes. 'How strange that she can stay away from you so long.' Natasha rolled her eyes. The woman was married, for goodness' sake and had kids – two or three of them. An aunty behaving like a teen. Ridiculous.

Vicky's fair face turned red. He continued in a boisterous voice that betrayed no discomfort, 'I'll surely bring her here before any other place! You guys are my best students.' He slapped his palms together with a resounding smack. 'Over for today, see you all next time!'

The class looked gratified. Natasha knew he probably said

that to all the students he had. How could one man have so much energy? She felt wiped out after just this one class.

Everybody was leaving, but as Natasha was about to exit, Vicky shouted, 'Natasha ma'am?'

She turned to look at him questioningly.

He grinned at her. 'I'm really glad you changed your mind. Bye!'

'Bye, Vicky.' Natasha laughed. He waved and went back to bending over his dumbbells, stuffing things into his bag. Her eyes lingered on his sweaty back for just a moment before she finally left the room.

It would be interesting to see how much energy the boy had in other areas, she thought. He wouldn't outdo her so easily there, she was sure. Too bad for the wife who chose to stick around in Lucknow. Not Natasha's fault at all.

FIVE

AND THEN THERE WAS RISHABH

'Deepesh, you really need to pull up your team.'

Deepesh fidgeted in his seat in front of Natasha's desk. He was the head of the Delhi-NCR sales branch, one of the old hands in the system. He was hard-working and had a very positive attitude. In fact, he was amongst the very few veterans who hadn't protested when Natasha was promoted to national sales head – despite the fact that she was five years younger than him, not to mention a woman.

Natasha had always liked him and treated him with respect. But now she was impatient. How many times was she expected to make the same point?

'Last week, when I went on the Noida sales calls, your guy, Sunil, told me he would meet me at Prisms Technology.' Deepesh nodded. Her entire team kept track of Natasha's whereabouts – she often made unplanned visits but the word spread quickly enough. Natasha opened her faithful little diary, found the right page and went on. 'First of all, he hadn't done his homework. We've discussed this before, he's not taking advantage of the new pre-sales team. He could have got so much more information: their hiring and retention rates, current sources used, existing HR technology solutions and need gaps. Then, he landed up five minutes late for the meeting – I arrived before him and was waiting in the lobby. And then, when we began, instead of spending any time understanding their requirements, our man just went ahead and started pitching the least appropriate solution. What's happening to your training procedures? This guy's been in the system for six months now, and his knowledge of our selling points is appalling, to say the least—'

Deepesh cut in, 'Natasha, we've had regular training and recently finished a refresher. He's not too shabby with around two closures a month and a good pipeline. He says he just got nervous, that's all. I spoke to him and he said he'd been stuck in a terrible traffic jam near Malviya Nagar. There was an accident…'

'Deepesh, we've *got* to stop making excuses for our people,' Natasha snapped. 'I expect better from you.'

He looked helpless, and ran a hand through his thinning grey hair. She said, 'Get another round of training in place. Let's go ahead and design that certification already. It should be a combination of hard-skill and soft-skill testing. We may actually have to bench people if they fail the test twice. And if they fail it three times, well, consider it a way of cutting the flab.'

'Natasha,' Deepesh protested, 'we've let go of six people who were performing just below average – there isn't any flab. We even have a couple of unfilled positions. The team is already feeling the pressure, and they're going to feel worse if we introduce the certification process right now. I suggest we keep the training going but make the certification optional with some incentives for performing well, and…'

'We're not a charity, Deepesh.' Natasha was irritated now. They usually saw eye to eye. 'If people are scared of fair assessment, they're the wrong people for the job. Are you with me?'

Deepesh didn't look happy about it, but loyalty, and his fundamental respect for hierarchy, kicked in. He sighed and nodded. Without meeting her eye, he rose from his chair and walked away.

Natasha watched with a frown. She almost called out to him, but decided to let him cool off. He'd come around eventually. Why couldn't these guys see that her way had been working well? It showed in their sales growth. And if they thought they could slack off now, they were wrong. It was time to push the pedal even harder. Sure, they had broken some initial resistance in the market after their product revamp, and more and more customers seemed to be accepting BizTech Smart HR as the better HR technology management solution, but the market was growing and they still hadn't tapped into the fast-growing SME segment. Thoughts began to buzz in her head about their sales structure. It was time to introduce another layer, which focused on different customer segments. Or should they just restructure completely by account type?

She snapped open her laptop. This would need more research and analysis, but she wanted to get her thoughts down as quickly as possible. She felt herself getting increasingly excited as her fingers flew over the keyboard. This would make so much sense. Team members could specialize by product solution sets appropriate to client industry. The geographic spread would need to be studied, of course, but this could potentially bring about some real efficiencies. She knew the kind of resistance the change would bring, but she would just prepare the counterarguments to the counterarguments. Resistance based on insecurities and egos was no match for logic. She had a clear idea about the skill sets she would need for the corporate team, and a couple of people immediately came to mind about taking leadership roles within that – she might as well go ahead and create a draft organizational chart, and…

'And this is someone very important, Rishabh – our national sales head, Natasha Patnaik.'

Natasha froze. That was Aman's voice, and the name he used had her immediate attention. Here already? She looked up at them. She gave Aman a tight smile – she knew the remark about her being important was well-meant but she felt it came across as a little condescending in front of the new guy. She didn't really want to stand up, and strictly speaking, a lady didn't have to, but she never went by that crap anyway. She rose from her desk to shake Rishabh's hand, trying to keep her face impassive.

He looked the same as he had in his LinkedIn profile. It hadn't been just a camera thing – he really was good-looking. Too good-looking, she thought, returning his bright grin with a polite smile. He was dressed sharply in a suit – goodness, he was even wearing a tie. She had never even seen Aman in a tie. She felt a little self-conscious about the relatively plain peach shirt she had chosen to pair with her beige pants. On days when she knew she was unlikely to make a sales call, she wore simpler stuff, reserving her killer outfits for time on the field. His gaze lingered on her and she returned it evenly as Aman went on.

'Rishabh, I'm sure Renu has slotted in plenty of time in your induction schedule with Natasha, but I thought you could get a head start in any case. She's been in the system almost right from the beginning. Five years, right, Natasha?'

Natasha nodded briefly.

'It's a real pleasure, Natasha.' Rishabh's voice was surprisingly deep. 'I'd love to get to know you better.'

What was with that glint in his eye? She felt a sudden burst of adrenaline coursing through her veins. Besides fear and suspicion, she felt a little flattered. She checked herself. She was far too experienced to fall for this kind of thing. Clearly, she needed to get laid soon – it had just been far too long. Anyway, as long as she was in control here, little else mattered.

'I'm sure you two will work well together. She's a real star.' Aman beamed at Natasha and she inclined her head to acknowledge his praise. 'Been the champion of our growth over the last two years. She'll take you through the sales strategy, the structure, the challenges and so on. You have time right now, Natasha? Renu'll be along with the induction schedule shortly, I thought Rishabh and you could have a chat till then.'

Natasha was grossly underprepared for this, but she wasn't going to show it. She would have preferred the time to make a formal presentation to Rishabh once she had gathered her thoughts about the current status and future strategy for the business – and she really wanted to get back to those new structural ideas. But still, it was important for her to come across as capable of rising to any request, so she said crisply, 'Of course. I would be happy to spend some time with Rishabh.'

Aman smiled and said, 'I'll leave him to you then, Natasha.' He smiled, slapped Rishabh lightly on the shoulder and headed towards his office, leaving them standing together.

That piercing gaze was on her again. Natasha coughed a bit. The discomfort in her throat was more acute these days. Maybe the smoking was exacerbating it. Recovering quickly, she indicated the conference room nearby and said, 'Shall we?'

Rishabh's smile hadn't wavered. Didn't his cheek muscles hurt? He suggested in his smooth baritone, 'Why don't we just take a seat in my office?'

Of course. Just two years older than her, a total noob as far as this industry was concerned, and he had an office. With walls. Hiding her displeasure, she nodded brusquely and started to walk in the direction he had indicated. Hmm. So, that empty office she had assumed was going to be a new meeting room had been reserved for this guy all along. She stopped in front of it and he opened the door with a familiarity that belied the fact that he had probably just been shown his room this morning. He held the door open and gave her a polite 'after you' gesture. She sailed in past him, clearing her throat again, wishing away the stupid cough.

He followed her in and the door shut behind them. After a couple of moments, everyone in the office, who had been pretending not to watch them, went back to work.

'What'll you have?' Rishabh asked Natasha as he picked up the landline and pressed a button.

What, was this the first thing this guy had picked up over here – how to order a coffee? 'Nothing,' she said distractedly. 'I'm good.' She cleared her throat again.

'I recommend some green tea – it's good for the throat.' He spoke into the phone. 'Would you please have someone send two cups of green tea to my office, just a hint of honey and lemon? Thanks, Diana.' He listened for a second or two and laughed. 'Wonderful. Thanks.'

Well. He had already made friends with Diana, the forty-five-year-old perennially grumpy executive assistant, who was supposed to be the group secretary for Aman and his subordinates, including Natasha, though she rarely asked her for anything. Natasha preferred to do these things herself, without feeling like she had a favour to return. It was clear that Rishabh was of the overly-smooth variety who made it a point to try and charm every woman who came his way. It certainly wasn't going to work on her.

Wait. Had he just ordered green tea for her? And right after she had refused. It was a different matter that she didn't know they even had green tea here. But to decide for her – unacceptable. Even though it could do her throat some good. That stupid cough threw her off a little – it felt like a disadvantage when you were trying to make an impression on someone. Not that she was.

'So,' she began, 'I can tell you about our basic structure first and some of the…'

She stopped short. He was shaking his head slowly from side to side as he leaned back in his chair, tie just slightly crooked. He looked like he had a good physique, impeccably maintained. He gave her a slow, disarming grin and said, 'Let's start at the beginning, shall we? Tell me about yourself, Natasha.'

That deliberate use of her name, with that slight emphasis. He had done the same thing with Diana. She took a deep breath and said coolly, 'That sounds like something out of an interview – with a management trainee … Rishabh.' She stressed his name. Just in case he was harbouring any hope of being called 'boss'. That she reserved only for Aman.

Rishabh's eyebrows rose slightly, but he didn't look unduly put out. 'Not at all, my dear.' Natasha hated being called 'dear', but didn't react. 'I just thought that we should get to know each other better since we're going to be working together. This sales-strategy-challenges-structure discussion can wait for our formal induction. This is just you and I getting to know each other. As people.'

Hoo boy. He was definitely one of those. Well, it had clearly worked well for him this far. Everyone had been gaga about Rishabh Sethi joining the leadership team. Apparently, the guy had quite a rep even outside the organizations he had infested.

'If you like, I'll start with myself,' Rishabh offered, but Natasha wasn't going to come across as unprepared.

'I've got fourteen years of experience now, and almost all of it has been in the sales function,' she rattled off. 'Eight years on the business-to-business side. I've been with this company for five years and have been leading sales for two years with 20 per cent revenue growth each year.'

Rishabh was listening with rapt attention, but Natasha knew he was waiting for something personal. Annoyed for having to give any of it away, she said, 'I'm from Delhi and have a management degree from IIM Cal.'

'What about your family?'

'I'm single. No family.'

This time, Rishabh did look surprised, as if he was going to say something further, but smoothly side-stepped, saying, 'And interests, Natasha? What do you like to do in your spare time?'

She looked at him for a moment. It was really nobody's business, but she didn't want to seem unidimensional by claiming not to have any interests outside of work. Why was this guy making her so uncomfortable? Why couldn't they just keep this to work-related stuff?

Luckily, the door opened and the oldest 'office boy', a man of about fifty called Jaggan, came in with a tray. Saved, thought Natasha, turning to smile appreciatively at Jaggan. A nice, clean tray, unusually posh, and two cups of green tea with a little dish on the side for the lemon and even a dainty pot of honey. Wow. Had Diana actually ordered new cutlery for this guy, and that too at top speed?

Jaggan was stone-faced as usual as he served them, and Rishabh gave him a charming smile with an 'Ah, thank you'. So the charm wasn't reserved just for the females, Natasha thought. It didn't appear to make any difference whatsoever to Jaggan, and Natasha found herself liking the old fart more for it. He exited the room without a word.

Natasha picked up her cup and took a sip, fortifying herself for the rest of this getting-to-know-you session. 'So, how about you?' She smiled at him, hoping to make him forget that she hadn't answered him about her interests. She added, 'I'd love to know more about you.' Did that sound flirtatious? Dammit. She just wanted to get him talking about himself.

It seemed to work. Rishabh gazed at her for a moment and then picked up his cup of tea and sipped. 'Hmm.' He leaned his head back and said, 'Well, I'm not going to bore you with my professional credentials. I'm sure you already got that from LinkedIn.'

Natasha started a little. How did he know? She felt off-balance again. She wondered if he had just said it casually because it was the norm to look up people on LinkedIn, especially if they were joining the organization as your boss. Or was it to do with the fact that he had a paid account?

Oh *shit*. She should have known – senior management professionals, not just those in human resources, tended to upgrade their accounts to see who was checking them out. How infuriatingly careless of her. She decided she hated this guy already, and it was a few moments before she could register what he was saying.

'. . .And I'm an avid sportsperson – especially fond of playing golf.' Shocking, Natasha thought sardonically. After all, it would help him creep up the corporate ladder. She feigned interest as he went on.

'And what else? I enjoy travel and reading, non-fiction mostly: history, evolution, philosophy . . . you know.'

Sure, she nodded, thinking: what is this, snob-central? He seemed to enjoy talking about himself and finished smoothly with, 'And I've been married for ten years now – Kirti and I have two children, Ayaan and Ayush. They're all going to move from Mumbai over the next couple of months when the kids' school term finishes.'

Ah, a family man. Successful professional, good looks, wonderful family. Good for you, thought Natasha grumpily as she nodded to acknowledge all that he had told her.

He leaned forward, resting his elbows on the table and said, 'And I'm just so happy to be here, Natasha. I really look forward to a great working relationship with you.'

There was absolutely nothing wrong with the words. It was maybe just the tone, or the fact that the glint was back in his eyes – it wasn't just flirtatious. She thought she read a hint of mockery, as if he knew he had the power to make her feel uncomfortable.

'So do I,' Natasha murmured and then quickly looked at her watch and said, 'Well. I'll tell Renu you're ready for your induction schedule.' She immediately felt pissed-off with herself for that – she had meant it to be a gesture of politeness, considering he was new and it was his first day and all. But judging by his handling of Diana, she had a feeling he pretty much had his own schedule in control – she didn't have to offer to do secretarial type of duties for him, for god's sake.

He smiled appreciatively, turning on the full force of his grin as he murmured, 'Thank you, Natasha. That's very kind.'

Natasha gave him the briefest of smiles, rose and left his room in a few brisk steps. She didn't like feeling out of her depth. And she certainly didn't like the thought that she might just have met her match, and then some.

SIX

CLENCHED

'Didi … *Woh* aunty *phirse aayi hai* … Chopra Aunty.' Natasha glared up at Jamuna from her position on the floor. She hated being interrupted like this. Last thing she needed. It was too early in the day to deal with cranky old fogies.

'Couldn't you have said I was sleeping?'

Jamuna looked sheepish. Natasha sighed. As if Jamuna, of all people, could think on her feet. Muttering to herself about the-help-these-days, she walked through the hallway and swung the door open with a smile pasted on her face. 'Good morning, Chopra Aunty.'

'For you, maybe.'

Natasha groaned inwardly. She should have known better than to greet her with that. Chopra Aunty began, 'I for one do not like being disturbed during my morning prayers.'

Natasha leaned against the doorway in defeat. 'And what exactly is disturbing you today, Aunty?'

'Water!' Chopra Aunty spat out the word. 'Great big, *fat* drops of water, dripping from your balcony on to mine. I was just sitting there in the middle of my puja, balcony door open for a little morning freshness, and you were pouring buckets of water for god-knows-what reason, without any thought as to—'

'Aunty, Aunty,' Natasha interrupted. 'That was Jamuna – she's bought some plants for the house, and I made her promise to take care of them. She was watering them and a drop or two must have spilt on to your—'

'A drop or two!' Chopra Aunty gasped. 'It was like a *downpour*. Do you know how it feels to be disturbed in the middle of a peaceful morning routine?'

'I can't even *imagine*,' Natasha said evenly, sarcasm lost on the Chopra.

'And I'll tell you something else about that maid of yours.' The old lady leaned forward. Natasha sighed and bent her head to get closer. Mrs Chopra whispered, 'I've been smelling smoke from your balcony too. It must be her beedi or something. It was disgusting, clearly something from the roadside, which only the lower classes could enjoy.'

Natasha sucked in a sharp breath. Her Benson and Hedges smelt nothing like a bloody beedi. She stared stonily at Mrs Chopra. 'Thank you for letting me know. I'll look into it and take corrective action.' *Like using your balcony as my new ashtray, you reedy old cow.*

Mrs Chopra didn't look like she was ready to be dismissed. 'Don't you think it is impolite to keep your neighbours standing outside? You have never invited me into your house…'

Oh lord. 'Aunty, my drawing room is such a mess right now, I wouldn't dream of having you in. You see, the lower cla—I mean, *Jamuna* hasn't even had time to begin cleaning it up. Rather early in the morning, you know,' Natasha said pointedly.

'Natasha?' a male voice called from inside the house.

'Just a minute,' she called back, and turned to bid the Chopra goodbye.

Why did that relic suddenly have a crafty look on her face? 'Oh. So I see. You have *company*. I saw a … gentleman making his way to our building from my window and when I enquired, the guard outside said he often comes here at odd hours. I didn't realize he was your…?'

Natasha felt her blood boiling. The nerve! She opened her mouth to clarify, although it was none of the Chopra's business. But then something stopped her. She threw her head back and laughed.

Mrs Chopra looked disapproving of this early-morning mirth and waited for her to stop laughing. Natasha breathed huskily, 'Can I speak to you frankly, Chopra Aunty? Woman to woman?'

Mrs Chopra didn't look sure about this, but Natasha went on anyway. 'You see, I do have basic needs. You've been there, I'm sure. You were young once?'

Chopra Aunty stiffened. 'What?'

'Oh come on, Aunty,' Natasha said affably. 'You've made it to this century. Might as well get used to it. Today, you can get everything – for a fee. And I mean *everything*.'

The full import seemed to sink in now.

'This is nonsense!' Chopra Aunty gasped. 'I should have you reported for this. It's people like you who bring down perfectly respectable neighbourhoods…'

'Don't get me wrong, Aunty,' Natasha said quickly. 'I didn't mean to imply that you're past your prime or anything. In fact, I can check with him if he can come to your place after mine.

Don't go by appearances, he's very good. Flexible enough to handle all sorts of clientele.'

Chopra Aunty looked apoplectic with rage. Natasha pretended not to notice. 'In fact, maybe he'll even give you a good rate, considering your age. In any case, I don't think you'd be able to go longer than maybe…' – she pretended to think about it – '…forty-five minutes?'

She batted her eyelids innocently at Mrs Chopra, head tilted to one side. Chopra Aunty turned on the heel of her chappal and charged down the corridor.

Natasha gazed after her, squashing her regret. The Chopra fully deserved that. Her heart still pounding, she shut the door with a bang.

'Natashaji, *aap aa rahi hain*?' the voice floated out into the hallway again, nasal and complaining. '*Aise toh poora time* finish *ho jayega…*'

'*Haanji, haanji,* sir.' Natasha shook her head to get rid of all things Chopra, and headed back to resume her yoga session in the living room.

'Natashaji.' Ramakant sir was not his usual calm self. In fact, he sounded positively frustrated. 'Not good!'

Natasha craned her neck to look back at him, straining in her dhanurasana. What more did the guy want? It was a perfectly respectable stretch – she was balanced precariously on her upper abdomen, her hands reaching back and holding her ankles. If she bent backwards any further, she would probably snap her spine. Still, she was a committed student and she strained further as she tried to raise her legs higher, rocking back and forth a little.

'No, no, no.' Ramakant got up from his position on the floor and came over and squatted in front of her, gazing into her face, his moustache twitching. 'You are not *here*.'

What was that supposed to mean? Natasha couldn't hold the stretch any longer, and gasped as she suddenly let go of it, hands and legs dropping to the floor in the clumsy release that she knew he disapproved of. She pushed her hair off her eyes and mumbled, 'I'm here only, sir.'

'No, you are not,' he insisted. He sat on his haunches, surprisingly at ease for a fat man in that position. But then, he was an experienced yoga teacher. He knew his stuff when it came to teaching, so what did she care about his paunch? She wasn't ever going to *actually* sleep with him, no matter what Chopra thought.

'Your body is here, but your mind ... Your mind is far away.'

Natasha sighed and had to stop herself from mouthing the words along with him – she had heard this one before.

'Yoga is not merely about a mechanical exercise ... It is about being present, being here. And you are not!'

Natasha murmured something about a stressful time at work, but she knew Ramakant sir wouldn't buy it. As far as he was concerned, everyone with a corporate job always had a stressful time at work, and that was because they were not properly committed to the practice of yoga.

He gazed accusingly at her. 'You are still not paying attention!'

'I am, I am.' Natasha stifled a groan as she sat up. Why was today's session harder for her than usual? Her heart just wasn't in it. Was it the Chopra's interruption? No. It was probably all of last week.

After his friendly act in their first meeting, Rishabh had asked to be taken through everything that had to do with the business. All the functional heads had to make presentations and these alignment meetings, as he had called them, took place every other day. She was suddenly seeing a lot more of her colleagues. Monday was the product presentation, Tuesday was marketing. For some reason, he had chosen to schedule even the HR presentation by Renu before Natasha's and that had irritated her. His emphasis on people was already beginning to annoy her. She was beginning to suspect he had more style than substance. And style he had plenty of. Most of the team members seemed impressed. Still, she couldn't think of him as her boss and was sore about his superficial comments during her sales presentation. He hadn't once expressed any appreciation of her talent or her ideas – he had just nodded through it all, making notes in his diary but not commenting on anything specific.

'It's too early for me to start making comments,' he claimed. 'I'm in the process of assimilating things right now.' The others seemed to fall for this show of humility.

She hated having to spend two full hours every morning in a presentation instead of working on her own numbers and reviews and calls. It disturbed her well-planned schedule, but Rishabh hadn't bothered to check with anyone – there were just curt meeting invites sent from his email by Diana day after day. She wished she could actually decline the stupid invitations, but everyone knew that wasn't an option when they came from your boss. Oh well, she hoped the daily meetings would soon turn into weekly meetings, and then hopefully once a month. And then maybe Rishabh would figure the office mirrors or something didn't suit him and leave. Hah. Wishful thinking.

'Surya namaskars – five!' Ramakant barked, as if he were on the verge of giving up on her. She stood up and started the twelve-step exercise, trying to execute each move exactly as he had taught her. But she couldn't keep her mind from wandering over the events of the week at work.

Rishabh wasn't the only new addition to the team. Aman had announced the organization's focus on new innovations to be developed alongside regular operations, and so Nikhil Katre had made his appearance two days ago. Vice president – innovations, it seemed. Great. Another new person who was clearly senior to her. He was reporting directly to Aman and was supposed to set up new product and revenue streams. He had a small team, which was expected to grow with the business, and in the meantime, the functional heads were to support him as and when required.

Well, Natasha wouldn't have much to do with him until he actually developed something for her to sell. On the other hand, maybe she would provide him some inputs on the market – she had a firmer grip on customer issues than the fools in marketing, who were preoccupied with creating useless pretty print ads. It made sense for her to cooperate with Nikhil, she realized – he was going to produce insights and products that would help the company stay relevant in the future, and she knew better than anyone that they needed this, what with technology and user preferences changing at such a fast pace. Besides, she wouldn't mind helping him along – he had sat through the last couple of presentations, and he looked the decent sort. He'd hardly said a word, preferring to sit quietly at the back of the room, an arm's length from Rishabh.

Natasha had observed him closely from across the room during the HR presentation. Renu had been bleating on and on. She had become more of a ditz now, as if she had a schoolgirl crush on Rishabh. Public speaking did not come naturally to her though, and she seemed nervous while making her presentations using charts that were impossible to read unless you happened to be carrying a magnifying glass.

Natasha had amused herself by stealing glances at Nikhil. He had been focusing on the screen, a slight frown on his face. Tall, dark and lean. He wore a simple clean-cut shirt that fit him well, and radiated a quiet self-assurance. Only once, when he had first met Natasha, had he given her a friendly smile that lit up his face. He had a tiny dimple, only on the right cheek – it showed up sometimes even when he wasn't smiling – like when he chewed his lower lip in deep thought. She couldn't quite place it, but there was something about him. An air of sadness? Well, it wasn't her place to ask. But yes, she wouldn't mind interacting with this new head of innovations.

The silly young girls in the office seemed a lot happier these days. They hadn't had too many good-looking men to ogle at until now, and apparently getting a Rishabh and a Nikhil together was an unexpected bounty. Natasha ignored it, but she had overheard a couple of debates at the vending machine – the ladies were arguing about which of the two new bosses was cuter; the consensus seemed to be Rishabh, given his flamboyance and charming way of holding the door open for all ladies. The tittering got to her, and she'd snapped her head around to glare at the girls, who were mostly from marketing and content. Thank goodness the few female members of her sales organization were sensible.

What was her own future in this company though, she mused in the middle of another surya namaskar. Aman could have at least asked her if she was interested in the position he had brought Nikhil in for – not that she would have taken it. But it involved less people-handling, which he had been repeatedly droning on and on about as being her weakness. She knew she could handle all sorts of people. Shekhar was a weakling. It was still embarrassing for her that he had left on such short notice. His team in Mumbai had gone ahead and given him a farewell. Not that she approved of the idea. Let someone try and send her the bill for it, she would show them what she thought of it. That reminded her – the position was still open, and stupid Renu had yet to send her a set of shortlisted applicants. Why couldn't people just do what they were supposed to? How did they get to rise in organizations despite their inherent lack of talent?

Ramakant's glare stopped her mid-namaskar. 'Am I doing something wrong?' she said a bit sullenly, well aware of what the answer was going to be.

'Nothing wrong at all,' he said, and she didn't like the sarcasm in his tone. 'It's just that I asked you to do five surya namaskars and you've already done twenty with no signs of stopping.' He sighed heavily. 'I'm telling you, Natashaji, you're not paying attention at all. What is the point of my coming all the way here if you're going to be like this?'

He waited for an answer and she bit back the one that danced around her lips: because it's your damn job and I pay you a freaking lot of money to come here and teach me yoga. She suddenly felt fed up. Maybe the yoga wasn't working for her, after all. He had been sporadic himself, showing up today after two weeks of absence, muttering something about an illness in the family. And now he was acting all demanding. There was rarely a murmur of appreciation from him even though she was a diligent student. She didn't need to start her day on a bad note. She looked at him coolly. The fitness classes going on with Vicky were workout enough, and Ramakant could keep threatening to leave her – maybe she would fire him well before that.

He sighed. 'I have been saying to you that the perfect time to do yoga is after three hours have passed from the time you wake up. But you insist I meet you at this early hour, and if you're not going to—'

She cut in hurriedly, 'Sir, your rule about three hours is unrealistic. I work till eleven at night sometimes. It's a tough job. I certainly can't get up at four to do yoga at seven – I have to get to office by nine, and that only leaves me with this window.'

'Yes, yes, you've told me all this,' Ramakant grumbled, scratching his potbelly in a manner she found particularly repulsive. 'Well then, the least you can do is actually listen to what I am saying. I come all the way from Delhi to Gurgaon. I could easily take on two or three new clients closer to my home.'

That was the last straw. Sixteen thousand a month for these lessons, and he was definitely charging her more than he did other people, to compensate for the distance. She was done with him making it seem like a favour.

A wicked idea entered her head. Before she could change her mind, she said sweetly, 'New clients … that reminds me, sir. The lady who came by a while ago? She lives on the ground floor, directly below.' She pointed downwards. 'Lovely woman, her name is Mrs Chopra and she was very insistent upon knowing your fee.' A part of her was shocked at what she was doing, but she went on, 'Perhaps, if it suits you, you could take her on as a client too? That should make the long trek out here worth your while.'

Ramakant looked somewhat mollified by this suggestion. Yes, she could see him thinking, it made sense to try and get more clients within this complex.

'She's an old lady, of course, but very pious and sincere. I'm sure you'll find her a wonderful client,' Natasha continued. A glance at the clock. 'Oh, we've overshot our time. Thank you, sir. I promise to do better next time.'

He grunted. Natasha waited for him to gather his bag and scooter keys. She knew very well there wouldn't be a next time. But who cared?

She saw him off at the door, waving cheerily. If only she could be there to see the Chopra's face when Ramakant showed up at her door, quoting a fee. But no, she had to get to that job of hers.

SEVEN

WHAT BEGAN ON THE TERRACE

Beep, beep, bee—

Natasha cut the call. It was Priya, trying to get in touch with her. She would call her back later. Right now she barely had twenty minutes before the next meeting and was hurrying to the terrace for a quick break. Her heels clacked up the dark, empty stairwell. It was a six-floor trek but she hadn't felt like taking the lift. It was good exercise and helped let off some steam.

She opened the door to the terrace, and was greeted by a cold gust of wind. Dammit, she'd been hoping for some sun, but it had turned cloudy – a grey and dismal winter day. Shivering a little, she walked to her favourite corner. There were some advantages to having designated smoking areas – it cut out the casual crowd and gave her more time and space alone. In fact, in the late afternoons, there was no one around at all.

She was still angry about her meeting with Renu. *Stupid, simpering HR idiot.* Two weeks since Shekhar had chickened out of the system, and Natasha still hadn't seen the shortlisted CVs. It wasn't some random junior position – it was critical, leading one of their largest regions. And Renu had smarmily cited the importance of the role when asked why finding a replacement was taking so long, adding that it was getting her personal attention at every stage. Natasha snorted to herself. *As if.*

Ever since Rishabh joined, Renu had seemed preoccupied with getting herself a makeover. These days the woman wore new and carefully planned outfits: fancy saris and skirts. To make things worse, she had been acting all soft and feminine lately and her eyelash-batting around Rishabh made Natasha sick. It was a pity Renu couldn't take as much interest in her work, which in her case meant sourcing good people, especially for sales.

And what the hell did she mean by saying she had emailed *Rishabh* for his thoughts on the position? Natasha stood frozen at Renu's desk, glowering furiously at her, unable to believe her ears. This was a position in a team that reported to Natasha, who wrote the job description, and Renu deemed Rishabh the best person to discuss the details with. It took all the self-control Natasha could muster to calmly say that she was better placed to offer inputs. Renu smiled affably and indicated for Natasha to sit down.

Natasha crossed her arms instead and Renu glanced around before saying, in a soft voice, 'Listen, Natasha. We know there's been a little *issue* with the way Shekhar left. I'm just trying to be sensitive to the situation. I felt it would be better to get our boss's input before we proceed further. He has already replied, saying we should discuss it, and we're due to have a meeting about it tomorrow. Of course, you'll be brought into the loop once we've aligned. It's just…'

Natasha's hands were tightly clenched, but otherwise, she didn't react. Was there a hint of condescension there? And that allusion to the 'little issue' with Shekhar. Nothing would delight Renu more than the ability to go one-up on Natasha for once. They had always disliked each other, with Natasha despising Renu for being less-than-efficient, and Renu resenting Natasha for being more centre-stage. Well, if she had been more dynamic like Natasha, she could have played a role in changing the organization's perception of the HR function. Of course, now that Renu appeared to be taking matters into her own hands, Natasha hated her even more.

'That's fine.' Natasha made an effort to sound neutral. 'When you and your boss…'

'Our boss.'

She muffled the urge to snap at her for that. 'When the two of you are ready to discuss this, let me know. Just keep in mind that each day the position is empty is causing serious harm to our revenue numbers. I would greatly appreciate your expediting this. And, of course,' she added craftily, 'we'll have to take into account the number of man-days lost and the motivational impact on the team, and revise our business targets accordingly for the rest of this quarter. Perhaps you should be presenting that section in our next review with the board.'

Renu's eyes widened. Natasha never used lack of people as a factor in her presentations to the board. Apart from Aman, she was usually the only one with a presentation at all – the rest of the functional heads only sat through and pitched in with a few slides when there was a special new product or marketing initiative. HR rarely got up to present and Natasha knew about Renu's fear of being in the hot seat, much as she craved appreciation.

Renu cleared her throat. 'Well. I was just going to say – there are a few CVs you could take a look at in any case, parallel to my conversation with Rishabh.'

Natasha raised her eyebrows. 'Are there now? What a good idea. Do email them to me.' She forced a smile and added, 'I'm under P for Patnaik.'

'I know,' Renu said mechanically. As usual, the sarcasm was lost on her, but when she did seem to get it, she let out the fake, tittering laugh she had been perfecting for Rishabh. Natasha grinned like a shark before walking away.

—

'Bitch,' Natasha hissed to herself as she fumbled with the lighter. She was settled in her usual spot in the corner, perched on a concrete slab between two large water tanks. The tanks offered just a bit of respite from the biting wind, and she lit up and took a long, grateful drag, feeling light-headed almost immediately. It had taken so much effort to control her emotions – she couldn't let Renu see she was getting to her. She took another drag and exhaled again, repeating louder, 'Bitch!'

'Natasha?'

She almost dropped her cigarette as she snapped her head in the direction of the voice. Her heart was pounding – she had been so sure she was alone.

Oh. Nikhil. He'd materialized to her right, on the other side of the water tank. What was he doing here? Well, smoking obviously, as a glance at the cigarette in his hand told her. She didn't know he smoked. Come to think of it, she didn't know much about him. He wasn't as open as that showman Rishabh.

She went a little red, hoping fervently that he hadn't heard her. She said as breezily as she could, 'Hello, Nikhil. Didn't see you there.'

His dimple showed in the easy smile he gave her. He walked closer, a good four or five inches taller than her, and leaned against the tank before taking a drag. She suddenly felt awkward, and stared straight ahead at the greying clouds.

They smoked together in silence. After a few moments of feeling self-conscious, but not uncomfortable, she felt the return of her mild curiosity about him. He seemed too easy-going and down-to-earth for someone in such a senior position. A senior vice president, same level as Rishabh, really. He didn't look much older than her – what was he, thirty-eight? Definitely not over forty. A quick glance at his dark brown hair revealed no greys, and he didn't look the sort to go about trying to conceal them. She wanted to say something, but hesitated, wondering what a safe topic would be – she didn't want to get personal. Maybe she'd ask how his work in innovations was going and at what stage he would be taking her inputs from sales' perspective.

He spoke first, though. 'How long have you been in Delhi?'

'Oh, many years. Grew up here.' She took a deliberately casual puff and turned back to him. 'You?'

'Bangalore boy, mostly.' He smiled at her, and the dimple reappeared on his cheek. She watched it distractedly while he went on, 'Should stop calling myself a boy, no?' He shook his head with a short laugh. 'I've lived and worked there most of my life. Delhi – it's only been work trips till now.'

'Must be quite a contrast,' she said.

'I love Bangalore,' he said, warmth in his voice. 'There's

something about the city. My family moved there from Mumbai when I was only five. My parents are still there and my daughter is only just about getting used to being away from them.'

Of course. She refused to allow herself even a twinge of disappointment. Good-looking, successful man – he was bound to be happily married. That sort always got snapped up early. Well, good for him, she thought. She smiled politely but wanted to avoid a family-centric conversation. 'And what is it about Bangalore that you like so much?'

'You've spent time there?'

'For work, mostly. I like the weather, but thought the…'

'The traffic is terrible,' he finished the sentence with her and laughed at her sheepish smile. He went on, 'There's so much more to the city than that. There's something very musical about it. It's as if every third person plays a musical instrument there. There's always something going on – concerts, shows, music festivals…'

'You play something, don't you?' Natasha guessed.

'Used to.' He exhaled a puff of smoke, looking straight ahead. 'Drums. I was in a band. Stopped after marriage, though.'

Yeah, I've heard many things stop after marriage. 'That's great.' She added somewhat ruefully, 'I've always wanted to play an instrument. Too late now, though.'

'Hey, it's never too late. What kind of music do you like?'

'Ah, all kinds. U2. Pearl Jam. Collective Soul. Old stuff, actually.'

'I love those guys too. Floyd?'

'You bet.' She gave him an open grin. 'You should see my collection. I wish CDs weren't going out of style. You think I'm old-fashioned?'

'Old-fashioned?' he protested. 'I have all my CDs too. But it is convenient, being able to get your music digitally.'

'Haven't got into all that yet.'

'Well, I'm not that heavily into it myself. My daughter's probably savvier than me!'

Obviously, that would keep coming up. They had been talking as if they were still in college or something. Well, they weren't. They were serious, working professionals. She straightened up a little, taking a long, deep drag. Neither of them spoke for a while, each lost in thought.

After a few moments, Nikhil said, 'So, I believe there's a New Year getaway being planned for the thirty-first? Will you be going?'

It was the first she was hearing of a 'New Year getaway'. This was clearly the work of none other than Renu. Trying not to look clueless, she gave a short laugh. 'Not my scene. I think I'll be travelling to Mumbai around then anyway. And besides,' she said, giving him a sidelong glance, 'aren't you supposed to spend New Year's with family or something?'

'Yes, but Renu said this getaway is planned *with* families – I'm not sure my daughter will enjoy it, but it beats hanging around at home. I don't know, though.' He looked at her again. 'You sure you're not going? Spending New Year's with family in Mumbai?'

Natasha stiffened. She glanced at her watch. 'Whoops, I'm running late for a meeting. See you later, Nikhil.' She dropped her cigarette and crushed it under her heel. She looked up once at his bemused face, unconsciously searching for his dimple. It wasn't visible.

It was almost time for that stupid meeting anyway: another

team catch-up Rishabh had called for – when was he going to stop these things and let people get on with their work?

She coughed and noticed Nikhil was watching her face closely. She gave him a self-conscious little wave before hurrying away from him towards the door to the stairwell. When she was about fifteen feet away, she heard him call her name.

She whipped around, shivering against the full blast of the cold.

'I just wanted to say I agree.' He was smiling at her – was it teasingly?

'What?' she said blankly.

He took a final drag from his cigarette and said, 'You know, the whole "bitch" thing.' And then he winked at her, before bursting into laughter at her expression, dimple flashing again.

She stared for a moment and turned away before he could see her go pink. He had no way of knowing who she had been talking about. Right? She went through the door. The sudden darkness after the bright light made her feel disoriented until her eyes adjusted to the change. Then her heels clicked loudly down the stairs as she tried to compose her thoughts, her expression, her heartbeat.

EIGHT

NO SAINT

'What's wrong with our renewal rates? Why are they stuck at 20 per cent?'

Natasha frowned at her laptop and looked up at Deepesh and his two branch sales managers. The men around the conference table sat rather stiffly on their chairs and the other ten-odd people, attending the call from their respective locations, were probably on the edge of their seats. This particularly sharp, enquiring tone from Natasha did not bode well for them.

'Our plan was to move renewal rates to 25 per cent this quarter and end the financial year at 30 per cent. You guys do know that keeping our existing customers happy is essential for sustainable success, right?'

Silence all around. Natasha repeated, 'Right?'

A murmur of assent but no further comment. Natasha waited a moment and then probed, 'So what do you guys have to say about this number? What's the problem?'

Deepesh cleared his throat and positioned himself closer to the speakerphone, as if to enlist the support of his brethren across the country. 'Er, Natasha, in the Delhi branch, we have that slight issue with headcount—'

'Deepesh,' Natasha interrupted, 'you know we're not discussing headcount. Our numbers are committed at the beginning of the year – we're not going to use manpower as an excuse in this room. If people have to stretch to cover up, make them stretch. We're not in the business of sitting pretty in corporate offices. We already have two working Saturdays in the month – I'll request all four Saturdays working if we have to find more man-days.'

Deepesh sputtered, 'But, Natasha...'

Vikas's voice crackled in from the speakerphone at the same time that Deepesh was speaking. He was the head of the south branch, and a relatively new member. Natasha raised a hand to silence Deepesh, and strained to make out what Vikas was saying. '...Product issues over here, especially in Chennai ... Customers are saying that the system isn't user-friendly enough, and...'

'Listen, Vikas...' Natasha cut in. 'There is no question of product issues "over there". It's the same product all across the country. There have been changes and upgrades over the last year and a half, and every attempt has been to make the system easier to use. So let's give up on blaming the—'

'South customers are different because the legacy systems here are different,' Vikas said, a hint of obstinacy in his voice. Natasha sighed. This was the problem with the new guys. She would have to make a trip to Chennai soon. She didn't want to have to force her point of view on her team – they had to learn that she was right and fall in line themselves.

'Okay, Vikas,' Natasha said, running her eyes over a few numbers on the Excel file open on her laptop. 'It says here that the south branch currently has the lowest number of sales calls per existing customer than any other branch – is it any surprise that your repeat rates are 18 per cent lower than the country's average? It's obvious your guys need to visit the current accounts more often than simply chasing new leads.'

'But, Natasha, that's an unfair comparison,' returned Vikas, and Natasha scowled at the phone. She thought she heard Deepesh suck in his breath sharply, but when she glanced up at him, he was expressionless. Vikas continued, 'We're a newer branch and obviously our customers haven't even had a chance to use the product, much less to renew – in fact, that's the reason our calls-per-customer is lower, a large percentage of the sales have just been closed in the last quarter and so…'

'Make up your mind, Vikas.' Natasha was getting fed up. Her throat was bothering her and she coughed once and went on, 'What is the real issue? Is it the newness of your branch that explains your low renewal rates, or the lack of customer acceptance? And, in any case, especially in the early stages, customers need more hand-holding, so that still doesn't explain your lower average call-per-customer.' She took a sip of coffee and made a face – it had gone cold. Deepesh indicated to one of his guys that he should go and ask for a fresh round of coffee in the conference room, and the fellow made his escape with alacrity. Natasha rolled her eyes towards the speakerphone. 'Time to choose your excuse.' Her tone was lilting, but the warning clear.

This time, Vikas didn't respond immediately. When he spoke, it was in a low voice. 'We'll look into the calls-per-customer issue.'

'Thank you,' Natasha moved on briskly. 'Anirban – there?'

Anirban, who was standing in as acting branch head for the west, said, 'Yes, yes, Natasha, I'm here, I'm listening, I'm here…'

Natasha rolled her eyes. This guy was overenthusiastic – perhaps he thought he had a chance at becoming the new branch head. Well, he thought wrong. He was too raw, barely in his early thirties or something, not nearly mature enough to handle the job.

'Your numbers this month are dismal, as expected…'

'Natasha,' came the over-eager voice on the line, 'it's also the holiday season, with the year ending, and many people have been in a festive mood and planning leaves. They aren't really open to entertaining sales calls, and…'

'Did I ask?' Natasha's voice was icy. 'I've had it with all of your excuses, guys! Anirban, I said your dismal numbers this month were *expected* – but let me clarify that it has nothing to do with the season. For your information, New Year comes around regularly and all across the country, there's no special trend in the west that calls for a dip of 15 per cent when everywhere else it's only 6.5 per cent. Your numbers are to do with the lack of a leader with any form of vision and direction.'

This time, Natasha happened to catch Deepesh's expression before he could hide it. He was cringing. She saw how Anirban might take her remark personally. It wasn't what she had meant, but it was not untrue. Why was everyone arguing with her today? She tried to modulate her voice to a more even tone. 'Anirban, I'll be visiting Mumbai the day after tomorrow, we can catch up then. I'd like to review the entire team individually. Please make a schedule and send it to me.'

'On the thirty-first?' Anirban's voice was tremulous.

'Yes.' Natasha snapped her laptop shut and paused. 'Objections?'

'It's … New Year's Eve, Natasha.'

'Anirban, in case you've forgotten, we're working that Saturday in sales. It's only the first of Jan that's off. What's the problem?'

'Well…' Anirban hesitated but then finished, 'Nothing… That's fine. I'll send you a schedule.'

'Good,' said Natasha crisply. 'Okay, that's it, guys. The New Year's coming up and I may not speak to some of you before then. It's going to be a big year for all of us. Hope you're planning to make a lot of resolutions. The only one I want us to make as a team is: no excuses.' There was a faint tittering, but no one laughed. Natasha had only been half-joking. She concluded, 'Let's make this a productive new year.' There were some murmured responses as Natasha rose, picked up her laptop and left the room.

A couple of seconds later, Jaggan appeared with hot cups of coffee steaming on a tray. Deepesh gave him a '*kya yaar*, so late' look, which had no effect on Jaggan's impassive face. Deepesh distractedly picked up a cup for himself anyway. He wiped his brow – end of December, freezing cold outside, but here he sat sweating.

'Is it true, Natasha? You're not coming for our New Year getaway?' Renu's voice irritated Natasha, particularly when she was trying to sound sweet and concerned.

Natasha looked up at her. 'No. I won't be coming.' She

added pointedly, 'I didn't know about it early enough, unlike the rest of the leadership team. For *some* reason.'

Renu smiled and settled on the chair in front of Natasha's desk. 'Really? Oops. I thought I sent out the mail to leadership as soon as we had the location confirmed. Must have missed you somehow – strange. Anyway, beautiful place, the Tree Top – just an hour and a half from here. Come on, Natasha, it's with family – it's important for all the team leaders to be there. It'll be a great bonding exercise.'

'We are working through the thirty-first in sales,' Natasha said pointedly. 'My team is not going to be there. It's more of a corporate getaway – the branches aren't involved.'

'The thirty-first is a non-working Saturday, Natasha.' Renu frowned. 'Why would sales be working?'

'Because we have something called revenue pressures, dear Renu.' Natasha's voice was dripping with sarcasm. 'It's the same reason we don't have a formal winter break this year. So I took the call last week that we'll all work the last day of the year. Everyone will be out on the field.'

Renu looked put out. 'As the head of HR, I'm supposed to be kept in the loop about these decisions.'

'Oops,' returned Natasha with a tight smile. 'I suppose I missed marking you on the email I sent to Rishabh. Strange.'

Touché. Renu had nothing to say to that. She just tossed her long ponytail and changed tack. 'Well, good luck finding anyone in office on the thirty-first to sell to. As someone representative of your customer set, I can assure you that 80 per cent of the HR department will be on leave – we're a hard-working lot and the year end is a time for relaxation for us.'

'Thank you so much for your feedback,' Natasha said sweetly. 'We hadn't thought of that. But actually, we're just going for the 20 per cent of the guys who are in the office. They're even *more* hard-working. Appointments have already been set up and they're likely to result in something, given that there won't be much else going on in many offices. It's an experiment, our year-end drive.' She recalled something. 'In fact, I sent you an email about setting up those face-to-face interviews for the branch head position.'

Renu threw her head back and laughed in her usual, annoying manner. 'You really expect people at that level to land up on two days' notice for an interview – on New Year's Eve – and that too, a Saturday?'

Natasha gave her a cool, appraising look. 'Yes. I expect them to know that it's a great opportunity for them to get in a meeting with the national sales director for the job they've applied for.' She raised an eyebrow. 'Surely, some of the candidates you've been lining up value their career progression over a mere celebration?'

Renu returned her gaze. 'I'll check. But don't get your hopes up, Natasha.' She stood up. 'We'll miss you *terribly* at the getaway.'

Natasha managed to turn her snort into a cough. This would be Renu's chance to get in some serious flirting-time with Rishabh – it would take work to do it with family around but Natasha had faith in her. She seemed jealous of the continued attention Rishabh gave Natasha. Well, he was the same with all women – holding doors open, putting on an exaggeratedly attentive face when a female spoke up. He had the ability to make any woman feel like a princess, and Renu seemed to want it all for herself. Well, she could have it. As if on cue, Renu added, 'Rishabh has confirmed he'll be there, of course. And Nikhil said he'd let me know today. Do tell me if you change your mind.'

Was there supposed to be some sort of meaning there? Whatever. Natasha didn't have time for this shit. With another over-sweet smile that mirrored Renu's, she said, 'Have a good time. Don't get too drunk and end up doing something silly. After all, your little boys will be there too, right?'

Renu looked annoyed, but Natasha rounded the barb off with, 'Give my love to them.' She then looked at her laptop and frowned as if concentrating on something. Renu finally stalked off and Natasha pretended she couldn't hear her muttering, '*Still* just one *daughter*.'

Natasha scrolled through the messages on her phone. There it was again, another missed call from Priya. She had been calling incessantly. True, Natasha was supposed to call her back, but she hadn't found the time. Priya would understand – well, she should, anyway. Natasha had sent her a text with: 'I'm in a meeting, SMS please.' All she had received was, 'Please call back when free.' Well, she would. Eventually.

It had been a particularly bad day. First that teleconference with her entire team, wherein everyone had been so unnecessarily argumentative; then the run-in with Renu; and then Rishabh had wasted an entire hour and a half in the afternoon, getting her to explain the status of all the key accounts. As if the guy cared. He had barely been on three customer visits since he joined a month ago. She had that kind of customer interaction in a *week*.

She sighed. She was lingering, but it was nice to have some time to herself, even if it was inside a loo stall. She was in the furthest one at the end, which was the only one she ever went into because, she believed, it was the least used.

She heard some girls come into the ladies' room. They were of the giggling, 'let's go to the loo together' variety. The holiday season made them even sillier than usual, Natasha thought. Their voices echoed off the tiled walls.

'Hope he asks me to dance at the getaway.'

'The other one's cuter. But he's too quiet-types! Don't even know if he'll come.'

'Madam will make sure he comes. Have you seen how she's started dressing? Suddenly very hot-types.'

'Hitler's the same, yaar. Good for us! I knew she was totally sexless. Reserves all her energy for scaring her poor team, no? Did you see them today?'

A lesser mortal may have cringed and sat through the nonsense quietly, waiting for the idiots to leave. But this was Natasha. She immediately stood up and flushed the toilet loudly, almost drowning out the surprised gasps from the girls outside. She unlatched the door and stepped out, throwing them a long, cool look as she walked up to the mirrors and started washing her hands. She watched their shocked faces in the mirror as they glanced at each other, clearly wondering how much she had heard. It was a girl from marketing and her little pal from, naturally, HR. Natasha didn't recall their names, but she knew she would find out easily. She'd remember their faces.

They stood frozen as she finished washing up in silence before walking towards the door. She paused for a moment at the door and then turned around and said, 'Enjoy yourselves at the getaway.'

The marketing one had recovered enough to stammer, 'T-thanks, Natasha ma'am … You, er, won't be coming?'

'I don't think so. I'll probably be busy. You know, practising my salute.' Natasha raised her right hand and barked, 'Heil!'

The two girls paled with horror and guilt. Pasting a smile on her face, Natasha promised, 'But I'll be seeing *you* in the new year.'

Leaving the two frightened young girls practically clutching each other for support, Natasha sailed out of the door.

'Natasha ma'am, you're not keeping up! Let's see some *energy*, come on!'

Vicky's words snapped her back to attention. But the word 'energy' took her back almost immediately to the previous day. *Reserves all her energy for scaring her team.* Stupid idiots. Sexless, one had said. Dumbasses, faffing around at their jobs, waiting to find men stupid enough to marry them.

She was anything but sexless. She checked herself out in the mirror. She was the slimmest, sexiest, best-looking woman in the room. Well, that wasn't saying much, considering the aunties in Vicky's fitness class. Still, she was glad for the workout, it took her mind off office stuff. She did miss Ramakant though. He hadn't shown up again, and she felt a bit ashamed about having pulled that little trick on him with the Chopra. Perhaps she would call him in the new year and convince him it was a misunderstanding, and coax him to come back.

Or maybe just get a new yoga teacher.

She turned her attention to Vicky while he put them through a rigorous cyclical routine – squats, followed by thirty reverse crunches, lunges and then interval running around the periphery of the room. The air-conditioning was on, and it was winter, but Natasha was sweating as she applied herself to each exercise. Vicky looked more approving, and she felt better.

After the cool-down stretches, she picked up her water bottle and towel and turned to leave. The rest of the ladies crowded around Vicky as usual, this time ostensibly to exchange New Year's greetings with him. He called, 'Hey, Natasha ma'am! Are you going without saying happy New Year?'

'Well, it's still a couple of days away,' she said. 'But okay, have a good one.'

'Wait, wait. I wanted to talk to you about something.'

The small group of ladies parted unwillingly to make way for him, throwing Natasha wary glances and less-than-heartfelt New Year's wishes. She waited near the door, wondering what he wanted to say to her.

He walked up with a big smile as he pushed open the door to let her out. 'Sorry, I'm all hot and sweaty, or I'd have given you a big New Year hug.'

'That's okay,' Natasha muttered. The sweat glistened on his powerful arms. She didn't exactly find it repulsive. In fact, she was a little flattered by his attention today.

'Listen' – he cleared his throat – 'I've been wanting to speak to you for a while now, but you're always in a hurry. If you're not doing anything right now, I was wondering ... You want to go for a drive or something?'

Natasha hesitated. She had to admit, she liked this guy, but she didn't really know him that well. They had a light, friendly equation and part of her wanted to keep it that way. Besides, he was a sweet guy, claiming he was devoted to his new wife.

She wasn't sure she'd ever be able to execute her plan for flings with married men.

Sexless.

Well, she wasn't the one who had asked him out. And she was no saint.

She adjusted the strap of her revealing, purple workout top. It was starting to get chilly, but she refrained from slipping on her jacket. She gave Vicky her most alluring smile as she acquiesced. 'Sure. Let's go for a ride.'

Hopefully, he'd keep calling her 'ma'am'.

NINE

FLIGHT OF FANCY

'*You may now use your mobile. Thank you for flying with us and we hope you will give us the opportunity to serve you again.*'

The tinny, recorded female voice rang through the airplane as it taxied to a stop. Natasha stretched and, to the surprise of the old couple sitting next to her, snapped open her laptop for a last-minute review of the numbers to date for the Mumbai branch. She ignored their sidelong glances and they shrugged and stood up, jostling around for their cabin baggage, like the other passengers. She always thought it was a stupid and uncouth thing, this hurry to be swept along with the crowd. Typical Indian thing. Not so different from the local trains she used to take years ago, when she was a management trainee in Mumbai.

She sat in the twelfth row, near the emergency exit. She'd listened, in a bored manner, to the special instructions that came with the seat. Yes, she would be okay with pulling the red lever to open the door in an emergency, and hopefully, be the first one out of the plane. She had heard it about a hundred times, but it was worth the window and the extra leg space. Of course, she was entitled to business-class travel, a privilege she had given up due to the number of flights she took in a year. Naturally, all her direct reportees, the various branch heads, had to give up the privilege too. She made it a point to travel with IndiGo airlines whenever possible because they were usually on schedule, and they didn't even have a business class. Who cared about stupid frills like meals being included and other so-called comforts?

The aisles were jammed as the other passengers waited for the plane doors to open. Natasha glanced up once in a superior manner at the lot of them, packed like sardines. She caught the eye of two flight attendants standing patiently near the front and they gave her polite smiles, which she returned with a brief one, and then she turned back to the numbers on her Excel sheet.

Last week's bookings had been particularly bad – she knew that Enthu Anirban would be vociferous in his defence that it was due to the holiday season. She tried to focus on the pattern the numbers showed by sub-region, but found her concentration wavering. Memories of last night's tryst with Vicky were coming back again. She closed her eyes, annoyed. She had spent the whole morning thinking about it, even while getting ready for her trip, and it had been on her mind during most of the flight too, despite her attempts to keep such thoughts at bay. She opened her eyes and scowled at the numbers with renewed vigour. But they soon blurred again and she felt her cheeks turning pink.

—

They were at Vicky's beat-up old car. He bounded into the driver's seat and indicated for her to get into the other side. Well, what was she expecting from this guy – some chivalrous opening-of-the-door-for-the-lady? Hah. She went around and opened the door, feeling a little nervous for the first time. They hadn't even showered. Why couldn't they have set up to meet somewhere later instead of going out together like this right after a hot and sweaty workout?

It was warm in the car – she realized only now that she'd been shivering. It was cold outside but she still hadn't put on her neon-pink, post-workout jacket – it was wrapped loosely around her shoulders.

'I love that colour!' Vicky remarked, grinning at her in a friendly manner, but with a sudden shyness.

'You love neon pink?' Natasha glanced down at the jacket sleeves and then raised her eyebrows at him.

'No, I mean it's just very … workout-y!' he finished. She couldn't help but laugh, and felt slightly giddy as he started the car and revved up. He sped up very quickly and she told him, 'Hey – keep it slow. There's a speed limit. Don't forget I live here!'

'I didn't forget that, ma'am!' He slowed down obediently before they reached the gate, and gave the guard an exaggerated namaste. The guard peered in curiously and then snapped to attention when he saw Natasha in the passenger seat. He gave her a salute.

'He saluted you!' Vicky said incredulously. 'He never does that to me.'

'Must be only for the residents,' Natasha murmured a little self-consciously. She was tough on these guys. In fact, this particular one, Kishan, had been pulled into her ongoing war with Mrs Chopra on more than one occasion. Such as last summer's dripping air-conditioner episode, a figment of the Chopra's imagination, of course. But she definitely didn't want to be thinking about the old crone tonight.

She felt a sense of anticipation as they reached the highway. Where was he taking her? Was she nuts to be going out like this with someone she didn't know? He was hot all right, but she couldn't smother the growing feeling of anxiety.

Was she ready to go through with this? It was definitely a little sneaky. What kind of man cheated on his wife, anyway? And was that someone she wanted to be with? Well, not in the long term, but then something like this wasn't meant for the long term. Besides, if a guy wasn't getting what he needed in his marriage, and it was something that she was craving too – there wasn't all that much harm in it. Right?

She watched him crank up the music – some Latino beat he was bobbing his head to – looking happier than usual, and that was something.

She'd never been with a typical jock before. In fact, she'd always been attracted to the intellectual kind. Had this guy even been to college?

'Which college did you go to, Vicky?'

'Huh? Oh. KMC.'

That wasn't bad. 'Sports quota?'

He looked at her to see if she was serious and then laughed loudly. She supposed that's why she liked him – anyone else might have been insulted. She realized it was a stupid thing to say.

'No. 80 per cent in twelfth boards, madam.' He added jokingly, 'You ladies all think I'm just a pretty face.'

He caught the embarrassed look on her face and guffawed. She wondered when he would make his move.

They reached a relatively empty stretch on the highway, and he slowed down.

'Natasha ma'am.'

'Yes, Vicky?'

'There's something … I've been wanting to tell you.'

'Go ahead,' she said in a soft tone, her breath slowing as her heartbeat sped up.

'I wouldn't want you to think less of me…' He looked troubled. 'It's something I have been … lying about, to almost everyone I meet. But I have some sort of … connect with you, and feel bad about letting you believe it too.'

Huh? What was this? She hadn't counted on a confession right now, and she definitely didn't want to deal with anyone else's shit. 'Well,' she began, 'maybe you shouldn't, Vicky…'

'Oh, but I have to!' He looked frustrated. 'I have to get it out of my system.'

Trapped.

'Go on then.' She leaned back, resigned.

'It's just that I … I'm…' Vicky started out uncertainly but then ended in a rush: '*Notmarried*.'

'Pardon?' Natasha wasn't sure she had heard him right. 'You're not … married?'

'No!' Vicky was almost shouting. He pulled the car to the side of the road suddenly, and she jolted forward, before being snapped back by the seatbelt. He switched off the engine and turned to her.

'I just couldn't take it any more, Natasha ma'am! I'm thirty-five years old, but I don't want to get married. I just want to be able to focus on my career. But these ladies! These aunties in my classes. They try to … to…' He finished in a rush again, and she could see, even in the dim light, that his cheeks were flushed, 'to take advantage of me!'

'I see.' Natasha tried to register what he was saying. She tried to look on the bright side: if he was telling her all this, she figured it meant that at least he didn't see her as an aunty trying to take advantage of him – never mind that she was, she thought guiltily. And *this* was why he had wanted some time alone with her? She felt the itchy feeling in her throat and coughed a little, and then managed—

'But … I don't get it … Why did you have to lie about being married? You even showed the class photos of some girl the last time.'

'My *cousin*, Bindu,' Vicky practically sobbed. She edged away a little in her seat, but he didn't notice. 'She's in Allahabad and she's the only person I know who's not on Facebook. So I just showed those aunties some snaps I took the last time I visited there. But it didn't make a difference! I thought, if I told them I'm married and deeply in love with my wife and just waiting for her to show up in Delhi to live with me, they would back off. But they don't back off, Natasha ma'am! They don't! They want it even more. Can you believe it?'

'No,' she assured him, thinking well, yeah. Nothing made a man more attractive to a horny aunty than the fact that he was happily married. It showed a certain dedication and sensitivity. She wasn't going to explain that to him, though. It would reveal too much about her own twisted thinking. She waited for him to calm down. 'Are you okay?'

He took a deep, shuddering breath. 'Yes. Thank you for listening, Natasha ma'am. It's just been too much to deal with. It's more in this colony somehow. My other students aren't like this.'

'Wait – aren't your other students … class five school kids?' Natasha recalled how he had introduced himself the first time.

'Yes,' he admitted. 'I've never had to deal with this type before! You're so … different, you know, Natasha ma'am.'

'I am?' Natasha decided she would have to settle for a little flattery tonight. Nothing else was going to happen.

'Yes.' He looked at her fondly. 'You act like a totally cold person, but I know you're not really like that. I feel some sort of bond with you. I knew I could trust you with this.'

Natasha tried to smile and he went on, 'Somehow, I've always thought of you as an older sister. Never had one, you know.'

Natasha's smile froze on her face.

'What?' she said through clenched teeth. He looked surprised and she continued, trying to keep her tone even, 'I'll have you know that I'm just thirty-five. Your age.'

'Is it? What month were you born?'

'Does it matter?'

'Whoa. Sorry, sorry…' He was fumbling for words. 'That's not what I meant … I mean, it's not about age. It's about the feeling. A *bond*.'

She was trembling with rage, but recalled her own stupid line about the sports quota. He hadn't been insulted by that, so why should she react now?

But even as the anger subsided, she felt incredibly stupid – he thought of her as an older sister. This was beyond idiotic.

She sighed and buried her face in her hands – her hands were a little cold and her face felt like it was burning. 'Vicky,' she all but groaned, 'you think we can head back now?'

'Already?' he said in a surprised, slightly hurt tone. 'But

we've barely been out twenty minutes. I was hoping we could get to know each other better.'

'What do you want to know?' she said with her hands still on her face.

'Tell me anything! Where is your family? Are you spending New Year's with them?'

Oh god. She lowered her hands and gave him a long look. 'Forget me, Vicky. Let's just focus on you. Have you thought about why you don't like women?'

'It's not that I don't like women!' Vicky protested. 'It's just that I'm not ready for a relationship.'

'So you've had relationships before, then?'

'Well … No. I wanted to … wait for the right one.'

'So,' Natasha said thoughtfully, 'you've been … saving yourself for the right one? The one you're going to marry?'

'Yes.' He looked a little ashamed but then his face cleared as she looked at him sympathetically. 'Most people don't understand. But I knew you were different.' His expression became almost loving. 'Natasha ma'am, can I call you didi?'

That did it.

'Vicky,' she said, ignoring his question, 'haven't you thought about it? Never having been with a woman; not feeling the draw even now…' She raised her eyebrows at him knowingly.

He frowned at her in confusion and then after a moment broke into loud protest. 'Hey! No! It's not like that! I mean, *I'm* not like that. I mean, it's okay and all, I have friends who are gay … But not *me*.'

She sat back with her arms crossed over her chest. 'Are you sure? How would you know if you haven't tried,' she said with a look full of meaning, 'either way?'

'Oh, I think I would know.' He let out an uncertain, wavering laugh that died quickly. He finished in a croak, 'Wouldn't I?'

Natasha shrugged. 'It's the end of the year. A good time for reflection.' She glanced at her watch. 'Sorry, Vicky, but I really have to get home now. Got an early-morning flight to Mumbai. And I know you've got a bunch of things to think about too!'

He stared at her for a few moments, and then nodded in a somewhat dubious manner. He started the car and swung it out on to the road. He was nowhere near his earlier, enthusiastic self, and a part of her felt sorry for making him feel this way. He'd obviously hoped to lighten his burden. Well, she wasn't a damn priest. And his hopes were not the only ones that had been dashed tonight. She stared out of the window stonily and unseeingly as he drove her home in silence.

Even now, she stared absently out of the plane window. It was only when she heard the polite 'Excuse me, ma'am' from the male flight attendant that she noticed the plane had emptied. She nodded at him and he smiled and went off. She hurriedly stuffed her laptop in its case and got up, straightening her navy-blue A-line skirt. She then reached up for her black travel bag.

She was facing the back of the plane, so she didn't notice the way the female attendant at the front smirked as she leaned over to whisper to the male one: 'Very lost today, Miss Corporate is. Didn't demand anything the whole flight.'

'Come on. She's not always that bad. I think she's cute,' said the young man, eyeing Natasha.

'What? She's horrible!'

He shushed her as Natasha turned around and made her way to the front of the plane, breezing past them. They called out their final goodbye of the flight in unison, 'Bye, ma'am. Happy New Year!'

This made her pause. She narrowed her eyes as she turned around and corrected them. 'Not yet.'

They hadn't received this response from any of the other passengers. They managed identical, sheepish smiles. The male attendant finally managed, 'Advance wishes?' but the words were addressed to her back as she stalked away with purposeful steps.

'See?' said the female attendant, giving the man a cat-like smile. He responded with a small shrug that suggested 'You win'. Then they both stepped aside to let the cleaners get into the craft.

TEN

RESOLUTIONS

'Is that it? No more?' Natasha demanded.

The HR lady Indu shook her head with a practised smile. She had just poked her head in to check on Natasha, now that the last candidate had left the conference room. She let herself in and took the chair opposite Natasha. 'It's New Year's Eve, Natasha! We're lucky that these many candidates showed up at all. Find anyone suitable?'

Natasha pushed her hair off her eyes. She hated the way the Mumbai weather made it all frizzy. She had straightened it this morning as usual, before leaving for the airport, but the humidity here was impossible, and just the taxi ride from the airport to the branch office had undone all her straightening. It made her feel dowdy and careless.

'No one remotely suitable,' she told Indu crisply. 'They didn't even meet half of the requirements for what we need in this role. Who's done the shortlisting anyway?'

Indu's smile disappeared at Natasha's brusque tone. 'Well, I did the first lot … and sent my shortlist to Renu, and she picked eight. You met the three that showed up today. Three said they were travelling for the holidays, and two raised issues about meeting at our office, saying they couldn't risk being seen and expected to meet at a more, uh, neutral location for such a senior position.'

'Well, I already told you that's nonsense. I'm not going to go waste time waiting in a hotel lobby for someone. It's an official meeting, it should happen at an official location.'

'Natasha, but it's the norm in most places now, for such senior positions, to meet at outside locations first...'

Natasha waved her objection aside, irritated. 'It's strange that you didn't get better matched applicants. You used our own recruitment management system, right?'

'Er, yes...' Indu didn't sound sure, and Natasha looked up at her sharply.

'You *did* use our own recruitment management system for this?'

'Well.' Indu looked unhappy. 'I did put up the requirement on our corporate job board and was going to post on BizTech Plus too, but then when Renu said you'd be coming on the thirty-first, I thought it would just be faster for me to get the team to manually pull people out of the existing database and call them up.'

'Our system promises faster results than any other, Indu. You know that.' Natasha's expression was incredulous. 'You're a part of the company, and you should be evangelizing it in your fraternity. If you aren't going to even use it...'

'I did use it. The team uses it regularly too.' Indu was looking obstinate now. 'But it takes time to figure out how to work the system and fill in the details, and we keep having so many upgrades that it's hard to keep up...'

'The product upgrades are always based on feedback from your brethren, and your team too,' Natasha pointed out, looking at her through narrowed eyes.

Indu was sullen. 'It keeps changing. And anyway,' she affirmed, 'we are lucky these guys showed up. I guess you'll just have to make another trip here in Jan to meet candidates more suitable to your needs.'

She got up somewhat abruptly and muttered, 'Happy New Year' to Natasha without waiting for her reply. 'Not yet,' Natasha muttered after her, on autopilot. She looked after her – she hadn't seen pleasant-faced Indu so miffed before. What was making her so grumpy? Natasha had just been making a valid point about her using the system that they were all supposed to be marketing as a complete HR management technology solution. She'd always thought Indu was a decent sort, but apparently all HR folk were alike. Who could help getting their brain addled if they reported to Renu for an extended period of time?

Happy New Year, she'd said. Why did people insist on wishing each other a week before, or into, the new year? What was the big deal? It came every year. And nothing changed. All that fuss about nothing, interrupting work for no reason. Holiday season. Bah!

Recognizing that she was teetering dangerously close to Scrooge territory, she shook her head. *Come on, I'm not that bad*, she told herself. She had finished the day's review early and had released the team members by afternoon. They were free to go home or go and party or do whatever they wanted. Of course, it hadn't been an easy review. They were missing a leader, but that meant they were expected to rise to the occasion and try harder. Anirban had clearly been nervous, and she hadn't had a chance to speak with him separately and tell him not to get his hopes up about getting to branch head any time soon. She wanted someone senior and mature enough for the role, and couldn't ignore how similar this was to the position she had been in when Aman announced the new business head role. Well, if she had handled being bypassed, so could Anirban. This was how it was in the corporate world. Things happened for you when the time was right, not when *you* decided it was time.

She stood up and drained her cup of coffee. Yuck. All cold now. She reached for her laptop bag, tired, and coughed a little. That stupid feeling in her throat wasn't going away no matter how much she ignored it. Anirban appeared at the door.

'You're still here?' Natasha was taken aback. 'I figured you'd left after the morning meetings. What happened to all the "plans"?'

Anirban was a fresh-faced young boy – man, really, not that much younger than her. His spirits were never crushed for too long, and she figured that would help him last in sales and get somewhere, someday. Maybe if he developed some political smarts. He was smiling shyly at her.

'I was just waiting to ask you if you'd like to join us – we have a team dinner planned for New Year's.'

'You too?' Natasha pushed her hair out of her face again, frazzled. 'What's with all the collective New Year festivities, anyway? Aren't you supposed to spend it with family?'

'Our families are going to be there. Some of us had plans for the corporate getaway but...' Anirban checked himself. She kept her face impassive – she knew what he had been going to say and was glad he hadn't. He finished on a different note, 'Anyway, we are also like one big family, right?'

Natasha looked closely at his face. She was tempted to laugh, but she could sense that Anirban really meant it. Strange. She nodded seriously, and then said, 'Well, you guys go ahead and have a good time.' She smiled at him for the first time that evening. This guy was all right. He was holding the team together pretty well. The others seemed to look up to him. He would do for the time being.

'Are you sure?' he pressed. 'You've got plans with friends … or family, here?'

Natasha's smile disappeared and she said airily, 'Well, go on. Quit hanging around. You seriously wasted time waiting for me? You could have just messaged and I'd have told you to carry on.'

Anirban looked taken aback. 'Oh, okay. I just thought … Okay. See you when you're here next, then?'

'Very soon,' Natasha promised him as she pressed a button on her phone and held it to her ear. 'Hello, driver? *Main aa rahi hoon neeche. Aap kaunse* gate *pe aayenge*?'

'Okay then,' Anirban said, clear that he was being dismissed as Natasha cut the call and frowned at the messages on her phone.

'Happy New Year, Natasha.'

'Yeah, er, you too, Anirban,' Natasha said with a forced smile, which disappeared as soon as he left the room. 'Not yet,' she added through gritted teeth. She waited until he had disappeared from view, out of the rapidly emptying office, and then finally picked up her things and exited the room.

She glanced at her watch as she took the lift down to the ground floor. Only 6 p.m. She could have actually taken an evening flight back and been home and in bed before midnight. Oh well. It was ridiculously foggy and crowded in Delhi because of New Year's so it was better that she was returning tomorrow. But what was she going to do for the next few hours?

The weather was sultry as she stepped out to wait for her taxi. Dumb, typical Mumbai weather – even now, when it was supposed to be winter in saner parts of the country. She took out a cigarette and lit it, the little cough back even before she inhaled. Her hair flapped in her face and she batted at it – bloody misbehaving mop – she couldn't stand it any more.

She knew how she would be spending New Year's Eve.

'You sure?'

The tall, curly-haired hairdresser pursed his lips as he surveyed Natasha's hair. He shook his head even before Natasha could reply, saying in a decided manner, 'No. You shouldn't.'

'What?' Natasha said sharply. 'What do you mean?'

'You shouldn't cut it short,' said the hairdresser. 'It won't suit your face. You have a sharp, pointy face, you should go for a more sensitive, feminine look with the hair. I can give it a little bob here, and you—'

'I want it short,' Natasha said, stern this time.

'No, you don't.'

Natasha laughed in disbelief. This would never have happened if she was back at her local salon in Gurgaon. Those guys knew better than to question her. But this fellow apparently thought that he was god's gift to fashion or something.

'Look, it's *my* hair,' she hissed. 'You cut it the way I want, okay? Or I will just take my business elsewhere.'

The guy had the temerity to yawn at this. 'It's New Year's

Eve, honey. You think you'll get an appointment that easily at any halfway-decent place? I don't need to be doing this right now, you know. It's almost closing time. I have a family to get to, too.'

Honey? She glowered at him in the mirror. 'Why don't you just go ahead and do your damn job quickly, then?'

'I'm the expert here, right?' He certainly had some confidence, this fellow. They were definitely bolder here, in Mumbai. 'And I'm telling you, it won't work.' He took a strand of her hair and examined it in a detached but slightly disgusted manner. 'And I've seen this before. You're a Delhi girl, you come here unprepared, without conditioning or spray, and can't take the weather, so you decide to blame your hair. Blame yourself!'

Natasha decided she'd had enough. She made as if to get up, and he changed tack quickly. 'Wait, wait. Why don't you just go in for rebonding, if you're so keen on straight and silky hair?'

'Kindly stop trying to maximize your revenue at my expense,' Natasha snapped. 'I'm not paying six thousand rupees to have my hair permanently damaged.'

'It's seven thousand five hundred here, and the damage is not permanent. You get new hair over time, you know,' said the impossible man.

Natasha had figured out how to play him. She turned around and looked him straight in the eye. 'Well, never mind. I guess it's not just anyone who can take up a challenge to make short hair work. It probably takes a lot of skill.'

The guy tilted his head to the side and looked at her appraisingly for a long while. He reached out and tucked a few strands of hair behind her left ear. She stood still, fighting the urge to bat his hand away.

'Okay. Fine,' he finally said. 'Sit down. I'll give you what you want. And I will find a way to make it work.'

Natasha plopped herself back down. The curly-haired man finally took out his scissors, rolled up his sleeves and went to work as his young trainees watched, awestruck, from a safe distance.

She stood on the balcony of her hotel room, a glass of wine in her hand. From up here on the tenth floor, Mumbai looked almost pretty. She gazed at the chain of yellow lights that surrounded a stretch of beach by the roadside, and she could see people crowded there in droves. Even more of them than usual. New Year's Eve.

The temperature had dropped and it was pleasant outside, much better than the balmy evening. The air felt cool on her neck and she reached up yet again, with a sense of surprise and wonder at the absence of her hair. The Curly-Haired Snob had actually done a fabulous job – they had both surveyed the results in the mirror with quiet satisfaction. She'd gazed at her hair, while he'd watched her face. A pixie cut, he announced, in fashion amongst all the Hollywood celebrities. Not that she cared. It looked great – it highlighted her high cheekbones, and somehow softened her overall look. 'You look like a fashion model,' he had declared.

'Let's not get carried away,' Natasha had muttered drily. But she gave him a handsome tip and they parted on extraordinarily cordial terms, given their rough beginning.

She lit a cigarette and decided it had been a good idea to avoid being at home on New Year's Eve. Christmas had been bad enough, with people having the gall to ring her bell and ask her to come down for the community celebrations. What bloody community celebration? She bet half the people out there didn't know what Christmas was even celebrated for, they were just trying to find another excuse to party and fool their kids with silly concepts like Santa Claus. She had refused the invitation from the club secretary, who apparently had nothing better to do than go knocking on people's doors. The friendly Mrs Jain was new to the post and had said, 'Oh come on – it's only you and Mrs Chopra missing. Everyone else is there. Come, come, I'm sure if you come, we can also convince her.' Natasha immediately feigned a bad stomach – the woman backed off only after Natasha confided she really couldn't be more than twenty feet from her loo, else the consequences would be disastrous. Natasha then directed her downstairs, saying, 'I'm sure Mrs Chopra wants to come – but please make sure you ask her many times until she agrees, she's the shy variety.' Natasha was sure Mrs Jain would know of Mrs Chopra's reputation, but it seemed worth a shot. The club sec looked like she'd had a few glasses of wine already, and Natasha put on a sad face. 'Such a wonderful old lady, Mrs C, and so misunderstood. She just needs a friendly person like you to drag her into the thick of things.' Inspired, Mrs Jain trotted off with a look of determination, wishing Natasha's stomach a speedy recovery.

Natasha leaned on the railing, a little light-headed with the wine and smoke. She coughed – dammit, when was it going to go away? She stared out at the convivial scene outside until she couldn't stand it any more. She put out her cigarette, went back inside and sank into the overstuffed chair by the bed. Much better being in a place where you couldn't be disturbed. She liked being by herself, especially on days like this.

Her phone beeped on the table, and she ignored it. Probably just Priya again. Why didn't she just give her a little more space? She had her own family, her little baby and parents and so on. Why was she so insistent on talking to Natasha? They didn't have anything in common any more – she didn't like hearing about the baby's exploits; and she didn't feel like explaining stuff about her own life either.

Her throat itched and she coughed again, clearing it a couple of times. The phone beeped again. Couldn't be anyone from work tonight. At this very moment, most of her colleagues would be at the stupid getaway, partying. Not that she cared in the least. Renu would be in her element, flirting with Rishabh. And maybe even Nikhil. She didn't like how she cared a little about that. Well, there wasn't much Renu could do by way of damage, Natasha assured herself, taking another long sip of wine. After all, their families were around. Families tended to hold you back. It was probably a bore being married, but it did keep things in check. At least, she assumed so. It was her decision that she didn't need a family of any sort. It worked. Things were simpler. She was just living for herself, and that was how it should be. After all, we come alone, and we go alone. Hah, she smirked at her glass of wine. Was she getting philosophical? That wasn't like her. No. Not philosophical. It was practical. Let the Priyas of the world go ahead and have their families in their bubbles – she begrudged them nothing. But that sort of thing wasn't for her.

Her phone continued to buzz. Probably just stupid New Year's messages starting to come in – silly, meaningless mass messages.

'Not yet,' she muttered, 'not yet.' It was her fourth glass of wine. The bottle was almost empty, and she would soon have to order another one. She closed her eyes and rested her head against the back of the chair. Room service was nice. Who needed anything else, or anyone else?

We come alone. And we go alone. It was true, and it suited her just fine.

PART TWO

ONE

SOMETHING DIFFERENT

'What's with the crowd today?'

Natasha was muttering to herself as she walked to an empty table. There was no need to keep her voice low; the group of delinquents at the far table – *her* usual table – were being too loud. What were they doing here? This coffee shop had always been more of a corporate joint, frequented by executives from the nearby buildings. In fact, at this particular hour on Wednesdays, she was invariably the only one here. She'd brought her laptop along, hoping for some peace and quiet. Maybe it was a spillover from the stupid multiplex which had opened next door.

Muthu greeted her in his quiet, courteous way, and she nodded her acknowledgement a little coldly – really, he could have given those kids any other table. She noted that the friendly young boy from Ludhiana was still haunting the place. Great. In a moment, he came up to her table with a cheery, 'Happy New Year, ma'am!'

'Too late,' Natasha said with a tight smile. It was the tenth of January. Why the hell were people still wishing each other?

Ludhiana Boy looked like he'd been expecting this reaction, and stood there with an all-too-polite smile that pissed her off. She raised her eyebrows at him and he said quickly, 'Your usual, madam? Cappuccino?'

His confidence was amusing, considering how he had messed up her order the last time.

'No. Just get me an espresso shot.' She needed something strong today. Besides, she'd been thinking of giving up milk in addition to wheat. She'd been feeling bloated even though she hadn't been eating much, and it was bothering her.

Of course, a lot of things were bothering her. She scowled at her laptop screen as she tried to find the file she was looking for. Where had she saved it? She was usually well organized, but it had been a bad week. Sales had been slower than usual – thankfully, customers and salespeople had finally decided to come back after their New Year's holidays. She would have to schedule a review soon and take stock of what was happening. Deepesh was to sit with her and explain the Delhi branch numbers and status, with the key accounts, and she planned to visit several key customers over the next week.

Rishabh had come back to the office yesterday, and in his usual manner, had already held an impromptu functional head review. He had greeted her affably, and his gaze had lingered as he complimented her on the new hairdo. She'd thanked him and turned the conversation back to the sales numbers and the immediate action needed to correct them. He had seemed to be half-listening, and had suggested they set up another meeting to review things in a day or two. She had managed to keep herself from rolling her eyes. The past several days, while he was on leave, had been enough to make her forget all about him. She hated being called in for his reviews – they achieved nothing. Status updates, status updates. What was this, bloody Facebook? Natasha had nothing to do with Facebook, and she refused to so much as open an account, even though everyone in the office was apparently active on it. In fact, even Aman had confessed to checking it compulsively on his phone these days. Wow. When did people actually work?

She was used to being the one asking for reviews, and hers served an actual purpose – to drive her team to achieve their targets. They needed to know someone was watching their numbers like a hawk. Rishabh's reviews were more like time-pass, each functional head giving what Rishabh called a 'high-level' overview. Renu loved these – it was yet another opportunity to gaze admiringly at him as he spoke, usually just paraphrasing and summarizing.

He was a skilled orator, and Natasha amused herself by watching Renu stare at him. The man knew how to use a lot of words without actually saying anything. Useful. For him.

Nikhil hadn't come into the meeting yesterday – just before New Year's, he had presented briefly on the approach being adopted for developing the Innovation Funnel, mentioning that the larger group would be involved in prioritizing the projects. She had listened with great interest and found herself impressed with his one neat slide – it laid out a good framework, very well structured – and yet she thought quite a few of the ideas themselves were breakthroughs. It hadn't escaped her notice that, in sharp contrast to Rishabh, Nikhil used the word 'we' a lot more than 'I', though he was equally self-assured. It made her wonder about her own style and she'd made a mental note to watch her language.

She'd been looking forward for another update and had felt marginally disappointed when he hadn't shown up yesterday.

Well, these meetings were optional for him, and she couldn't blame him for often opting out. But she had been wondering where he was. She hadn't seen him on the terrace either, though she had made it a point to go there for her smokes at exactly the same time she had run into him before. Oh well, maybe he wasn't back from his New Year break yet.

She finally managed to find the latest file with the regional sales update, and tried to concentrate on the trend lines.

'Madam, your espresso.'

She frowned and nodded, indicating for Punju Boy to place it on the table. He did, but continued to hover annoyingly.

She looked up and he was gazing at her with a smile. She snapped, 'What?'

'Nothing, madam. I just wanted to tell you that your new hair is very nice. Top class! Like a model!'

Natasha narrowed her eyes. The gall. The cheek. Who the hell was this guy to interrupt her work with such a personal comment? She opened her mouth to tell him exactly what she thought of him, but at that exact moment, one of the delinquents called out, 'Oye, boss! "*Dhoom Machale*"! Turn up the radio, ya? I love that song.'

Friendly Punju Boy grinned at him and hurried away towards the radio. And Sunidhi Chauhan's voice filled the café as the teenagers laughed and pushed their chairs around, as if they hadn't been loud and obnoxious enough already.

Natasha gritted her teeth. This was ridiculous. There was no way she could work here with so much noise – besides, she found Sunidhi Chauhan's voice particularly nasal and all her songs very irritating. She looked around for Muthu and caught his eye. He looked on in a helplessly apologetic manner, and gave her an eloquent shrug. The message was clear. The riff-raff were not his preferred clients, but they were customers all the same.

She turned away, exasperated. She would stop coming here. This place was going to the dogs. The kids burst into a round of wolf-whistles and howls at some private joke, possibly aimed at her. *Dogs.*

She took a sip of her espresso and almost gagged. No milk, no sugar. Why would anyone *do* this to themselves? Well, it had been her choice and she certainly wasn't going to give that idiot boy the satisfaction of serving her the cappuccino he'd suggested and which she so badly craved right now. She forced down another sip, and couldn't wait to get out of here. Bloody waste of time it had turned out.

She felt a little better when the caffeine hit her. It had been a bad night – she didn't know why she was so restless of late. Those weird dreams she had been having over the last ten nights were taking their toll. It was strange – she usually didn't have dreams, or didn't remember them the next day if she did, but these recent ones were both vivid and confusing. They featured a little girl who looked about nine or ten, with curly brown hair and big eyes. Strange, but she was choosing not to think too much about it. She would just have to start taking pills if this went on for much longer. It might start affecting her productivity at work.

She bravely drained the remnants of her disgusting beverage. She had intended to sleep in this morning, but that idiot had come and rung the bell at 7 a.m. She'd rolled out of bed, cursing Jamuna for coming in an hour earlier than usual, and had opened the door, shivering in her nightgown, to discover it was one of the guards. Suddenly conscious that she was braless, she had crossed her arms over her chest, demanding to know what he wanted. He kept his eyes on her face, and murmured that he had been asked to investigate who was feeding Kalu. Bleary-eyed and infuriated, she enquired as to whether he was feeling quite ready for the mental hospital yet. He explained that Kalu was a stray dog who had been hanging around the colony and seemed to show a particular proclivity to this building.

Ah. Natasha had noticed the mangy black mutt hanging around the building entrance a few times – he wagged his tail whenever she passed him. She liked dogs, but wasn't going to encourage strays, and so always just walked past him. The guard had some nerve implying she was the one feeding him. And that too, so early in the morning! She snapped at him, saying she had no idea what he was talking about and that he would do better to ask his stupid questions at a more decent hour. He protested, saying he had seen the dog slipping into the building just a few minutes back, but Natasha slammed the door on his face. She went back to bed, but it was too late. There was no way she was going to get any sleep. She tossed and turned and fretted and fumed until Jamuna rang the bell.

She stood up and picked up her things, leaving two hundred-rupee notes on the table. Not that the guy deserved the tip, she just didn't feel like seeing his face as he brought back the change. Ignoring Muthu as well, she swept out of the café, certain she would never go back.

The cold of January hit her hard after the toasty warmth of the café. Adjusting her laptop bag over her shoulder, she fumbled in her coat pocket for a cigarette. She lit up and took a long, grateful drag. The smoke calmed her, but within a few seconds, it was irritating her throat and she coughed.

She suddenly remembered that Priya had first pointed it out at this very café, months ago. Shit. She *still* hadn't called her back.

She was just stubbing out the cigarette when she saw someone approaching her with long strides.

'Hey. I *thought* it was someone I knew!'

It was Nikhil. She was surprised to see him – but then, the office was only five minutes away, and she wasn't the only one who walked over here for breaks. It had only been a couple of weeks since they had seen each other, but somehow it felt like ages. His hair was a little longer. Was he looking even more handsome now? He came up to her and grinned, the dimple back in his cheek. She smiled at him, self-conscious.

'Happy New Year, Natasha,' he said warmly.

'You too,' she murmured. It was the best she could do, certainly better than her usual snarky response.

'And nice hair,' he said, and for the first time since coming back to work, she felt really good about her new haircut. It had elicited mixed reactions in the office, even though she'd tried to make it clear that she didn't care for feedback. Rishabh had handed out his fake compliments about how it was so professional and yet so feminine; while Renu remarked snidely that her husband had stated his preference for long hair on *her*, but how nice it was that Natasha could afford to be so daring since she didn't have anyone to please but herself.

Nikhil smiled down at her. 'You look cute.'

Cute. Natasha laughed out loud. 'What?' said Nikhil, eyebrows raised.

'I don't know.' Natasha felt a little light-headed. 'Can't remember the last time someone used that word for me.' She shook her head. 'I'm way past that age.'

'What are you talking about? You're young. I just turned forty.'

'Wow.' Natasha looked at his face closely. 'That *is* old.'

'Thanks.'

'No, I mean,' Natasha fumbled, going red, 'I meant, it's just – you certainly don't look that old.'

'Oh, good.' His eyes crinkled at the corners as he smiled.

Natasha looked away for a moment, feeling a little silly. Then she said brightly, 'Hey, you want a smoke?' She fumbled in her pocket again and then paused, wondering if he was the Benson and Hedges type. Obviously not. Which one had he been smoking that day on the terrace?

He shook his head slowly – he really had a warm, lovely open grin. His eyes almost closed when he smiled widely. Forty or not, this guy was hot. 'I've given up, Natasha. New Year resolution.'

Oh. So she wasn't going to run into him on the terrace again. She felt a faint sense of disappointment. Why did that matter? 'That's great, Nikhil.' She tried to sound enthusiastic.

'Yes, well, my little daughter emotionally blackmailed me. I don't know where she gets it from. She's all of seven.'

'An inborn trait?' Natasha suggested lightly. 'Or perhaps she gets it from her mom?'

'Unlikely.' Nikhil's smile turned wistful. 'She never knew her.'

What? 'Umm … really?' It wasn't the most sensitive reaction. This was difficult territory for Natasha. Personal conversations made her uncomfortable.

Nikhil sighed. 'Well, my wife died giving birth to her. It was a haemorrhage and they couldn't control the bleeding.'

He saw the shocked look on Natasha's face and paused. 'Sorry, you didn't need to hear the details.'

'No, it's ... *I'm* sorry,' Natasha said in a hoarse whisper, feeling sick to the stomach.

'I know.' Nikhil nodded. 'Well, it was a long time ago. It was difficult when we lost her, but I had my hands full with Tisha. I decided right away I wouldn't let her feel the lack of a parent – well, as far as I could help it. She's doing really well, though. I'm a pretty good single dad, you know.' He was grinning proudly now and his eyes twinkled, but she was unable to smile back.

Tisha. This was the first time he'd said his daughter's name. It somehow made her more real. Tisha. Little girl without a mom. She instinctively knew Nikhil meant it – he was probably a fabulous dad. But it sounded absolutely horrible, what he had been through. She found that she couldn't say anything yet.

Nikhil looked closely at her face. 'Wow. I just realized I haven't spoken to anyone about this in, maybe, years.'

Natasha nodded. She had noticed he wasn't any more open about his personal life than she was. Not in public, at least. Now she was beginning to understand why.

'Must have been interesting, answering questions at the New Year thing, then,' she managed, trying to keep the conversation as light as Nikhil seemed to want it to be.

'Oh, I didn't go for that.'

'You didn't?' He hadn't been with Renu and company on New Year's after all? Natasha tried to ignore how ridiculously happy this made her.

'Nope. Stayed home and watched Doordarshan with my

kid.' He laughed. 'Sad, right? But we enjoyed it, although Tisha fell asleep at 11 and I had to tuck her in.' He looked straight into her eyes. 'And you? Partied in Mumbai?'

'Hah. Well, kind of.' She was flattered he remembered where she'd been on New Year's Eve. 'Sat alone in a hotel room getting drunk.'

'Really?' He was laughing. 'Hey, that might actually be sadder than mine!'

'Than DD?' Natasha laughed teasingly. 'Nope. I think that honour is all yours!'

She shivered unconsciously and coughed again.

'Hey, you've still got that cough?' He sounded concerned. She shook her head but couldn't reply because of another bout that came over her. Pesky thing, why was it ruining the moment?

'It's cold,' Nikhil said gently. 'I guess we better go back.'

'Sure.' Natasha's eyes were watering with the effort of trying to control her cough. 'I've been out for too long anyway. Let's go.'

They walked back towards their office building in comfortable silence. Natasha's mind raced as she tried to digest all that she had just heard. She felt a sense of warm admiration for Nikhil's strength and spirit and positivity; his unfamiliar blend of empathy and curiosity. Amongst other things.

Somehow, laughing and talking with this guy was just so easy. That was it – he put her at ease and she knew she was on the verge of letting her guard down with him. The way he had with her.

She stiffened at the realization and started to walk a little quicker. She barely registered his surprise as he increased his pace to keep up with her, but he didn't say anything and she made sure she stayed half a step ahead of him.

She would definitely have to watch out for this one.

TWO

DARNED DOG

'Didi?'

Jamuna's soft voice was always over-polite and tentative, which got Natasha's goat. As usual, she was interrupting Natasha's busy morning routine, probably with a stupid question about what to cook. Natasha had just finished dressing and was in the middle of applying some light makeup in front of the mirror. She was also mentally preparing herself for the day ahead, running through the various tasks she had lined up. She turned to the door and saw Jamuna hovering uncertainly and got all the more irritated.

'What is it now?' Natasha said curtly. 'I've already told you not to disturb me in the morning with silly things. What?'

Jamuna lowered her eyes and looked as though she would withdraw, but then held her ground, repeating, 'Didi...'

Natasha put down her lipstick with a sigh, crossed her arms and waited. Jamuna found the courage to go on. 'Didi, Preeti was saying ... about finding a job...'

Natasha's eyes narrowed. Jamuna's young daughter had come to the flat on two occasions when Jamuna was ill. She was about fourteen but looked younger, and Natasha had felt uncomfortable when she offered to clean up in lieu of her mother. Natasha had refused, asking her to go home and just tell Jamuna to hurry up and get better. She'd sent the girl away with five hundred-rupee notes both times, pressing them into her hand, muttering, 'For medicines.' She liked the look of her – she was slight but stood straight. She was neat and clean in the simple hand-me-down clothing she wore, and had bright, intelligent eyes. Jamuna had told her that she was doing very well in school. It was clear that a lot of importance was given to her education, despite her being a girl. Well, since she was the oldest of four sisters, Natasha supposed the family didn't have much choice. So why a job now?

'Are you making her drop out?' Natasha asked sharply.

Jamuna hesitated. 'Didi, she is the oldest. Her father lost his job, back to the drink again. He gave me another beating last night.'

Natasha winced. She was wary of getting too involved in Jamuna's many problems. It would just open the floodgates and she wouldn't be able to help her out anyway. Jamuna went on, 'We were running short of money, and so Preeti was asking if there is any job in this colony; she can come with me in the morning and go back when I finish work at the other houses at about 7 p.m., so—'

Natasha cut in, 'She is not going to get a job. She is too young.'

'Nahin, Didi,' Jamuna protested. 'She turned fourteen last month … At fourteen, it is *allow*.'

Natasha wasn't buying it. 'It may be "allow", but it still isn't right.'

Jamuna opened her mouth to argue, and Natasha said,

'Look, I'll loan you some money. Take your salary six months in advance, and you tell her to stay put in school.'

She turned back to the mirror and picked up her brush to do her hair. The nicest thing about this new pixie cut was that it just took a few careful strokes and all was in order.

Jamuna wasn't done, though. 'Didi, thank you, but I cannot take the advance.'

Natasha was not used to defiance from Jamuna, so she looked at her in surprise. 'What? Why not? It's not that large an amount. Just take it from me and tide over the next few months.' She realized almost instantly that it *was* a large amount as far as Jamuna was concerned.

Jamuna stood very straight, reminding Natasha of the way little Preeti stood. 'Thank you. But we do not take loans.' With that, she turned and withdrew from the room, leaving Natasha uncomfortable and a little ashamed for some strange reason.

She shrugged and resumed getting ready. What were her top three tasks for today? She wasn't able to concentrate. She stared at her reflection. Was it her imagination or were those dark circles under her eyes? She'd always had effortlessly smooth skin, but her face was looking a little patchy. It had been a year since her general health check-up. She supposed she should set up another appointment. There was the cough, although she was getting used to it by now. It was more the lack of sleep – she felt drained more easily these days, despite the increase in her caffeine intake. And those damned dreams. She'd had another one last night; her head was heavy by the time her alarm went off. Who *was* that little girl she kept seeing? She couldn't remember meeting any of her friends' kids who looked like that. And yet, she looked familiar. Why did she figure in all her dreams now? She made a decision. From tonight, she would start taking Calmpose. That should put the light out on weird, night-time mind-wanderings.

A shriek from outside made her jump. What was Jamuna doing? Must have seen a mouse or a cockroach. Natasha hated any sort of drama. She came out of her room, fully prepared to tick her off. She stopped in her tracks when she saw what had made her yell.

That mutt. The one the guard had come enquiring about. Kalu. What was he doing at her doorstep? He peered in through the open door, his tail wagging in a friendly manner as he looked from Jamuna to Natasha and back again, as if to say: 'Well, aren't you going to invite me in?'

Jamuna was frozen to the spot, about six feet from the open door. She said in a high, frightened voice, not taking her eyes off the dog, 'Didi, I just opened the door to shake out the mat, and he was lying there, and he got up and I thought he was going to bite me...'

'He's not going to do anything,' said Natasha. 'Your shriek probably scared him as much as it scared me. Just shoo him away and shut the door, will you?'

Jamuna said in a soft, quivering voice, 'Shoo. Shoo, doggy.' The dog seemed to think this was a nice little game, and he let out a friendly woof that echoed loudly in the hallway, making Jamuna back further away from the door with another little scream.

Natasha rolled her eyes and stalked up to the door. She wasn't afraid of this mutt. 'Out,' she ordered.

The dog looked up at her and wagged his tail even more vigorously, mouth hanging open. She saw he had very clear, brown eyes. He didn't look all that mangy. He was definitely well-maintained compared to the other strays. Almost like he had been groomed or something. That was strange.

'Go!' Natasha said, and this time, the dog seemed to realize she was serious. He turned around and disappeared down the stairwell.

Natasha stared after him, frowning. He had looked like he expected to be invited in, to be welcomed. It reminded her of something, and she couldn't quite place what, but she suddenly thought she knew what was going on.

The Chopra would have some explaining to do.

'I hope you don't mind that I decided to join you at the last minute,' Rishabh said smoothly. It looked like he was trying to check himself out in the rear-view mirror, but then he gave her his friendly smile, suddenly attentive.

They were in the back of the cab that Natasha had hired for her client visit. Natasha gave him an indifferent look. 'Why would I mind? I've been the one requesting you to visit customers.'

But not with me, she fumed inwardly. She had been waiting at the elevators when Rishabh walked past, and he had asked her where she was off to, and then announced his impromptu decision to come along. Well, it was something that he seemed ready to get his precious little ass out of the office, but her idea had been for him to go and visit customers with members of her team, in order to get some perspective on the market, and also perhaps give her some feedback on her guys – for whatever his opinion was worth. She hadn't meant for him to shadow *her*.

Rishabh seemed to take her words at face value, which he tended to do whenever it suited him. He preened a little. 'Well, don't worry, Natasha, after all the year-end madness, I'm now relatively free to turn my attention to the sales function.'

What year-end madness, Natasha wondered. He'd been on leave for two weeks even though he had joined only recently, and had been partying away on New Year's Eve. From what she had heard around the office, he had been the life of the office getaway, dancing and flirting and making many silly ladies very happy indeed. It seemed he hadn't brought his family to the New Year getaway so that he could focus on getting to know his new colleagues. Whatever. What did she care?

'So who are we meeting?'

'Aventure,' she said shortly. 'One of our key accounts.'

'I know that.' He smiled. 'I meant, what is the name of the person we are meeting?'

'Oh. Sudha Virmani – she's the head of HR for all-India. It's a team of about twenty people, mostly concentrated in the corporate office here. They've been using our product for the last ten months, and they're fairly happy. I set this up because I wanted her to upgrade to a newer package, which is likely to give them better ROI.'

'Which package are they currently on?'

'They're on the BeckittPro,' Natasha said, 'like most other key accounts. But I analysed their usage patterns, and figured they could actually do a more efficient job if they transition to the multiple-user-account version of SmartSilver.'

Rishabh frowned. 'But don't we make higher subscription fees on the Pro?'

'Yes, of course,' she agreed. 'However, we've seen that a lot of the renewal rates are determined by the actual returns our clients get, and they usually make that calculation at the end of the year. Now's a good time for us to showcase how they will get a better result from the Silver, so our chances of long-term retention and recommendation are much higher.'

Rishabh pursed his lips. He seemed to be mulling it over, but only said, 'Let's see how it goes.' Natasha was fine with that. Rishabh rarely talked actual business with her, and she had already given up expecting much by way of input from him.

It bothered her that he was just operating as a layer between her and Aman, but she had been in the system long enough and could make her own decisions. She didn't need a boss. Even Aman had fallen a little in her eyes after he'd brought in this guy, after all that sensitivity crap. Just because of that bloody Shekhar.

That reminded her – she had to call Anirban for a review. He'd better be ready to answer for the post-New Year's sales, which still hadn't picked up to match the levels of the other branches. She thought she'd call him to Delhi for a couple of days – they could have a joint all-day session with Deepesh. He was much older and her right-hand man, he would fill in the gaps in Anirban's training. Of course, either way she would make sure a new branch head was brought in by March. She was still reviewing CVs sent to her by HR, but hadn't found anyone who looked suitable.

They had almost reached their destination. The cabbie parked the car in front of the building's entrance. Natasha smoothed down her green dress over her beige stockings and then opened the door to let herself out. Rishabh got out from the other side and brushed himself off, as if the cab had been covered in dust or something. He was in a suit as usual, with a snazzy blue tie. He looked good, she admitted. It's just that he was way too full of himself for her to actually think of him as good-looking.

They walked into the building together. It was a large office complex like their own, and there were crowds of people milling about. Some of them threw glances their way, and Rishabh gave two young girls a winning smile as he passed them. Natasha stalked straight ahead, leading the way to the elevators.

She pressed the button for the twelfth floor, and they waited in silence. She felt her cough rising up and tried to suppress it, but failed. She hoped he wouldn't ask her about it. No danger of that happening, she realized – there was too much noise, and besides, he appeared to be checking out his reflection on the large steel doors of the elevator. Prissy fellow.

The lift doors opened and she sailed in, with him close behind. They were alone, and she tapped one foot impatiently as the elevator climbed. He remarked, 'That's a very nice dress, by the way, Natasha.' He gave her his friendly grin, but suddenly, it looked sharkish. She didn't like how he'd looked her up and down as he said it. There was no real hint of innuendo, and it was a perfectly normal thing to say, but she felt uncomfortable. She adjusted her jacket and crossed her arms over her chest as she replied stiffly, 'Thank you.' She knew perfectly well she would have reacted differently had the compliment come from Nikhil. Perhaps she was being a little unfair.

The elevator reached the twelfth floor and she walked out first. She had been here at least five times before, and hoped they would get to meet the MD, Suresh Wadhwa – he was the one whom she had actually initiated contact with at an industry meeting. He had been a key participant in their initial presentations. Sudha, the HR lady, was a little demanding, but they managed to keep their relationship cordial, if a little cold.

The guard let them into Sudha's office, where she was gazing at her laptop as they entered. 'Hi, Natasha.' She looked up, noticed Rishabh and immediately looked flustered. 'I didn't know you were bringing someone else.'

'Hi, Sudha. Actually, Rishabh – our business head – made a last-minute decision to join us.' Natasha noted that Sudha wasn't actually looking at her – she seemed to have eyes only for Rishabh and rose slowly to her feet as he approached to shake her hand. 'I did message you, of course,' she muttered, but Sudha wasn't listening now.

'Rishabh Sethi.' Rishabh had enveloped Sudha's skinny, fair hand in his larger one. He said warmly, 'It's a real pleasure to meet you, Sudha.'

Natasha couldn't believe the way Sudha was simpering under his gaze. They continued to hold hands until Natasha coughed, this time on purpose, and it appeared to break the spell.

'Why don't we move into a conference room?' Sudha's voice was smooth again. This room is too small and a little too … warm.' She smiled at Rishabh. 'Please give me a moment while I arrange another space, won't you?' Indicating the two chairs in front of her desk, she went out of her room in a flurry.

Natasha watched her leave. She had never seen Sudha act this way. Rishabh was clearly turning on the charm, full blast. Well, she didn't like it. She looked at him – he was giving her an innocent smile. She quickly averted her eyes.

After a few moments, Sudha poked her head in and said, 'Please come. The boardroom is free.'

Rishabh stood up and so did Natasha. He gave her his

usual, polite 'After you' gesture, and she almost rolled her eyes. Sudha led them down the hall to a room at the far end of the office, which Natasha hadn't seen before. A really fancy place, clearly reserved for the most important meetings. *She* hadn't ever been brought in here. There was space for twenty people, but apparently just one Rishabh was enough for Sudha to roll out the red carpet.

Natasha took a chair while Rishabh politely waited for Sudha to sit down across from him. He then seated himself next to Natasha. She had already pulled out her laptop. It was time to get down to business.

'So, are you having a good start to the New Year?' Rishabh asked Sudha.

She actually blushed. 'Well, do you mean business-wise or personally?'

'Both, of course.' Rishabh smiled. Natasha stared dubiously at him and then at Sudha and then back at Rishabh. *Hello? I'm still here. Can you quit the flirting now?* She decided she didn't dislike Rishabh mildly after all – she *actively* disliked him.

'So,' he went on, 'did you go somewhere for New Year's?'

Before Natasha knew it, the two of them were discussing their respective holidays with keen interest. She gritted her teeth. Could they get on with it?

'I'm so sorry.' Sudha was laughing breathlessly. Natasha squared her shoulders. Finally. But Sudha continued, 'I didn't even ask what you'd like – tea or coffee?'

Rishabh politely waited for Natasha to go first. She was itching to get started, but realized she really needed a coffee. 'Black coffee, please.'

Rishabh said a normal coffee would do just fine for him, and

Sudha picked up the telephone in front of her and murmured the order into it.

Natasha cleared her throat. 'Shall we get going, Sudha? I have here a presentation with a full analysis that I've got done for your account's usage. I have a few suggestions about changes that we could make to get you better results. If I could just set this up?'

She looked around for a cable to the projector. Sudha seemed to have come down to earth a little because she said, 'Well, Natasha, before that – I just wanted to give you some feedback on what I've noticed in the last quarter.'

'Go ahead,' Natasha said, and Rishabh leaned forward in his chair, all agog.

'You know we've been using your product for the last nine months.'

'Ten,' Natasha corrected on auto-pilot.

'Ten, perhaps.' Sudha inclined her head. 'But while I am actively pushing the system's usage, there's still some resistance from my team on the recruitment segment. They are saying that they still prefer the user interface of the other portals that we've been using, and it takes more time to fill in the details of your job posting form—'

'Sudha,' Natasha interrupted, 'it's a matter of a refresher training for your team – that's all. There were some upgrades to the system recently and your guys just need to get familiar with them – there are some really important enhancements. And the reason our system takes more time to get going is that we need to capture more information for better results. It's part of our promise. Let's just set up another training next week, your branches can join in.'

'I don't know, Natasha.' Sudha looked doubtful. 'The

feedback has been pretty strong. Those guys don't really want to have to learn a new system.'

'But it's something that will integrate with every other aspect of the recruitment process workflow – in fact, as you know, there are lots of other features which integrate into subsequent stages, and—'

'I know all that,' Sudha argued. 'But my team's problem is that they're still not comfortable. They tend to continue to use the other portals, and then I have to convince them to post on your system, and then there are still so many calls that they have to make to shortlist people, so—'

Rishabh spoke up for the first time. 'So sorry to interrupt, Sudha. But I assume the calling is a very time-consuming part of the process?'

Sudha blinked and then answered him in a warmer tone, 'Well, yes. The issue is that there are so many people who don't answer the first few times; then we have the problem of their not being able to take calls during office hours. A lot of manual effort goes into actually being able to narrow down to a workable shortlist.'

Rishabh nodded, and Natasha glared at him, wondering where he was going with this.

'So what if we take that process off your hands? We've been contemplating the idea of setting up a call centre exclusively dedicated to the needs of our larger clients. In fact, we would be happy to handle all your tele-calling requirements, not only the candidates that you are viewing on our system.'

Sudha looked interested, but Natasha was filled with a growing rage. This was the first she was hearing of any such plan that 'they' had regarding a call centre. How was that even feasible? It had nothing to do with their core offering.

How dare Rishabh even make such a suggestion to *her* client, especially when she had told him of her plan to get them to switch to another package? She knew her solution was much better, it would have taken some more convincing, but Sudha would have got it eventually. But now, Rishabh was taking the conversation off on a total tangent.

She opened her mouth but Sudha spoke first. 'Now that sounds really promising … Rishabh. Please, tell me more.' She was ignoring Natasha completely. Natasha felt her face grow hot, but gave away no emotion whatsoever.

The office boy entered and served their coffees. Natasha stared at her cup and found he had put milk in hers and probably sugar too. Sudha may not even have mentioned her preference for black coffee.

Rishabh was busy holding forth, explaining his idea to Sudha, but Natasha couldn't concentrate. She only heard things like 'holistic' and 'one-stop solution'. She took a sip of the too-sweet, too-milky coffee, somehow not gagging. She waited stone-faced for a chance to get a word in edgewise. It didn't look like it was coming any time soon.

No, she didn't actively dislike Rishabh. She hated his guts.

THREE

AS SUSPECTED

Bastard. Sonofabitch. No – Bastard.

Natasha swerved into her parking spot, brakes screeching. She'd been seething the entire day about Rishabh's behaviour during their meeting with Sudha. A couple of the colony guards had waved at her to slow down, which she did when she remembered how many little brats came cycling down here. Her mind continued to race though, and she sat in the parked car, trying to calm herself.

How could he? Aventure was her most important win. One of the most difficult ones to crack, and she had built the relationship, personally monitored their usage and the system's performance, and had pushed for upgrades which she knew would benefit them. And Rishabh had ruined it all with his 'one-stop solution'.

She'd tried to tell him in the cab on the way back that setting up a call centre was not and should not be on their priority list. They were in a different space, using technology for more efficient handling of HR processes. Where did a call centre fit in? He had smiled at her winningly and said that she looked a little perturbed, and perhaps it would be better to get a cup of coffee to talk it over. Knowing she was on the verge of telling him how hare-brained his intervention today had been, she bit her lip and suggested, since it was getting late, that they discuss it tomorrow. She'd then stared stonily out of the window all the way back, wishing fervently she had driven her own car to the meeting. As soon as they reached the office, she had gotten out of the car with a curt goodbye, and without a backward glance, headed straight to the basement for her car.

It was dark now, and she sat and stared out at nothing. She finally picked up her things and got out of the car. It was freezing cold, but for once she didn't feel it – she was burning with rage. Her cough returned, a reminder that nothing but a cigarette could make her feel better. She couldn't wait to get to her apartment and light up again. She was now at six a day, but it was all under control. Not yet an addiction. These were stressful times, after all.

She approached her building and suddenly noticed something moving up ahead. It bounded up the ten steps that led to the ground floor, the light from the hall revealing what it was: none other than *that* Dog. The overfriendly, overfamiliar mutt better known as Kalu. He was wagging his tail so hard it was a mere blur. Asinine canine. What was the purpose in being so senselessly cheerful?

The dog trotted off towards the left. Good. At least he wasn't off to her floor. She might end up kicking him today. No, she thought as she went through the doorway, she wouldn't go that far. Definitely wouldn't ever kick a dog. Wouldn't mind kicking Rishabh, but not a dog. She liked dogs, it's just that this one was…

This one was…

She turned to look at him again. He was at the far corner of the hall, right outside Mrs Chopra's house. She suddenly remembered her suspicions. She took two steps back into the building's doorway, and waited quietly, holding her breath. She heard some low whining and when she strained her ears – the sound of the dog scratching the door. She heard the door opening and a voice whispering, 'Not now! Not now! Oh, come in, silly fellow. Shh.' And then the sound of the door clicking shut.

The hall was completely quiet and Natasha let out her breath. So that was it. The old woman wasn't just feeding the dog on the sly – she was actually taking him into her house. As if he was some kind of part-time pet. How ridiculous. Who did this old lady think she was? Pretending to be all pious and proper and talking about the standard of the neighbourhood being brought down by the young ones like her – all while she violated the regulations of the society. Encouraging strays to hang around the buildings was not allowed at all. She decided that it was the perfect opportunity to get back at the Chopra. That would be a satisfying end to a terrible day. She could report her right away.

Now, where was the nearest guard?

But what if the mutt disappeared by the time she got a guard over? She wanted to catch her in the act. She chewed on her lower lip. It would mean delaying her smoke, but it would be worth it. The Chopra's hypocrisy had to be exposed. And after all, what was a good camera phone for? Some might have said selfies, but no, a better use would be capturing damning evidence against annoying neighbours.

She tiptoed to Mrs Chopra's door – it wasn't easy, given the concrete flooring and her killer heels. She took a deep breath to prepare herself and then rang the doorbell officiously, pressing it long and letting it chime loudly. There. That should give the Chopra a minor heart attack.

She could make out a muffled yelp and then some panicked scrambling. She waited just another moment before ringing again. Come on, old lady. I'm sacrificing good cigarette time for this little exposé.

She was about to ring a third time when Mrs Chopra's voice rang out crankily, 'Coming, coming. Who is it at this hour? Making an old woman get up and come to the door…' The grumbling continued, getting louder and louder; the old lady was shuffling towards the door. Natasha couldn't help smiling. This would be fun. She put on a friendly smile as the door finally opened a crack. Mrs Chopra poked her grey-haired head out and peered at Natasha with suspicious bluish-grey eyes.

'Hello, Aunty.' It was the first time she had actually addressed her like this.

Mrs Chopra stood there in her trademark plain sari and blinked, confused. Natasha had never paid her a visit before. 'Yes?' she enquired.

'Sorry to bother you. Were you doing something … important?'

Mrs Chopra soured instantly, saying in her cranky manner, 'I was in the middle of my evening puja. What is it?'

'Oh, Aunty.' Natasha had already formulated a plan. 'It's so silly. I've left my keys at the office. Someone is bringing them over. But in the meantime, it's so cold outside. I thought I could use your bathroom for a minute?'

She hopped on one foot and then the other, trying to make it look urgent. 'I'm sure you understand, Mrs Chopra.' She had a burst of inspiration and added, 'It's a bit of an emergency. Woman thing. You've been there. Right?'

As expected, this embarrassed Mrs Chopra so much that she fumbled, opening and closing her mouth like a fish. By the time she opened it again to protest, Natasha had sailed in past her. 'Thank you, Aunty. You're so kind.' She went through the hall and looked around the sparse drawing room. 'Don't worry, I won't disturb your … puja?' She deliberately emphasized the last word as she scanned the house, as if making an effort to see where the fictional puja had been taking place.

Mrs Chopra came shuffling behind her and herded her towards one of the rooms, saying, 'You can use that bathroom in there. Please hurry. The auspicious hour for my puja is almost up.'

'Oh, which calendar do you follow, Aunty?' Natasha feigned polite interest as she allowed herself to be shepherded into what was apparently the guest bedroom – it looked completely unused. Natasha had heard that the Chopra had no children. She never had house-guests. Well, except the four-legged kind. She narrowed her eyes as she walked into the bathroom. Where was he?

She heard Mrs Chopra's scuttling footsteps fading away. Now was her moment. She quietly tiptoed back and waited at the doorway to the guestroom. She poked her head out and saw the old woman disappearing into the main bedroom at the end of the hall.

Within about five seconds, the black mutt came bounding out, spurred on by the whispered, 'Shh … Shh … Out!' from Mrs Chopra. He caught sight of Natasha standing with her arms crossed, and an accusing look on her face. He seemed a tad surprised to see her there, but clearly thought, 'The more, the merrier,' because his happy tail started wagging so fervently that it looked ready to fall off.

'So!' cried Natasha, addressing the shocked Mrs Chopra. It was difficult to maintain her stern and accusing demeanour with the dog sniffing around her dress in that ridiculously friendly manner. 'Shoo! Shoo! Go away!' she snapped at him, but he paid no heed whatsoever.

Mrs Chopra was the very picture of guilt. She had clearly thought Natasha would be busy in the bathroom and those precious couple of seconds were what she had been counting on. She put on a confused face. 'Ooof! That dog must have followed you in here.' Making a disgusted face, she screeched, 'Get out of my house, you dirty … dog!'

It was an unconvincing act at best because the dog bounded back up to Mrs C, and jumped up and pawed her, pulling her sari pallu askew. Natasha laughed incredulously. She held up her iPhone and, taking a step back, snapped a quick series of pictures of the dog and Mrs Chopra.

'What are you doing?' asked Mrs Chopra in a belligerent tone, trying to fend off the dog.

'Collecting evidence.' Natasha put the phone into her purse. 'Thank you so much, Mrs C. Now we know who's been encouraging this complete menace to society to come and terrorize our building.'

The dog was still wagging his tail, and Natasha continued, 'To think the guard came and accused me of feeding the mutts. Ridiculous. They should be removed. And so should residents who stealthily feed them and encourage them to come into their houses! Goodnight, Mrs C.'

She turned to sweep out of the house, but Mrs Chopra said, 'Wait.'

Something in Mrs Chopra's voice stopped her. She really wanted to get to her cigarette now, a sick feeling settling in her stomach already. This detective work just wasn't her thing. The dog wasn't that bad, and she knew that somewhere deep inside, she had a soft spot for dogs, which was clearly a feeling shared by the Chopra. But still, Natasha was strait-laced about such matters. She turned reluctantly and looked at Mrs Chopra.

'He's a good dog,' Mrs Chopra began. 'He was much smaller and weaker when he started to come here a few months ago…'

Natasha gasped. 'You've been doing this for *months*?'

'He was hurt,' Mrs Chopra protested. 'He had a limp. I bandaged it and then he became all right. He's very friendly and he would never hurt anyone…'

'Look, Mrs Chopra,' Natasha said, arms crossed over her chest, 'if you like him so much, you should have just taken him in. Why didn't you do that? It's unfair to have him roaming about.'

Mrs Chopra's wrinkled face quivered. 'But he would hate to be on a leash. He's a free spirit. He doesn't even sleep here on most nights, only when it's really cold.'

'He sleeps here?' Natasha couldn't keep her pitch down.

Mrs Chopra seemed to realize she needn't have given that away. 'It's cold these days,' she mumbled in a low voice that Natasha could barely hear over Kalu's heavy panting.

For the first time ever, she couldn't help but feel sorry for the old lady. 'Look, Mrs Chopra, you know this is wrong. The society rules state that all pet dogs are to be kept on a leash. You can't be doing this – what if he goes and hurts some kid or someone else? Some old person—'

Mrs Chopra interjected, 'I'm the oldest resident here and

I know he wouldn't hurt a fly. He stays away from the kids, some of them throw stones at the strays. I'm telling you, he's...'

Natasha was done hearing about Kalu's virtues. She leaned against the wall, suddenly drained and weak, a dull ache beginning to spread through her head. It had been a terrible day, and this wasn't turning out to be the satisfying conclusion she had hoped for.

'Are you all right?' Mrs Chopra sounded concerned. Natasha looked up sharply. Concern from Mrs C was a first. Was it an act?

Natasha gazed at her and didn't answer for a few moments. The dog wasn't bad, and this old lady probably wasn't all that bad either. She had some spunk. Natasha was amused at the thought of Mrs C keeping the guards fooled this long. She shook her head to clear it, but Mrs C seemed to take this as an answer to the question about Natasha feeling well. She added somewhat tentatively, 'Would you like to have a cup of coffee?'

Mrs Chopra being hospitable? Definitely another first.

'Er, no,' Natasha managed to say politely, 'I think I just need to turn in for the night.'

Perhaps it was the faint disappointment on Mrs C's face as she nodded, a little too quickly – or the fact that Natasha genuinely felt sorry about snooping; but somehow she found herself adding, a little tentative herself, 'But thank you ... Maybe some other time.'

FOUR

LUNCH DATES AND DIMPLES

'What is wrong with men these days?'

Natasha muttered the words to herself as she took a final, shuddering drag of her cigarette. She almost didn't know where it had gone, she had smoked it so fast.

She stood alone on the terrace, at her favourite spot near the water tanks. It was the only place she could hope to find some privacy. She needed a few moments to compose herself. She lit up again.

Crying. It was something she wasn't used to handling.

But what had led to Anirban's little breakdown? If he wanted to become a branch head, he needed to be able to take everything that a branch head usually did, and that included having to answer questions about where the numbers were going. And here he was, a fully grown man, blubbering like a baby. All because of one tough review.

She sighed, thankful that he had waited until Deepesh had left the room. Deepesh had been giving him worried glances towards the end of the review, which had distracted and irritated her further. She had asked him to sit in on the discussion and assess Anirban for his training needs. As soon as the meeting was concluded, Deepesh had made his exit, as if aware that something uncomfortable was to come. And then it had happened – Anirban asked Natasha if he could have a word and, in the next moment, he had burst into tears.

'I'm sorry,' he'd blubbered. Then he blew his nose into a white hanky. 'I shouldn't have tried out for this role.'

Natasha had hissed at him to keep his voice low. The walls of the conference room were made of glass, and the two of them were already attracting some curious glances. She shoved a box of tissues towards him and tried to soften her tone. 'Look, Anirban, don't you think you're taking all this a little too personally?'

But he wasn't listening. 'It's just that … I thought I was ready. But I'm clearly not.'

Privately deciding that Anirban was, indeed, not the best choice for acting branch head for Mumbai, Natasha tried to comfort him by reaching out and touching him on the arm. He gasped, almost recoiling. She froze and then said in the gentlest possible tone, 'Anirban, I'm sorry you feel this way. Please try to calm down. My intent was not to hurt you, but to help you improve your performance. After all, you want to grow, right?'

Anirban just snorted into his wet hanky, and then hung his head miserably. She patted his wrist and said, 'There, there. It's all right.' It felt fake, especially since she had never used those words like that before. This guy was incredibly low on self-control. Would he have taken the same words as badly if they'd come from a male boss? For god's sake, she'd heard that her predecessor, the previous sales head, was famous for asking his team to shape up and deliver the numbers, lapsing into Hindi to explain how he was 'now hanging by his last pubic hair'. Or something. Yuck.

'Natasha.' Anirban looked up again, his eyes red. 'Do you think you could … give me a moment?'

'Of course.' She quickly rose from her seat. 'Take your time. See you later.' She had walked out and straight up to the terrace, ignoring the curious looks from her colleagues. She had to get away.

Her second cigarette was already over. Oh hell. It was lunchtime. She usually made it a point to work through lunch or grab a salad at her desk, but since there was a visiting team member, it was only appropriate to take him out for lunch. Especially now that she'd made him cry. A long, deep breath to fortify herself came out as a hacking cough. She leaned against the parapet to steady herself – she wasn't feeling well. Must be the lack of sleep. And food. She couldn't remember if she'd had breakfast. Oh yes. The green juice. She'd left it halfway because she couldn't stand the taste, not the way Jamuna made it. The woman didn't know what spices to add to the concoction, and Natasha hadn't had time this morning to do it herself, so she had left it on the dining table and walked out.

No exercise of late, either. Both the yoga and the fitness boot camp were now out for her. She told herself she needed to try something new, but hadn't got around to it. She sighed, knowing that she should get something to eat, even though she didn't feel like it. She made her way back to the stairwell, her feet heavy although her head was light. She was a little dizzy, she realized.

Entering the dark stairwell, she paused for a moment. The sudden blackness could take a second to get used to. As her eyes adjusted to the dark, she caught a glimpse of something and her heart skipped a beat. She just about managed to keep from crying out in surprise.

A little girl, in what looked like a white nightgown, stood grinning up at her cheekily. About seven or eight years old, curly haired. In an office building? Where had she come from and what was she doing here? But in the blink of an eye, she was gone. Natasha reeled and sat down heavily in the doorway to the terrace.

What was going on? There was a rational explanation for everything, even for what she had just seen. She had to be hallucinating, probably because of some vitamin or mineral deficiency. Or could the lack of sex do strange things to your mind? With her head in her hands, she squeezed her temples, applying as much pressure as possible to make the spinning stop. It was all okay. It was all okay.

'Natasha?'

This time she did cry out. But it was a shriek that died quickly in her throat when she saw it was Nikhil. Her heart was pounding. She stood up and almost lost her balance.

'Whoa ... hang on.' He caught her and helped her straighten up. 'Got up too suddenly? Are you all right? You look like you just saw a ghost.'

She looked up at his face. He was standing very close to her, and it made her a little nervous – not that she disliked it. Not at all. She said as steadily as she could manage, 'Yes. I'm fine ... You, you just er, startled me.'

He looked at her closely. 'You don't look so good, Natasha.'

'Thanks.' She rolled her eyes. 'I live to hear that from strangers.'

'Stranger?' The dimple was back. He took a step back and said teasingly, 'I thought we were colleagues. Maybe even friends.' Natasha looked at him uncertainly and he continued, 'In fact, I thought you might be here. I came up to check if you want to get lunch at this new Italian place? You haven't eaten yet, have you? I've never seen you in the office cafeteria!'

Natasha bit her lip. She hadn't been expecting this, but it was kind of flattering. He had come out of his way to seek her company for lunch. It wasn't the kind of thing that happened often. Everyone else seemed too afraid to ask. That was only part of the reason that she ate at her desk, of course. She supposed she could just leave Anirban to Deepesh, and good old Deepesh would help the younger man sort himself out. It might actually be a lot better that way.

'So, coming?' Nikhil said, tilting his head. 'Sometime … today?'

'Of course. I was just taking a moment to compose myself,' Natasha said with as much dignity as she could muster. Yes. She would just send Deepesh a message to take Anirban out – maybe even for a calming beer.

'Yes, you do look a little decomposed,' said Nikhil with a concerned face. Her sharp glance made him laugh. 'Sorry. I tend to make bad jokes, usually at all the wrong times. Just one of the things you'll discover about me.' He chuckled softly and indicated the dark stairwell. 'Shall we, mam'zelle?'

His French accent was pretty bad, but for a change, she didn't feel the urge to tell someone how it was supposed to be pronounced. She just stared at him and let out a little laugh, half-disbelieving. It was the first time she had laughed all day. Together, they headed down the stairs, and she felt suddenly lighter.

Natasha looked around at the red-and-black décor, and then across the table at Nikhil. 'This is the new Italian place you were talking about?'

Nikhil looked innocently at her. 'Yes. You've been here before?'

Natasha leaned across the table, hissing, 'Very funny.' This guy was weirder than she'd thought. 'As if you didn't know this is Pizza Hut.'

Nikhil frowned, his mock-confusion faltering before he burst into laughter at the look on her face. 'Oh, come on, Natasha. It was supposed to be a joke.'

She continued to stare at him through narrowed eyes and he said more apologetically, 'Okay, next time, we'll go to a fancy Italian place of your choice. I assumed you wanted to get back to office really quickly, in your usual business-like manner.'

She felt the colour rising in her cheeks, but wasn't going to give him the satisfaction of seeing it, and quickly picked up the menu, hiding half her face behind it. He was being rather overfamiliar, she decided. In a huffy manner, she said, 'You're assuming there will be a next time.'

He laughed out loud, as if it had been a joke. She couldn't help but smile behind her menu-shield. It was true, she *didn't* mean it. Right now, Nikhil was probably the only person in the world she wanted to be with.

Whoa. Where the hell did that thought come from? She tried to concentrate on the menu. Salad, salad, where was the salad ... Ah yes. 'I'll have the veg salad,' she announced, and put down the menu. She looked for a glass of water and took a sip, just to have something to do. Now that they were here, in this public place with all its bright lights, she felt even more self-conscious. This building was right next to the office, what if someone saw the two of them together? She rarely went out with anyone and didn't like the thought of people gossiping about her, although she always told herself she didn't really care.

Now it was Nikhil's turn to stare. 'A salad? At Pizza Hut? What's wrong with you? Come on, share a chicken-and-cheese pizza with me. We'll add a lasagne to that.'

Natasha wrinkled her nose. 'Yuck! All that fattening, greasy cheese. And anyway, I'm off wheat.'

'Eh?' Nikhil frowned at her. 'So what do you eat at home?'

That suddenly felt like too personal a question and she reddened visibly. Why did Nikhil think he had the right? She drew herself in a little, repeating, 'I'll have the salad.' She hoped he wasn't the kind of guy who thought he could order women around.

He smiled good-naturedly. 'Okay. Done.' He turned his head to signal to the waiter, who landed up with his little writing pad. 'One chicken-and-cheese pizza, no olives please; and the lady will have a veg. salad. Anything to drink?' He turned to Natasha and she shook her head. He smiled at the waiter. 'Just a Coke for me please, then.'

The waiter smiled back. Nikhil's was an easy-going and genuine smile. It felt so different from Rishabh's affected friendliness – and her own cold treatment of waiters. She felt a little ashamed about how she had glared at that overfriendly Punjabi waiter and even poor Muthu back at the café. She hadn't been there in a while now. She missed it.

'So I'm guessing you're not a fan of aerated drinks?' Nikhil said. 'Too … bubbly?'

Natasha sighed. 'Are we going to keep talking about my food choices?'

'No.' Nikhil smiled. 'I was just wondering; you seem very health-conscious.'

Feeling like she was being more distant than she intended, Natasha acquiesced. 'Well, yes. I try to take care of myself. I'm usually particular about exercise and I'm careful about what I eat.'

'Well, that's great. What kind of exercise do you do?'

'Umm, this and that. Yoga … some group training.'

'That's cool. I can only play squash. But I find it tough to get a partner ready to wake up early and play with me.' He smiled at her. 'Do you play?'

'What, squash?' Natasha laughed. 'Never touched a racket in my life.'

'Well, there's always a first time,' Nikhil insisted. He paused. 'But I'm not sure you're strong enough for it.'

'What?' she snapped. 'I'm very strong. What is that supposed to mean? I'm totally fit…'

She saw his face and realized he had said that just to get a rise out of her – again. 'Ha ha,' she murmured. The waiter brought Nikhil his Coke – he picked it up and offered it to her, but she just made a face so he shrugged and started sipping from it.

'On a serious note,' he said after a moment or two, 'you're not looking too well.'

'On a lighter note,' she retorted, 'don't ever tell a woman that.'

'Come on.' He rolled his eyes. 'How's that cough?'

'What cough?' She could feel it coming up again. She tried to suppress it with another sip of water, but ended up coughing into her glass. 'Shit,' she murmured between coughs and shook her head.

'So, you really don't eat wheat?' he pressed. 'You should come home one day for breakfast. I'll make you my world-famous aloo parantha and you'll come running back to the wonderful world of wheat, faster than you can say—'

'Aloo parantha!' she gasped. She couldn't think of anything unhealthier. 'Let me tell you something.' She drew herself up. 'I've read several books on nutrition, and one of the worst things anyone can do to themselves is to start the day with a heavy carb-ridden breakfast. In fact, eating nothing till noon is preferable to having the wrong stuff.' Warming up to the subject, she added quickly, 'And also the mixing of proteins and carbohydrates strains the lymphatic system, leading to all sorts of complications and toxicity. If some simple corrective measures are taken, we can all be healthier. But no one even bothers!' She sat back, feeling a little drained. But it was worth it to spread awareness.

He looked more amused than enlightened as he said, 'Natasha. We're in India.'

'What?' she said suspiciously.

'India.' He leaned forward, and added in a conspiratorial whisper, 'Don't be fooled by this fancy Italian restaurant.'

She frowned, knowing fully well that he was making fun of her, and he added with his usual easy smile, 'Come on! This is the land of dal-roti. We've grown up mixing carbs and proteins, and there's nothing wrong with us.' He looked at her appraisingly. 'Well, with me, anyway.'

She scowled. He was senior to her in the organization, and she was mindful of that, but he was the one who had asked her out and now he was constantly taking potshots at her. Luckily, the waiter came up at exactly that point to place their food on the table. She picked up a fork, ready to attack her salad, while Nikhil served himself a big slice of pizza, a look of satisfaction on his face.

She realized how hungry she was as she downed a mouthful of salad. Hmm. Just about tolerable. Maybe she should have ordered the chicken version. She looked over at his pizza and was surprised by how tempted she was.

'So,' he said through a mouthful of pizza, 'you still haven't told me a thing about yourself.'

'Not much to tell,' she said shortly. She took another bite and said, 'Some ups and downs these last couple of months with sales. Oh, but I have been meaning to tell you my comments on the Innovation Deck you circulated.'

'Natasha, believe me, I need your inputs, okay? You're the one out there with the customers more than anyone else. ' He smiled. 'But we should do that properly at the office with my team, when we can actually take notes.' He leaned forward and whispered, 'Besides – this is a break. Remember?'

She blushed harder. Why was it that she had nothing else to talk about? Had she suddenly become *that* socially awkward? What did she talk about with her friends? She still hadn't called Priya back, and now the calls had stopped coming. Was Priya her only friend? She racked her brain for something to say. 'Okay, why don't you go ahead and tell me some non-work thing about you?'

Nikhil laughed. She watched his dimple as he smiled broadly. 'Well, as I've already told you, I'm a single dad, and so my life pretty much revolves around my daughter. It's not been easy settling in here, but the schools in Gurgaon are great. She's settling well into Scottish. She loves the extracurriculars – sports, art, elocution. She's suddenly reading everything she can get her hands on, which is great.'

Natasha noted, with some amusement, the warmth and pride as he spoke about his daughter's achievements. He went on, 'And also, I've got this great lady now.'

She looked up at him a little too quickly as he clarified, 'Maid. Help. Domestic worker. Very important when you're a single parent.'

She smiled, faintly relieved, and he continued, 'I'd like you to meet Tisha sometime.'

She was confused for a moment and then realized he wasn't speaking about the maid any more. Yes, he'd mentioned his daughter's name the last time they talked. She nodded politely. Somehow, she sincerely doubted that either she or the seven-year-old daughter that he doted on would mutually benefit from meeting each other. She wouldn't know what to say to a kid. She busied herself with her salad again.

Nikhil leaned forward and said, 'Here's the thing, Natasha. I don't know why, but I feel comfortable talking to you. But that doesn't mean you have to feel pressured to talk about yourself or tell me anything you don't want to. Okay?'

'Okay,' she mumbled. That made her feel a little better.

'But,' he said, 'you should know that if there's anything you ever need at any point…'

She wasn't good at this kind of conversation. Hell, apparently she sucked at every kind of conversation. It was all she could do to nod and murmur, 'Yes, yes. Thanks.'

She popped another forkful of salad into her mouth, barely tasting it. What did he think, anyway? That she was some kind of damsel in distress?

If there was one thing Natasha was sure of, it was that she would never need rescuing – not by anyone. Dimple or no dimple.

FIVE

IN SICKNESS

Buzz … Buzz…

Natasha knew her phone was ringing, but she couldn't get up to answer it. She was in the middle of a dream. A whole bunch of scruffy kids milling around, and of course, there was that curly-haired imp too. They were all gathered around a tree. A mango tree. The boys were trying to climb it, but the branches were too high. The little girl was standing to the side, and then when the boys gave up, she ran up and scrambled against the trunk until she got a foothold. The others cheered as she made it up to where the mangoes were. She started to pluck and throw them down to her friends, but Natasha saw that she was keeping the best ones for herself. It didn't matter. She was clearly the hero of the group. Little show-off, Natasha murmured, smiling in her sleep. The mangoes looked juicy and she wondered about the taste. Her mouth felt dry.

Buzz … Buzz…

She cracked open her eyes and reached for the phone. Where the hell was it? And what time was it, anyway? Goodness. It appeared to be daylight outside, which on a winter morning in Delhi meant it could even be 9 a.m. Had she forgotten to set her alarm last night? Why had Jamuna not woken her up with the bell this morning?

Still groggy, she felt around for her phone and found it under her pillow. She gasped to see it was 9.35 a.m. It was Jamuna who was calling. What the…

'*Kya hai*, Jamuna? Why aren't you here?' Natasha snapped.

Jamuna's voice sounded strained. 'Didi, I have a problem…'

'You're *always* having problems.' Natasha leaned back on the pillows, her head spinning. 'Are you not coming today?'

Jamuna was silent for a moment and then said, 'I'll send Preeti. She will at least be able to clean up…'

Natasha didn't want to hear this. 'No. It's okay. Don't send her,' she said shortly. 'But come tomorrow.' There was a note of warning in her voice. She knew Jamuna didn't skip work without a reason, but it was going to be a tough morning without her. She was feeling unwell, and would have liked Jamuna to bring her coffee. She was used to that. Well, good, she thought, shouldn't have to get used to anybody. Just get up and face the day, she told herself.

Buzz…

This time, it was Priya. Shit. She didn't want to talk right now – her stomach felt a little funny. Or was that guilt from ignoring her calls for so long? She bit her lip and then picked up the phone on the fifth ring.

'Hi.'

'Hello, Natasha.' It was a cold greeting. 'Glad you finally decided to pick up.'

She sounded mad and Natasha knew why. Still, given how she felt right now, Priya's tone annoyed her. She cleared her throat and returned in an equally cold voice, 'Hey. What's up?'

'Nothing.' Priya's voice was equally stony. 'Just that I had this reunion party for all our batch mates last month as a little New Year's do – and *almost* everyone in town made it.'

Oh. That's why she had been trying to reach her. Natasha opened her mouth to apologize, but ended up saying, 'Well, I was busy. You should have messaged me.'

'Messaged you? The fact that I was calling you like, a dozen times a day didn't tell you anything?'

Natasha couldn't resist saying, 'Anyway, I wasn't even in town that evening. I really don't have time for these things, Priya.'

'These things.' Priya's voice was ice. 'Meaning, friends. Right?'

Natasha was silent. She didn't want to explain herself. It's not as if she felt the urge to hang out and reminisce with their old school buddies. She coughed and her stomach hurt.

'That's what I thought.' Priya's voice was harder than Natasha had ever heard it. 'Don't think I haven't picked up on the vibes, Natasha.' She was using her full name, Natasha noticed. 'I guess you're just too busy and too successful for the rest of us now – including me.'

'Look, Priya,' Natasha began, 'you're making a big deal out of nothing. I—'

'It's never been easy, trying to be your friend.' Priya didn't seem to want to listen. 'But I kept trying. I'm always the one who calls, remembering your birthday, inviting you over. But you act like it's all a favour you're doing me. And I don't need favours any more, Natasha.'

Natasha sighed and closed her eyes. She waited for Priya to finish.

'And just so you know, it's never been easy to like you.' Priya's voice was low now. 'The one who always did better, would always do better. I brushed all the comparisons aside. Well, you're welcome to your success, Natasha. I've got a family and real friends to focus on. So don't worry, I'm not going to be interfering with your journey to the top. '

Natasha held her breath. She didn't have the words to respond anyway.

After a long moment, Priya whispered, 'Bye,' and hung up.

Natasha let out her breath. Fine. *She* wasn't the one trying to hang on to old relationships that had lost their meaning. It was Priya's decision, and Natasha tried to feel relieved.

Instead, she just felt a weird sensation in her stomach and had a sneaking suspicion that she had eaten something bad. Well, maybe it would just go away.

She willed herself to get up, but a sudden weakness overcame her. She lay back and coughed. Ouch. That hurt. She coughed again and felt a sharp pain in her chest and stomach. Oh god. She couldn't afford to get sick.

Could she just take the day off? Natasha never approved of sick leave – not for herself, not for any member of her team. Now, though, there was no denying how she felt.

She thought about it for just another moment before pulling out her phone and sending a message to Rishabh: 'Need the day off – have woken up feeling sick.' She hated having to inform him about this, but he was her boss. She forwarded the message to Aman, whom she still considered her 'real' boss, despite his decreasing involvement in her work. Immediately after she pressed the send button, she felt worse. Why did one more person need to know about this silly thing?

She pulled the covers back over her head and closed her eyes. The coughing started up again and she winced in anticipation of the pain. She closed her eyes. She knew she'd be better by the end of the day.

Evening found her considerably worse.

She groaned softly. The pain in her stomach was excruciating. She had already been to the bathroom four times, and couldn't bring herself to even think of food. She figured that her stomach needed the rest; and in any case, there was no way she could work up the strength to fix something to eat. She regretted rejecting Jamuna's offer of sending Preeti – at least she would have been able to fetch her a hot-water bottle right now. She bit her lip to keep from groaning again and broke out into another bout of coughing that left her gasping for breath and clutching her belly. She curled into the foetal position, glad no one could see her now. This was the tough Natasha who took great pride in not having ever called in sick in the last two years.

She was never eating out again. That limp Caesar salad at the so-called stupid Italian restaurant. Natasha knew it had been her choice to pick one of the few uncooked items on the menu, but she felt an irrational annoyance at Nikhil for having taken her there. He had savoured that chicken-and-cheese pizza. Her stomach rumbled at the thought. Maybe she was hungry after all. No way she could keep anything down right now though.

Her phone buzzed again, and she started a little when she saw who it was. Weird. She had just been thinking about him.

It was just a stupid coincidence, these things never meant anything. She contemplated ignoring his call, but since the phone kept ringing insistently, she held it to her ear and said, in as normal a voice as she could manage, 'Hello?'

'Hey, what's wrong?' His voice sounded concerned. 'I heard from Aman you're sick?'

'Uh, only a little.' She coughed and grimaced. Had he been asking about her? 'Did you need something? I can log on to my mail—'

'You have to be kidding.' His laugh was incredulous. 'Do *you* need something?'

'No … I'm fine.' Natasha tried to sound fine.

There was a moment of silence on the line.

'You know what?' Nikhil said. 'I'm going to swing by and see you. You live at Greenwood, right?'

Had she told him that? 'No way.' Natasha was firm now. 'I just need to be alone. I'm resting, and I'm going to be fine by tomorrow. It's just an upset stomach – must have been the food at Pizza Hut.'

There was another pause and then his voice came on the line. 'Yeah, that settles it. *I* made you sick. And now you're alone at home? Do you have someone over?'

'Uh…' Natasha was tempted to lie, but it was something she couldn't do with him. 'No,' she admitted, but added quickly, 'I don't need anyone, and…'

'Okay, Natasha. Noted.' Nikhil's tone was brisk. 'You don't need anyone. Ever. For anything. So I'm going to be on my way, and it would be very nice if you could message me your flat number, otherwise the guards at Greenwood might have a problem with me ringing random doorbells. Okay?'

What? What was his problem? If it had been anyone else,

she would have suspected them of wanting to get into her pants. After all, she knew the type – those who thought that being a single woman basically meant being available. But she instinctively trusted this guy even though this fuss was unnecessary.

'I make the meanest, cleanest vegetable soup,' he informed her. 'Lots of greens. Fresh.'

He obviously sensed that she was weakening.

She growled, 'Fine...'

'Great. Text me right now.' His voice was warm. 'Bye.' And then, he was off the line.

Fine, she thought as she stared up at the ceiling for a few moments. And then, she began to type out an SMS with her address.

'Wow.' Nikhil let out a low whistle.

Natasha stood shivering in her pyjamas. She had managed to wrap a shawl around herself and creep to the door to let him in. She had been drifting in and out of sleep over the last hour, and knew she looked dishevelled. Well, she was hardly going to dress up for him in this state.

'What?' she asked weakly. The hallway swayed around her.

'Hey, hey ... you're in bad shape.' Nikhil sounded alarmed.

'It's just an upset stomach,' Natasha said. 'Come in,' she said and turned to lead the way into the drawing room. She caught a glimpse of herself in a hallway mirror, and suddenly realized what he was talking about.

Her face was drawn and haggard, her eyes looking sunken. She was white and frail and suddenly a lot smaller. Oh god. She looked like the 'after' version in some anti-smoking campaign, which was, she realized with another painful cough, rather fitting. But it wasn't the occasional cigarette that could have done this to her all by itself.

She reached the sofa in the drawing room and indicated to Nikhil that he should sit down. And then she proceeded to practically fall into it herself. She looked up, trying to pretend this was always how she took a seat here and croaked weakly, 'Well, sit down.'

Nikhil's mouth was a tight line. 'What have you been eating?'

'Lousy Caesar salad.'

'Today.' Nikhil didn't seem to be in the mood for jokes.

'Nothing,' Natasha said. 'I tried drinking water to avoid dehydration. But even that's been making me throw up. Guess my stomach just needs a rest.' She looked at him hopefully. 'You mentioned soup?'

'You'll get your soup. But right now, I want to get you to a hospital.'

'What?' Natasha growled at him. 'I don't need…'

'Natasha,' Nikhil said as if he were talking to a child, 'you've got food poisoning. You just said you aren't able to keep down water. What hope have you got of retaining soup?'

'I didn't say I would retain it.' She was trying to sound dignified, but it was next to impossible in such a conversation. 'I just felt like having it anyway.'

'Come on. Get a coat.' Nikhil seemed to be losing his patience now. 'Let's go. Privat is the closest. We just need to get you a shot of Perinorm. I've done this lots of times with my daughter.'

'I'm not going.' Natasha set her jaw. *And I'm not your daughter, for god's sake.* Weak she may be, but there was no way he was going to force her into leaving her home for no reason.

He stood staring at her, and crossed his arms over his chest. And waited.

A coughing fit came over her, bringing with it another bout of sharp pain in the stomach. She doubled up and groaned, unmindful of the fact that she now had a witness. This bickering was just making it worse. She wished he would just go. Or not.

'Natasha.' Nikhil's voice was soft now. She looked up at him, her eyes bleary with unwanted tears brought out by the cough. How mortifying. He didn't seem to notice. 'Please?'

He held out his hand. His face was still worried, but he gave her the tiniest of hopeful smiles with a brief hint of the dimple.

As if in a dream, without knowing what she was doing, Natasha reached out and took his hand.

His grip was warm and strong. She allowed him to gently pull her up off the sofa, feeling as light and confused as a feather in a storm. And yet, suddenly, a whole lot better than she had felt the entire day. Or perhaps many days.

SIX

ONE SMUG LITTLE PROBLEM

'You're *what*?'

Deepesh looked a little embarrassed as he answered her in a slightly louder voice, 'The call centre solution project that—'

'I *heard* you,' Natasha interjected, glaring at him across the conference room table, 'I just don't *believe* you.'

Deepesh sounded both apologetic and defensive. 'But Natasha, Rishabh said it would help provide a more—'

'Holistic solution to our clients,' Natasha finished in chorus with him. Deepesh looked sheepish. She muttered, 'I don't believe he's ... and while I was out sick for, what, two days?'

'He called us all in on Friday.' Deepesh wiped his forehead. 'He said it was important to get our buy-in.' He added quickly, 'The other branch heads were in the call too.'

'And you actually bought in?' Natasha narrowed her eyes. 'Or should I say – you actually *bought it*?'

Deepesh protested, 'Well, Rishabh was very convincing ... He said we had to bring some new vision into the business.'

'New vision!' Natasha snapped. 'What's wrong with the old

vision that was getting us 25 per cent year-on-year growth? Did you think of asking him that?'

Deepesh looked uncomfortable and Natasha went on, 'Or was your own vision clouded by the glorious light Emperor Rishabh radiates when he takes the floor?' Deepesh squirmed. Natasha knew him well enough to know he had figured it out for himself by now – the call centre solution had nothing to do with what they were about as a company. But either way, it was inappropriate for her to be discussing her boss like this with a reportee – it didn't matter that the boss was new and the reportee old and familiar. She sighed and changed tack, saying in a tired voice, 'So I suppose none of you actually raised any objection?'

'Natasha,' Deepesh ventured, 'Rishabh said that *you* had already bought into the whole idea – he said that you proposed it jointly at the Aventure meeting and they loved the idea…'

She stared at him for about thirty seconds.

'Okay,' she finally managed. She knew she was on the verge of losing it, and didn't want to take it out on poor Deepesh. She tried to sound less snappy as she said, 'So what does this mean for you, as newly appointed leader of the project?'

'Well,' Deepesh hesitated, 'Rishabh said it should take about 30 per cent of my time for the next quarter, since I'm going to be coordinating for—'

'And what about your regular numbers?' Natasha cried. 'You're already stretched. A third of your time? That's just…' Realizing she was not doing a good job of controlling herself, she said abruptly, 'Forget it, Deepesh. I'll talk to Rishabh and let you know.'

Deepesh took it as a dismissal and couldn't hide the relief on his face. He got up and left the conference room, wiping his sweaty brow again. Natasha continued to sit and stare at the table for a few minutes, seething.

That Bloody Rishabh. He was a real piece of work. Until now, he had displayed a remarkable lack of interest in trying to understand what the market was actually like, preferring to spend his time in internal meetings and reviews, holding forth on theoretical business models. Now that he had met barely four customers, he had concluded that he knew the business. And how could he misrepresent her point of view on the subject – she had made it clear to him that she did not support the idea. To go ahead and announce it as a project in her absence to her team, and that too, appointing her most important guy as the leader … It was all too much.

She rose from her seat and took a second to steady herself. She was still a little weak from that bout of illness, although she tried not to show it. She had made it a point to avoid Nikhil from that day. She knew it had helped immensely to be driven to the hospital and given that Perinorm injection, but she hadn't asked him for it, and she hated feeling obligated. It had been his idea that she take another day off, even though she'd felt much better. That was Friday, the day that Risbabh announced his grand plans.

She knew she was far too angry for a sensible conversation with Rishabh right now. It would be better to cool off and approach him with a more rational argument.

Screw it.

Her heels clicked loudly through the office as she stalked up to his cabin. She poked her head in and said, in a cold and professional voice, 'A minute?'

He looked up from his laptop, blinked and then smiled broadly. 'Ah, Natasha – you're back! All well now?' His white teeth shone in his handsome face. She wanted to take a swing and see how many she could break in one go. 'Come in, come in. Have a seat.'

She walked in and stood in front of his desk, fists clenched. She made an effort to speak.

'Sit down,' he urged. 'You're not looking too—'

'I'm fine,' Natasha snapped. But she abruptly pulled back a chair to sit down. She took a deep breath, and, for once, didn't know where to start. No one got her goat like this guy. She hated, *hated* having to report to him.

'Natasha,' he said, leaning forward, 'I'm sensing you're not too happy about something.'

Genius. Considering that she probably looked like she was going to burst a vein, that was quite a deduction. Natasha bit back the sarcasm and said, 'Yes. I need to talk to you about—'

'Wait.' He held up his hand. Natasha noted the smooth, clean cuffs. Bloody sissy. If he spent as much time in the market as he did dressing up, he might actually learn a thing or two. 'First … Green tea?'

'No!' Natasha said it so forcefully that Rishabh looked surprised. She leaned forward and hissed, 'You started the call centre *project* without discussing it with me? As a business-wide initiative?'

'Calm down,' said Rishabh, looking nervous for the first time since she had met him. His eyes darted around as if to see if someone outside was watching them. 'It's something that we had already discussed that day at—'

'And I told you I thought it was a *bad* idea. Besides, that conversation was about doing it for *one* account. What's all this about making it a core offering for all our key clients – do you know how much effort it's going to take, and that too for something that's nowhere near the core of our business?' Natasha trembled with anger and knew she was losing control. In the last few years, she had built a reputation for being cold and emotionless. Why couldn't she keep emotions out of it right now?

Rishabh's face twitched and then suddenly froze in a neutral expression. 'Natasha,' he said in a cool voice, 'I think you're forgetting something.'

'What?' she said with clenched teeth.

'It's *my* business. And I decide what's core to it.'

Now it was Natasha's turn to freeze. In all the time that she had been here, no one had spoken to her like that. *My business*. This was what she had slaved to build. She was the most senior person in the team. The market scoping, strategy, product enhancement ideas, customer feedback processes were built painstakingly by her and her team, one step at a time. There had been plenty of long days and sleepless nights and there had never been any doubt in her mind that it was all worth it. Until now.

My business. What a megalomaniac. In spite of her own ego and firm belief in the critical role she played in building the business, at no point had she ever said or even thought of it as 'her' business. And this guy had just waltzed in and taken over. Emperor Rishabh. It was true, the guy was out to build his empire. And this project was some crazy scheme to prove that he had the ability to shake it all up and generate additional revenue – no matter what the cost.

She sat rigidly in her seat, staring at him. It was no use. He was pulling rank on her. More importantly, he had the advantage of being cool and emotionally detached right now. Why couldn't she have used her best weapon, cold sarcasm, to make her point? She had always thought emotional outbursts were for losers, and now she felt like one. What was going on with her? Why had things changed so much?

It took every ounce of self-control she possessed to compose herself. 'I'm sorry. I don't feel like myself right now, Rishabh. We shall have this discussion in a more rational manner at another time.' She added with exaggerated politeness, 'At your convenience, of course.'

He smiled again, but there was no warmth in it. 'I understand, Natasha. You haven't been well. And it's not always easy to accept change – particularly when your way of doing things has done well for the company so far.' He paused. 'Don't think I have forgotten that. You continue to be my most critical ally as we go forward.'

She had to smile at that. So much condescension. Bloody windbag. If he got any more gas in there, he would start floating a few inches above his seat. The thought tickled her funny bone. Drawing some strength from it, she rose from her seat. 'We'll reschedule this.'

He nodded, and she swept out of his room, aware that he was watching her with the same polite smile that didn't quite reach his eyes.

Natasha drove home on auto-pilot. No matter how hard she tried, she couldn't help thinking about everything that was going on. And going wrong. The stunts that Rishabh was pulling – was he trying to edge her out? No, he couldn't be that stupid – she was too important to the business's growth. He was just trying to show everyone who the new boss was. His Mr Nice Guy mask was slipping, and he wasn't as dumb and clueless as she had initially assumed. He was just about smart enough to be dangerous. He knew how to throw her off balance, and she hated that it was working.

She'd been waiting near the lift when Nikhil had appeared and tried to get her attention. Ignoring him, she'd hurried to one of the lifts opening at the far end, despite the fact that it was already overcrowded. She squeezed herself in, causing everyone to step on each other's toes. No one dared tell Natasha the lift was too full. She also tried to ignore how claustrophobic she was feeling as the lift went down. But the image of Nikhil's confused frown played on her mind – she knew instinctively he just wanted to know how she was feeling.

Well, she felt sick about everything, but it was no one else's business. No one could solve her problems but herself. Priya had also had enough of their so-called friendship. Not that she would have called and expected Priya to understand anything as complicated as her workplace dynamics. Still, she would have liked the option of calling her. They may have had their differences, and sure, they had grown apart, but Priya had stood by her through some really difficult times. Well, it was over and she wouldn't think about all that now. But there was a sinking feeling in her heart as she drove home – the solitude she often took comfort in was pressing down on her heavily tonight. She had to admit that, for once, she did not want to be alone. Not that she had a choice, of course.

Pulling into her parking spot, she noted that the light in the ground-floor window was on. She paused for a moment and bit her lip. Clearly she was going nuts.

Mrs Chopra poked her head out and looked up at Natasha suspiciously. 'Oh. You.'

'Hi, Mrs C.' Natasha tried to sound breezy, but she felt uncomfortable and adjusted her purse strap over her shoulder, just to have something to do with her hands. 'It's been a few days, so I thought I should check in on you. All well?'

'Fine.' Mrs Chopra still looked a little surprised. But Natasha thought she sensed an undertone of guilt.

She ventured, 'Kalu's in there, isn't he?'

Mrs Chopra looked uncertain for a moment but then she remembered that Natasha was sort of an ally in this matter. 'Yes,' she admitted. 'He's been coming in a little early because of the cold...'

She looked at Natasha, who shifted her weight from one foot to the other and tried not to seem nervous. She suddenly felt unwelcome and very self-conscious. She was just about to bolt when Mrs Chopra opened the door all the way and said, 'Well, come on in for that coffee, then.'

Natasha sat in the drawing room, sipping hot coffee. Kalu was curled up at her feet, his warm body pressing against her leg. He appeared to be asleep, but gave a low growl of protest every time she moved her foot. She had to admit, his presence made her feel better. He had given her a riotous welcome, jumping up and pawing her, with Mrs Chopra saying, 'Hush, Rocky!' Natasha had raised her eyebrows but said nothing about Mrs Chopra's apparent love for Sly Stallone. She still thought it was inappropriate to be harbouring him like a fugitive, but she wasn't going to comment on that now.

Mrs Chopra came in from the kitchen with a plate of biscuits and namkeen. 'Aunty, you didn't have to take so much trouble.' The 'aunty' rolled off Natasha's tongue with ease this time. 'I just wanted to stop by for a little chat and find out how you are.'

'I see.' Mrs Chopra lowered herself on to the sofa. Natasha had the uncomfortable feeling that she wasn't buying that. They looked at each other a bit uncertainly.

'So,' Natasha said, clearing her throat, 'how've you been?'

'So-so.' Mrs Chopra sighed and Natasha suddenly noticed that she looked older than the last time – strange. 'My maid has stopped coming. You can't retain any help these days.'

Natasha knew Mrs Chopra was notorious for not being able to retain anyone. She was too fussy and idiosyncratic. She wisely refrained from mentioning this, saying, 'I can put the word out – what kind of help do you need?'

'Just someone to come in the morning and handle the cooking and cleaning. I don't like the thought of someone hanging about all day.'

Natasha could understand – she felt exactly the same way. She nodded. 'Okay. I'll ask my maid, Jamuna, if she knows anyone.'

'And tell her to be careful with the watering of those plants.' Mrs Chopra was in her element when she got around to complaining. 'I still get drops sometimes on my balcony.'

'Okay, I'll tell her.' Natasha grinned – for once, she wasn't irritated by the complaining. She realized she might actually *like* this cranky, spunky old lady.

After a brief silence, Mrs Chopra said in a softer tone, 'I've been thinking about what you said – about adopting Rocky. But I think I'm just too used to living alone.'

Natasha took another sip of coffee. Curiosity compelled her to ask the question she hated being asked, 'Do you have any family?' She bit her lip – she certainly wasn't ready to answer that question if Mrs C asked her in return.

'None,' said Mrs Chopra defiantly, almost proudly. 'My husband and I decided not to have any children after...' She paused for a moment and then said more quietly, 'We almost had one.'

'Oh.' Natasha had not been expecting that. As always, this kind of conversation made her terribly uncomfortable. 'I'm ... sorry.'

'It's all right,' Mrs Chopra said. To Natasha's surprise, she went on, 'I was eight months along. It was a horrible experience.' She raised her chin a bit. 'After it was over, we decided that we would never put ourselves through that again.' Her eyes became a little misty. 'We were very happy together anyway, the two of us. But then he went and died. Silly man!' She seemed to be trying to snap out of it and smiled, exposing her neat dentures. 'My belief is simple – we come alone and we go alone. In the in-between space, how does it matter?'

Natasha almost choked on her coffee. It was the same thing she had told herself – in almost the exact same words. Uncanny. No, she reminded herself, it meant nothing. She tried to write it off. But it was obvious she had a lot more in common with her old neighbour than either of them had ever suspected.

'What about you?' Mrs Chopra probed. 'Are you planning to get married? You are not so young yourself.'

Classic, frank Mrs C. Well, she owed her an answer now. She said nonchalantly, 'Aunty – it *is* actually an option these days for people to choose not to marry. I'm one of those who believes it wouldn't work for me.'

Mrs Chopra gazed at her. 'I see.'

I see. It wasn't something you could react to, but Natasha knew it meant Mrs C wasn't buying it. She went on defensively, 'I'm fine by myself – I have my career. I'm an independent woman, and I have my health.' Involuntarily, she coughed. She tried to stop it, but the effort made it worse and she had to put down her cup. She would need to cut back on the smoking.

Even though her eyes were a little watery when she looked up at Mrs Chopra again, she could make out the twinkle in those old grey eyes.

Mrs C didn't say it again, but Natasha could clearly read the amused, disbelieving 'I see'.

SEVEN

AND DOWN GO THE WALLS

'A word, Natasha?'

Natasha looked up from her laptop. She was tempted to say 'Sure. How about beeyatch?' but instead, she just nodded curtly and indicated Renu should sit down.

Renu took a seat, her sari rustling. She appeared to have straightened her hair. It looked good. Natasha felt like kicking herself for the pixie cut; she should have gone with the rebonding. But then, on a good day, her cut made her feel really modern and corporate and somehow, powerful. Besides, some people appeared to like it, including Nikhil. She wanted to kick herself again for that thought.

Renu had her concerned HR face on, brows furrowed. 'Natasha – I was told the meeting with Anirban last week didn't go … very well?'

Ah. One of Renu's little HR spies had found out. Man, those creatures were everywhere. None of their bloody business, of course.

'What do you mean?' Natasha's tone was sharp. 'Has anything been raised to HR?'

'Oh no.' Renu leaned back with another silky rustle. 'It's just that there seemed to be some tension.'

Natasha looked her in the eye. 'Yeah. So?'

Renu was clearly not equipped to handle straight talk. She looked a little flustered. 'Well, it's … It is a part of HR's job to monitor team dynamics across functions, and—'

'Let me tell you something, Renu,' Natasha said, crossing her arms over her chest. '*I* monitor the dynamics in *my* team.'

'Well, now, Natasha,' Renu said with a tight smile, 'we know about the issues with Shekhar. I'm just worried that Anirban shouldn't go the same route.'

'He needs grooming,' Natasha said shortly. 'We're taking care of it.'

'I see. I just hope someone is taking care of *him*.'

'He's not a baby,' Natasha snapped.

'Then why was he crying like one after his meeting with you?' Renu said with the air of someone playing her trump card.

Natasha was silent. She had been naïve to believe no one would notice. Everybody always noticed everything here. They all loved office gossip. And it seemed to be encouraged by Madame HR Head. But she had to admit, Renu had the upper hand for now. Natasha settled for: 'He needs to be stronger if he actually hopes to take over the branch someday.'

Renu watched her for a few moments. Then she said, 'Natasha – can I speak to you as a friend?'

'Go ahead,' Natasha said, trying to look less hostile.

'As we get more senior in our respective roles,' Renu began, 'I think it is upon us to actually become more and more humble – after all, humility is a tremendously important quality in a leader, right?'

Natasha narrowed her eyes. Renu was pushing her luck. It was only a series of clever political moves through which she had got promoted last year, planting herself at the same level as Natasha. But for her to actually preach in that smarmy, know-it-all tone?

Deep inside, Natasha knew that maybe, just maybe, Renu had a point. But it was the delivery of the lines and the person who was saying it that made it ring false, an empty statement delivered with a flourish. And one thing Natasha couldn't stand was unnecessary drama.

So she put on a smile. 'Well said, Renu. I must agree with you there. But,' she said brightly, as if the idea had just occurred to her, 'it's also true that it just comes easier to some people than to others? As in – they just have so much *more* to be humble about?' She said it innocently, waving her hand in a sweeping gesture that included Renu.

It worked. The mask dropped for a moment and Renu's nostrils flared. Natasha watched her put the neutral expression back on; she had clearly decided that she couldn't beat Natasha when it came to words. Renu rose from her seat with as much grace as she could muster, and said, 'Well. I'm glad we had this little chat.'

Natasha looked at her with dislike. 'Yes. Always a pleasure, isn't it?'

Renu turned and walked away. 'Beeyatch,' Natasha murmured, trying to focus on the email that she had been composing to send to her team.

Renu's tittering laugh rang out, and Natasha all but groaned. Madame HR had obviously not gone very far. There she was, throwing her head back and laughing at something that someone had said. Oh. Nikhil. Was Nikhil joking around with her? Natasha couldn't believe the stab of jealousy she felt. How idiotic. She had no claim over him at all. She just wished Renu would keep her claws off him and keep her attention on her hero, Rishabh. Not that it was her business. She wished she could shake the feeling that Renu knew this bothered her. Had she picked up on something from when Nikhil and Natasha had hung out? Ridiculous. Especially when there was nothing to pick up on. Natasha would need to be more careful – she usually took care not to be associated with men at work. She tried harder to focus on the email, muttering, 'Where was I … Upgrade seventeen point one requires a … Da-da-da-da-da … Customer training plan and to that end, we are going to be rolling out a programme on the eighteenth…'

'Hi.' It was Nikhil's voice. Did her heart just skip a beat? Stupid woman, she told herself as she looked up, deliberately slow.

'Oh, hello.' She tried to sound surprised, as if just becoming fully aware of his presence.

He grinned. 'Just thought I'd check on how you're doing. Health-wise.'

'Am good. Health-wise.' Natasha indicated the chair, ignoring the fact that her heart was beating fast. She was still a little weak from the after-effects of the stomach episode, but she wasn't going to show it. The giddiness his presence seemed to bring about wasn't helping though.

He sat down and smiled. The dimple made her more nervous than usual, so she ended up blurting out, 'So what was so funny back there?' She tossed her head towards where Renu and Nikhil had been standing a few moments ago. Dammit. She was supposed to have just noticed him.

'Actually,' he leaned forward to whisper, 'I have no idea. Renu just stopped me to ask how things were, and I replied they were as good as they could be post-vacation.' He looked mystified. 'For some reason, she found that really funny. Is it funny?'

'Hilarious,' said Natasha dryly. So she had been right. Renu had done it deliberately.

'Is there something going on between the two of you?' Nikhil ventured.

'Nothing more than the occasional flirtation.' Natasha gave a sardonic smile.

'*I* bet,' he said. 'You've been using that sarcasm of yours with her.'

Natasha turned a little pink. 'So?' she said defiantly.

'Nothing.' His tone was light. 'But you know what they say about sarcasm being the lowest form of wit, right?'

She looked stone-faced, but felt a little ashamed. He was right, of course. She didn't need to stoop like that. Why did she let Renu get to her? Maybe she was just...

'Maybe she's just doing her job?' Nikhil continued. What, now he was reading her mind? She shifted in her seat uncomfortably. He grinned at her again. 'Anyway, glad you're better. And I'll be setting up time with you. You should take a look at the final version of the innovation pipeline before we get into execution.'

She nodded slowly, but his words about her sarcasm were still playing on her mind. Somehow, she couldn't think of his mild criticism as his lecturing her. It was the light tone, and the fact that he seemed to know when to stop. He stood up and turned away and she felt her heart sink. She suddenly realized she might just be driving yet another person away. She thought about Mrs Chopra's knowing smile. Yup. She was going to end up just like the old lady.

'Hey.' She tried to say it nonchalantly. He turned to look at her, eyebrows raised.

'Lunch? My turn to get you some food poisoning.'

He looked surprised but then smiled broadly. 'Sounds like a plan.'

They sat on opposite sides of the table at the new Korean restaurant that had opened up near the office.

'Been here before?' Nikhil looked around.

'Nope,' said Natasha, picking up the menu and scanning it with a frown. 'I just thought we should try it out.'

'Cool,' Nikhil said. Something in his voice made Natasha look up.

'What? You don't like Korean food?'

'No, no,' said Nikhil, 'it's just that I remembered only now that I had brought food from home.'

'You get a tiffin?' Natasha stared.

'Hey!' cried Nikhil. 'When *you* get your little salad box in an airtight container, it's called a box lunch. When I get my dal-parantha, dahi and sabzi, it's a "tiffin" – and what's wrong with that, miss?'

'Okay, okay.' Natasha couldn't help but feel a little flattered that he noticed what she got for lunch. She smiled. 'I just didn't think business heads brought their lunch to work.'

'You don't know anything because you never step into the cafeteria while people are there! Why is that, by the way?'

Natasha studied the menu again, murmuring, 'Actually, I don't think I'll take any chances with my stomach – maybe just the soup.'

'Natasha the Recluse,' Nikhil remarked, and when she looked up, he had a twinkle in his eye. There he went, taking liberties with her. Well, she supposed it didn't feel all that bad.

She sighed and put down the menu card. 'Nikhil, it may surprise you but I already know pretty much what I am. I even know everyone refers to me as Hitler. And that's fine. Because I don't believe that you have to be popular to be effective.'

'I'm not denying that at all,' said Nikhil, leaning forward. 'But neither is it true, Natasha, that the two have to be mutually exclusive.'

She flushed. It didn't feel too good when he put it that way. He was right of course – she immediately thought of Aman. He was benevolent but when it came to work, he was a visionary with a sharp mind. Well, except in his hiring decisions. She hardened her heart. Her way was better. She knew how to weed out the wrong people. She said a tad defiantly, 'Are you going to launch into another lecture? Perhaps you'll start pulling rank on me next?'

Nikhil grinned. 'No lecture. And we're outside the office. No question of pulling rank. I don't believe in that crap anyway. And I certainly don't think that way about you.'

They gazed at each other as the waitress came up. Natasha ordered the chicken coriander soup and Nikhil struggled for a few minutes and finally ordered a bowl of seafood noodle soup. As the waitress walked away, he said, 'Hey … are they really Korean in here?'

'Don't tell me you're one of those they-all-look-the-same-to-me types.' Natasha narrowed her eyes.

Nikhil laughed. 'You need to lighten up a little, Natasha. And by the way, with your eyes narrowed like that, even you look…' He trailed off.

'Don't say it,' she growled. 'Yes, they're Korean. This place is supposed to be really authentic. Meant for Gurgaon's growing Korean population.'

'It's really expensive, too,' Nikhil said breezily. 'I'm glad it's your treat.'

'Of course,' said Natasha stiffly. Just because she was a woman and earned less than him didn't mean she couldn't foot the bill.

Nikhil rolled his eyes. They sat for a few more moments in silence and then Natasha said a little guardedly, 'So. How's … Tisha?'

He seemed surprised. 'Well, she's fine. We're doing really well. Good reports from her teacher, and she enjoys sports. I'm also glad she's doing well with her piano lessons. I always wished I could have done more with music myself.'

'Drums, right?' she remembered.

'Yeah. Anyway. That was a long time ago.' His eyes crinkled as he smiled. 'So yes, Tish has been good – except, well, she's been having these quiet phases where I get the feeling she's thinking about something and not telling me what it is.'

'Hmm.' Natasha never gave unsolicited advice, but she couldn't stop herself. 'Well, she's almost eight, right? She's growing up now. Maybe she doesn't have to tell you everything she's thinking.'

'I know,' said Nikhil, but he looked troubled. 'It's just that no matter how hard I try, there are these little failures. The other day, because I had to travel to Mumbai, we got late with her homework – and then in the morning rush, she actually left it at home. I drove over with it but they refused to let me in – they said it's part of teaching kids about their own responsibility or something.'

There was a moment of silence and Natasha said, as gently as she could, 'And?'

'And nothing,' Nikhil admitted. 'Her teacher told her it was okay and that she could bring it the next day. But I felt like a failure.'

Natasha leaned forward. 'Hey, Nikhil. I'm no expert on parenting, but even I know that this kind of thing happens all the time. Are you seriously saying that leaving some homework behind by mistake makes you a failure?' She leaned back and crossed her arms, adding, 'That's a lot of pressure on little Tisha, isn't it?'

Nikhil blinked, a frown on his face. Then the frown cleared and the dimple showed itself. 'You're right.' He shook his head. 'Sometimes I take these little things too seriously. A little forgotten homework! It happens, right?'

'So I'm told,' said Natasha solemnly, liking the fact that she had actually made him feel better.

'You should come home and meet Tisha sometime,' said Nikhil, his voice full of warmth. 'Will you come next—'

'Oh good, food's here,' Natasha said with so much enthusiasm that a Korean couple sitting at a nearby table looked over at her with some censure. The waitress gave her a polite little smile and Natasha eagerly helped her get the soup and noodles off the tray. She then busied herself with tasting her soup. 'Mmm…'

By the time she stole another glance at Nikhil, he was eyeing his thick, murky seafood noodle soup suspiciously. He picked up a fork and smiled bravely at her as he stuck it into his bowl.

That was close, she thought. She could no longer deny the attraction she felt towards him. It was just that she wasn't into accepting package deals.

EIGHT

RISHABH BEING RISHABH

'Deepesh. At my desk, please?' Natasha demanded.

Deepesh stopped in his tracks, just outside Rishabh's room. He'd been sitting inside for what seemed like forever.

She had spotted him in there as soon as she returned from lunch, and had gritted her teeth while waiting for him to come out, unable to concentrate on anything else. The nerve of Rishabh, calling in her team member directly. And was that a presentation that Deepesh had been showing him? She led him to her desk, sat in her chair, crossed her arms and looked up at him.

Deepesh smiled nervously as he took a seat. 'Hi, Natasha.'

'Hello,' said Natasha. 'Pleasantries over?' she hissed. 'What were you doing in there?'

Deepesh looked around to see if anyone was listening and then wiped his brow. 'He just called me in out of the blue – said he needed an urgent review of the call centre project. He wasn't convinced I've been spending 30 per cent of my time on it and...'

'But why would he call you in without at least informing me?' Natasha was frustrated, knowing Deepesh couldn't answer. Clearly Rishabh wanted a rise out of her. She'd told him in no uncertain terms what she felt, and in their last meeting, Rishabh had assured her that he would keep her in the loop when it came to matters involving her team members, even on his precious project.

Deepesh was looking worried. Natasha said in a tired voice, 'So how did the review go?'

'Well, it was okay.' Deepesh sounded guilty. 'I don't know if he was really listening. He seemed a little distracted and just kept saying "hmm" and "good" throughout. But he made me go through the entire approach note and said he'll be wanting to track this daily through a thirty-minute review meeting at 1.30 p.m.'

'Daily?' Natasha couldn't believe her ears. 'During lunch hour?'

'Well,' said Deepesh, 'he said that's the only time he's going to be able to pull out, and asked me to adjust.'

'And of course you didn't protest. Or say you would check with me first.' Her voice was icy.

Deepesh sat up straight. 'No,' he said in a dignified tone. 'I said I would adjust.' He was a man who rarely questioned higher authority. Natasha realized that he had been caught between two authority figures here, and Rishabh outranked her. So much for loyalty.

He seemed apologetic again. 'Shall I send you the review presentation and his comments?'

Despite her irritation, Natasha couldn't help but feel sorry for him. She shook her head. 'Don't waste your time. Don't you have a call with Stellar Systems this afternoon?'

'Yes, I better get going.' Deepesh couldn't hide the relief he felt at this dismissal, and quickly got up and left.

Natasha thought she'd give herself a few moments to cool down, but why bother? She got up to go and see Rishabh in his lair.

He looked up as she opened his door.

'Oh, hello, Natasha.' He sounded surprised but she knew he had been expecting her. She walked in without waiting for an invitation and sat down in front of his desk as he said, 'Back from lunch?'

She frowned at him. What was that supposed to mean? Since when did he notice or care about her lunch plans? She decided to ignore his small talk and get straight to the point.

'You just held a review meeting with Deepesh?' Her tone was cool but sharp.

He blinked. And then, as if he had just remembered, said, 'Oh yes. Of course. Good progress. That Deepesh is quite a—'

'A member of *my* team, Rishabh,' Natasha interrupted. 'And we've already had a discussion about this. We agreed that we would let him lead this … project, but under my supervision.'

'Yes,' said Rishabh, acting innocent. 'And you've been doing a wonderful job, as always.'

Natasha ignored that too. 'So why would you hold a separate review meeting with him while I'm out to lunch? And you're talking about setting a daily discussion up during lunch hour? Why?' She couldn't hold back the frustration. Remembering how he had got the upper hand previously by retaining his cool, she tried to make an effort.

'Natasha.' The condescending way in which he drawled out her name caused her hackles to rise even further. 'It's just a little informal catch-up session. You have other priorities. This project is something important to me from a business-direction perspective, and I wouldn't want to pull you into every single discussion. It shouldn't become an issue if I have to speak to Deepesh about something in your absence. Surely, you know you need to be comfortable with skip-level discussions.'

'Yes, but an actual *review* is something that I shouldn't be left out of – it's not just a little chat in the corridor, Rishabh, and—'

'I notice,' Rishabh said as if she hadn't been speaking, 'that you are making an effort to establish relations with other departments. That is good, of course. It's always nice to be on good terms with different teams.' Natasha frowned, trying to figure out what the hell he was playing at. He continued, 'Of course, it would perhaps be nicer if you also paid attention to establishing such good relationships with a wider set of people.'

It took Natasha a moment to figure it out. For the last few days, she had been going out to lunch on a regular basis with Nikhil. He would swing by her desk at about 1.15 p.m. and they'd head out together. It had become routine. She took a deep breath. 'Are you implying there's something wrong with my having lunch with Nikhil?'

'Always so direct, Natasha.' Rishabh laughed. She hated his loud, self-confident and utterly fake laughter. 'And yet, so off-target. Aren't you listening? I said it's wonderful that you're actually coming out of your shell…'

'I was never in a shell,' Natasha corrected him. 'I don't like the cafeteria food and prefer to eat elsewhere.' *Not that it is any of your business, you jerk.*

'And now you have a lunch companion, and that's nice.' Rishabh smiled at her broadly. 'It's just that I thought I'd give you feedback about making a similar effort with other team members; including your own peers, of course.' She stiffened. He was making a point about Nikhil not being her peer – because he was at Rishabh's level. 'For example, there have been at least three occasions in the last month where I've asked you to join the other functional heads with me, over a team drink, and you've always said you're too busy. What does that prove?'

That you're a frickin' waste of time, thought Natasha. Out loud, she said, 'Rishabh, what I do after office hours is a matter of personal choice. And I don't think that at our level, we need to be given lectures about team-bonding practices.' She had stressed 'our level' to indicate that she didn't consider herself junior to him just because of the reporting relationship. What he was saying was bullshit. She was furious.

'I see.' Rishabh changed tack. 'So, speaking of team bonding … I received some feedback about your review meeting with Anirban.' Now it was his turn to get straight to the offensive. 'Is it true that you caused him to break down?'

Who had told him? *Deepesh*? Of course not. 'Let me guess,' Natasha said in a dry tone, 'a little HR birdie just flew by and whispered in your ear?'

'There's no room for sarcasm in a professional discussion, Natasha,' Rishabh said crisply and she had to bite her lip to keep from snapping. 'As a senior member of my team' – he emphasized the word 'my' – 'I expect you to understand it is HR's job, and indeed mine, to keep an eye on what is going on within the different teams across the business…'

'Oh, yes, I remember,' Natasha said with all the sweetness she could muster. 'Across *your* business.' She wished she could just tell him to stick it. 'Well, it's true that Anirban got a little … emotional. But he's been fine subsequently and I'm keeping a close eye on him.'

'Good. Good.' Rishabh leaned back and eyed her. 'I've also been thinking that we should make a trip to Mumbai. You know, combine a market visit with an internal team review.'

'Together?' Natasha did not like the sound of this.

'Yes, yes,' Rishabh said a bit impatiently. 'As two of the most senior leaders in the business, we should show them that they have our support and attention. It will be a show of strength if we go together, rather than do separate trips.'

Natasha opened her mouth to protest, but couldn't find any real flaw in his logic. Besides, if she was there, she could influence his point of view, rather than live in constant fear that he would return with some other hare-brained scheme to increase short-term revenue.

'Okay,' she said. 'We'll plan that out. But coming back to the point.' She narrowed her eyes at him. 'May I request that you cut down the frequency of the review with Deepesh to twice a week, and push it to post-lunch, 2 p.m.?'

He returned her gaze and then smiled. 'Of course, Natasha. You're my right hand. We should both be comfortable with each other.' He leaned forward and said earnestly, 'After a point of time, it's all about trust, right?'

Natasha hesitated. He had given in a little too quickly. Still, she supposed that the calling of a truce would only help her focus on more important matters at work. She was still angry about his comments on her lunch habit – but she hoped she had set him straight about staying clear of making remarks of a personal nature. It only cemented her desire to hang out with Nikhil, since it seemed to annoy Rishabh for some strange reason. For now, it made sense to walk away with a small victory. So she nodded slowly. 'Right.'

Managing a tight smile, she stood up and turned away.

At 6.30 p.m., Natasha found she could barely keep her eyes open. She sighed. Just a couple of months ago she had so much energy she could barely contain it. The fitness sessions, and even the yoga, had made a huge difference, she realized. She was less fussy about her diet since Nikhil had been teasing her at lunchtime about choosing to eat 'ghaas-poos' all the time. But she somehow knew the real problem was the lack of a good workout. Oh, why couldn't she just go to the fitness sessions again? Hmm. She picked up her laptop bag. Today was a Wednesday. She decided she would drop in and surprise Vicky. It had been several weeks. Besides, there was no real reason to not see him. That ride had been a little uncomfortable, that was all. No big deal.

She felt a little better as she drove on and parked near the club. Still five minutes to go before 7, but she thought she would drop in and find Vicky early to tell him she was going to get changed for the session. He was always here fifteen minutes early to 'mentally prepare' as he put it. But the room designated for the classes was locked. Hmm. She stood there, disappointed. Had he stopped coming just because she had told him she thought he might be gay? What an overreaction.

One of the aunties, whom she recognized as being from the class, was passing by. She asked Natasha, 'When is Vicky back? We've been waiting to resume classes since Christmas!'

Natasha shrugged – how would she know? She coughed a little and then started to head home. Even though her enthusiasm was now dampened and she would have liked nothing more than to crawl into bed and go to sleep, she paused at the base of the stairwell on the ground floor. She had taken to dropping in to see Mrs Chopra once in a while. She secretly enjoyed the old lady's cantankerous complaining and also liked playing with Kalu on the evenings that he was there. Maybe she'd stop by for a quick visit – it felt kind of nice to come home to someone, even if it was a cranky old woman with a mangy mutt. Natasha couldn't help but smile and shake her head as she rang the doorbell. Clearly, she was getting old.

She waited but no one came to answer. She listened for the sounds of either the old lady or the dog, but there was nothing. She rang again. Strange. She knew Mrs Chopra was home – the door wasn't bolted from outside.

After another couple of moments, she heard something. She let out the breath she hadn't realized she had been holding. The shuffling was slower than usual today. Mrs Chopra opened the door and looked out, dazed.

'Ah,' she said. It was all she could manage. She winced and tried to hide it but Natasha noticed immediately.

'What's wrong, Mrs C?' Natasha stepped forward. 'You're not well?' She took the old woman's hand without thinking about what she was doing, and realized that it was very warm. 'Do you have fever?'

'I don't know,' Mrs Chopra said irritably and Natasha was glad to see her spirit appeared intact. 'I was sleeping when you rang the bell.' She turned, freeing her hand from Natasha's, but gently. 'Come in, come in. I've been sleeping a lot these last couple of days.' She walked into the drawing room a little uncertainly, and Natasha followed, noticing how weak she looked. 'Perhaps I do have fever,' Mrs Chopra concluded as she reached her sofa and sank into it unsteadily.

Natasha continued to stand. 'Shall I make you something? A cup of tea? What have you eaten all day?'

Mrs Chopra looked up at her. 'Arrey, I don't want anything. And why will you make me a cup of tea?' She looked suspiciously at Natasha, but there was a twinkle in the grey, tired eyes. 'Have you ever made a cup of tea in your life?'

'A few times,' Natasha murmured. She felt like she should be doing something, but couldn't quite figure out what. Mrs Chopra looked really tired and frail. Natasha said, 'Should I get a thermometer? We should check your temperature.'

'Oh, nonsense,' Mrs Chopra said. 'What will we do with that? These things happen once in a while.' She winced again.

'What's wrong?' Natasha said as she sat down next to her. 'What's hurting?'

'Nothing,' said Mrs Chopra and then admitted, 'just my back. I think I might have strained it while washing clothes.'

'You wash your own clothes?' Natasha stared at her. 'Why? I thought you've at least got that lady who comes in for two hours in the morning.'

'Yes,' said Mrs Chopra, 'but I'm not going to let her wash my … my…'

Oh. 'Unmentionables?' Natasha concluded for her.

Mrs C gasped and then winced again. Natasha was seriously worried now. 'You know, you really should get someone who can stay with you longer,' said Natasha.

'No,' Mrs Chopra protested, 'I've told you, I like to be alone.'

'Even when you're sick?'

'It's just a fever,' said Mrs Chopra bravely. 'Do you want a coffee?'

'You must be joking,' murmured Natasha.

'I didn't mean I would make it,' said Mrs C. 'I just thought if you're making yourself a cup, you'll make me one. It's simpler than tea.' Natasha smiled and got up, glad to have something she could do. 'Anyway, I'm tired of sleeping all day.'

Something finally struck Natasha as a little odd. 'Where's Kalu?' He clearly wasn't in the house. 'He wasn't here last time either?'

'Oh,' said Mrs Chopra, a little too carelessly, 'he hasn't been coming these last few days. Must have found some other place. Ungrateful little mutt.' She chuckled but then winced again, and grunted, 'Good riddance.'

Natasha looked at her for a long moment and said, 'Yes.'

She turned to go into the kitchen. She had a feeling she knew why Mrs Chopra was like this, but the old lady wasn't going to admit it.

Once more, Natasha had the feeling that the two of them were cut from the same cloth.

NINE

TISHA

'Hey. You didn't get your car today, right?'

Natasha looked up. How the hell did *Rishabh* know that? Did this guy have her phone tapped or something?

'Yes,' she said warily. 'Sent it for servicing.'

He grinned. 'I saw you getting dropped off in a cab this morning and figured I'd give you a ride back home. Gives us a chance to catch up too.'

Natasha bristled. Did he actually think that after everything he had done, she was going to accept a favour from him? Truce or no truce, this was above and beyond the call of duty and she had no interest in 'catching up' with him. 'I'll call an Uber, Rishabh. Please don't bother.'

'Why?' He frowned. Clearly, he wasn't used to hearing 'no'. 'Come on, you can take a few minutes to wrap up. It's already seven.'

Out of the corner of her eye, Natasha saw Nikhil – he had his laptop bag slung over his shoulder and was walking out of the office with one of his team members. She suddenly had an idea. If her simple refusal had thrown Rishabh off, she couldn't wait to see what this would do to him. 'Oh, is it? Thank you for reminding me! I had clean forgotten – I'm supposed to be getting a ride home with Nikhil! Oh, and there he is, leaving already. I'm supposed to meet him downstairs.' She quickly started gathering her things and stuffing them into her bag. 'Bye, Rishabh.'

The pro that he was, Rishabh didn't let the surprise show on his face. She knew that somewhere behind his polite smile and nonchalant shrug was a bruised ego. He walked off to his room with rather stiff shoulders. She chuckled quietly to herself before running towards the lift, heels clacking loudly in the empty hallway.

'Nikhil,' she gasped. He had just been about to enter the lift and paused when he heard her. He threw her a surprised glance and then exchanged goodbyes with his colleague, who disappeared behind the closing lift doors.

'What's up, Natasha?'

'Nothing.' She swept a lock of hair from her eyes. 'Uh, I was wondering,' she said, looking up at him, 'could you give me a ride home?'

'Uh…'

She couldn't believe she was hearing doubt in his voice. Suddenly, she felt as if all the wind had been taken out of her sails. Well, served her right, she supposed. Now she knew how Rishabh felt.

She turned away from him, muttering, 'Forget it. Stupid of me to presume…'

'No, no, Natasha, wait.' He laughed and she turned back. 'It's just that I have to drop Tisha off at a sleepover and I'm already a little late. But if you don't mind the extra thirty minutes, I'd love to give you a ride home.'

'No. Seriously, it's okay.' Her cheeks were burning. 'You don't have to inconvenience—'

'Yeah, yeah.' He laughed as he caught her by the elbow and steered her towards the lift as the doors opened again. 'Let's go. This way, you'll also get to meet Tish.'

Not that it had been on her agenda, she thought as Nikhil called his driver to bring the car around. They walked out of the building together and Nikhil's driver politely held the door open for Natasha.

'Ramesh,' Nikhil said when they were both seated comfortably in the back. '*Pehle ghar jayenge. Phir tum nikal jaana, main* Tisha *ko drop kar doonga*.' Ramesh nodded and they were off.

After a few moments' silence, Natasha remarked, 'Sleepover, huh? Didn't know they happened outside of America.'

Nikhil laughed. 'We have a new single parents' club here that I'm a part of. There are a couple of moms with whom I do the sleepover thing a lot. It's a real support, especially on … What?' He noticed that Natasha was trying to smother a smile and then realized what he had said. He looked embarrassed. 'You know what I mean, right?'

'So are there other single dads in the group?' pressed Natasha.

'No. I'm the only one,' he said. He looked like he was going to say something more but didn't.

'And you're hot property in the group, right?' she guessed. He looked even more embarrassed now, and murmured something about how that was not the case. She looked out of the window, not wanting to push this further. She didn't like the thought of him hobnobbing with the single moms anyway.

They pulled into his complex, which seemed to have only row houses. 'Wow. Posh place. And not even five minutes from work,' exclaimed Natasha, looking around at the fountains and the carefully manicured trees and bushes.

'Yep, we're lucky.' Nikhil got out of the car and the driver held the door open for Natasha. She got out slowly. It would have been rude to suggest that she wait in the car. Nikhil led her to the door of his house and rang the bell once. A small woman opened the door and he said, 'Smitha, Tisha *ne khaana khaa liya*?'

The lady said, '*Haan, Bhaiya*,' and gave Natasha a polite 'Namaste, Didi.' Natasha felt uncomfortable as she tiptoed into the drawing room behind Nikhil. He called, 'Tish? Tish?'

'I'm right here, Dad,' said a voice that made Natasha jump. It sounded so grown-up, almost teenage. But it emanated from the little figure curled up on the sofa with a book.

'Tisha,' Nikhil ordered, 'get your feet off the sofa. And your nose out of the book. Say hello to Natasha aunty…'

'Just Natasha, please,' whispered Natasha. Tisha finally looked up and Natasha nearly had a heart attack. She looked so much like the little girl from her dreams. Curly hair, bright eyes, impish, pretty face. Natasha told herself to calm down, it *wasn't* the same girl. She distinctly remembered the hair of her little dream-invader was longer and less bushy, and her eyes were dark brown – Tisha's eyes were grayish green, and her skin much fairer. Something about her mouth and nose reminded her of Nikhil.

Natasha said, 'Hello, Tisha. Pleasure to meet you.'

The little girl looked surprised, and Natasha realized her greeting had been rather formal. But she returned in a serious tone, 'Pleasure to meet you, too.' Then she turned to Nikhil and said, 'Who is she?'

'Tisha,' Nikhil said with a warning note in his voice, 'we're not supposed to talk about people as if they aren't in the room, remember?'

'Oh, come on.' Natasha laughed. She was going to add, 'she's just a kid,' but something made her think better of it.

'Come on, T,' said Nikhil. 'You're all ready to go, right? Packed your toothbrush?'

'Umm. I think so, Dad.' Tisha frowned as if with deep concentration and Natasha had to smile at that. Nikhil sighed and said to Natasha, 'Will you please sit down for just a minute? I'll just look through her things once and we'll be off.'

He went into the bedroom and Natasha hovered uncertainly before sitting down on the sofa next to Tisha, who went back to reading.

The maid brought her a glass of water, which she accepted gratefully. She hadn't realized how thirsty she was. She took a long swig of the water and it felt good in her parched throat.

She put the glass down and looked around the room. It was a well-maintained house – not fancily decorated but the furniture was tasteful – combinations of white marble and wood all around. She liked it. It was kind of like Nikhil. Good-looking without making a fuss about it. She then noticed Tisha peeping at her and their eye contact sent the girl right back into her book. Natasha bit her lip and then said, 'So. What are you reading, Tisha? Enid Blyton?'

The little curly head shook from side to side and the book went up a little higher to reveal the title. *Pippi Longstocking*.

'Oh. What's that?' Natasha had never heard of this one.

'Pippi! You don't know Pippi Longstocking?' Tisha's face

came into full view as she cried, 'Really?' Apparently, she had never been faced with such astounding ignorance before.

Natasha managed to keep a straight face. 'Is it a girl?'

'She's not just a girl.' Tisha was scornful. 'She is the strongest girl in the *world*.'

'My goodness. Really?' Natasha was less intrigued by Pippi than by Tisha's excitement. She hadn't made conversation with a seven-year-old since she was about seven herself. It wasn't proving as hard as she had thought.

'Yes!' Tisha affirmed solemnly, curls bouncing up and down. 'She has a horse and a monkey and she lives alone in Villa Villekulla and has two friends, Tommy and Annika, and is always saving people and having adventures.'

'That sounds like an interesting life.'

'Yeah!' Tisha agreed wholeheartedly. 'I love Pippi. She's funny too. She hates multiplication and calls it plutipication.' She giggled.

'That *is* funny.' Natasha was enjoying herself now.

'Yes, but she lives without her parents, and I don't like that.'

'Hmm.' *Uh-oh,* Natasha thought. *Danger zone.*

'...But in this one, Pippi's sure she's going to be meeting her father. She hasn't seen him for years because he was a captain and got lost at sea, and everyone thinks he's dead, but she's sure that he's not dead.'

Natasha was at a loss for words. She hadn't counted on discussing death with the kid. She looked at her watch. Wasn't it getting late? 'Nikhil?' she called out, but there was no reply.

Tisha continued as if there had been no interruption, 'But her daddy will come. I know it!'

In spite of herself, Natasha asked, 'How do you know? How can you be so sure?'

Tisha frowned. 'Because a daddy isn't supposed to die!'

Natasha stared at her. She struggled to react, but the bedroom door burst open just then and Nikhil came out lugging a Barbie suitcase. 'Let's go, girls.'

Tisha sprang up off the sofa and said, 'Yay!' Natasha took a moment to compose herself and got up.

Tisha tugged at her skirt – she looked like she wanted to say something.

Natasha instinctively bent down to her level and Tisha whispered into her ear, 'Also, also, also, I've already *seen* the movie!'

TEN

FINALLY

'How come *I* can't sit in the front?' demanded Tisha.

Natasha took a step back from the car but Nikhil said, 'That's okay, Natasha. She never sits in the front

anyway.' He frowned and looked at Tisha. 'What did we talk about earlier? Not being rude?' His voice trailed off. Tisha raised her little nose and got into the back seat.

Natasha reluctantly strapped on her seatbelt while Nikhil got into the driver's seat. He murmured out of the side of his mouth, 'We have a rule – the front seat is no place for a kid.'

'How old are you, Natasha?' Tisha said in a sweet voice tinged with curiosity.

'Tish!' Nikhil warned, shaking his head. He looked at Natasha apologetically and started the car, glaring at Tisha in the rear-view mirror.

'Hey, it's okay.' Natasha laughed. She was not at all self-conscious about her age. She looked back at Tisha and smiled and said, 'I'm thirty-five.'

'Whoa!' Tish exclaimed and Natasha laughed again as

Nikhil rolled his eyes. 'But that's not as old as Daddy – he's forty, right, Dad?'

'Yes,' Nikhil said calmly. 'Thank you, Tisha. And you're a seven-year-old and not at all bratty. Now we all know how old everyone is.'

Tisha's voice floated in from the back. 'I can't wait to be thirty-five … Then I'll get to sit in the front.'

Nikhil rolled his eyes again and Natasha hid her smile as she looked out of the window. She had thought it would be uncomfortable, but this wasn't bad at all. They were really cute together, father and daughter. She settled back, content to listen as their banter started up again.

In twenty minutes, they reached Tisha's friend's house. Nikhil unstrapped his seatbelt and told Natasha, 'Back in a moment, okay?'

'Bye, Natasha,' Tisha called as she scrambled out of the car, slamming the door behind her.

'Bye, Tisha.'

As they walked off, Natasha could hear them bickering: 'You really should call her Natasha aunty.'

'She *said* to call her Natasha. Come on, *Daaad*…'

'I'm sorry about my daughter's behaviour.' Nikhil spoke again for the first time since they were alone in the car. 'She's not used to meeting any friends of mine.'

'Nikhil, will you please stop apologizing? I thought she was a hoot.'

This made him chuckle. 'She is, isn't she? I like that she's clearly got *my* sense of humour, even if all else is…'

His voice trailed off as he checked the traffic in the rear-view mirror before taking a turn. Natasha leaned her head against the window. Now that it was just the two of them, she felt self-conscious again. Why had she demanded that he give her a ride today? It would have been easier to just call a taxi. No more playing games just to amuse herself with Rishabh, she vowed.

The Gurgaon traffic honked outside, muted by the glass of the window. It was a little too quiet inside the car. Tisha's energy had been infectious. Her questions and non-stop chattering had kept them on their toes. She suddenly sat up straighter. That gave her an idea. Why hadn't she thought of it before?

Nikhil glanced over at her. 'What?'

'Hmm?' Natasha said, her mind still racing.

'You just thought of something, didn't you?'

'Oh.' She was always a little surprised by how he seemed to read her mind. 'Well, yes,' she admitted.

'What is it?'

'Nothing. You won't be interested.'

'Try me.'

She hesitated. 'It's nothing, really. There's this old lady who lives in the flat below me ... She's a widow and, uh, hasn't been well. I just realized that I know someone who can probably help her out – a young girl.'

'That's nice. Sounds like you really care about this old lady,' said Nikhil.

'Well...' Natasha wouldn't go *that* far. 'No, it's just that ... Mrs C doesn't have anyone else. So I'm just being ... neighbourly.'

'Always good to be neighbourly.' Nikhil nodded in a serious

way. She knew he was making fun of her in his usual gentle manner, and it made her clam up.

'Hey, don't worry, Natasha,' Nikhil said, glancing at her again after she had been silent for a few moments. 'Your secret is safe with me.' She frowned in confusion and he went on, 'No one in the office will ever figure out that you're really just an old softy at heart.'

'An old softy?' she cried.

'Sorry, a young softy,' he backtracked and then said teasingly, 'a mere thirty-five. So young. Ah.' He leaned back in his seat. 'I was thirty-five once ... The world looked so different then.'

She snorted. 'Of course. So long ago.' She coughed a bit.

'You've still got that thing?'

'What thing?' She wished he wouldn't keep pointing it out.

'Never mind,' he muttered. 'So tell me more about this Mrs C.'

This, Natasha could talk about. 'She's a cranky old lady, and I never really liked her – she was always complaining and putting everyone off. But I've figured out she really isn't so bad. She's actually quite ... kind. Well, to dogs, anyway.'

If this description confused Nikhil, he didn't show it. He just nodded. 'Hmm.'

Natasha went on, 'I think when you lose someone close to you, you change in ways that other people don't get. You know?' She paused and then looked over at Nikhil. 'I'm so sorry.'

'Not at all, Natasha,' Nikhil said as he pulled the car in through her gate. The security guard looked like he was going to stop them, but then caught sight of Natasha and straightened up with a smart salute. Nikhil didn't comment – he appeared to be thinking about what Natasha had said. And she felt like an idiot. Of *course*, he would know what it was like.

He pulled the car to a stop near her apartment. He switched off the ignition and then turned to her with his full attention. 'So I know what it's like to lose someone. And so does Mrs C,' he said in a quiet tone. 'I just don't know yet who it is that you've lost.'

There was a long moment of silence. He didn't say it as a question and Natasha knew that she wasn't expected to answer.

'My father.'

The two words were whispered so softly she didn't know if he had heard her. But he clearly had, because after a few moments of silence, he reached out and pulled her to him in a warm, intimate hug that she didn't bother resisting.

They sat there together like that, in the dark, for what could have been any length of time. She breathed in the faint scent of his aftershave and he ran his fingers through her hair.

She wasn't sure who started the kissing but it was most likely her.

PART THREE

ONE

WHEN IT FINDS YOU

'Where you going and *why*?'

Natasha had to smile at Nikhil's sleepy protest. This was a ritual that didn't change. They were lying in her bed, his arm and leg wrapped around her. Her alarm had already rung twice. She tried to slip out from underneath his arm again, but he tightened his grip. She wriggled around a little and gave up for the moment, turning to face him instead. Gratified, he pulled her closer so that her cheek was nestled against his neck.

'It's 4.30, you know,' she murmured softly.

'An ungodly hour if there ever was one,' he murmured back. 'Best not to be awake when it comes.'

'You're the one who has to get home before people wake up, remember?'

'Huh.' He dismissed it, but Natasha knew he was just procrastinating. It wasn't pleasant for her either, having him leave so early in the mornings on the two or three days in the week that he did manage to stay the night. But it had to be done. Well, she supposed a couple of minutes couldn't hurt.

She ran her fingers lightly over his arm, enjoying its weight on her. It was strange because she had never liked being pinned down – with others, she'd needed her space after sex. But things were different with Nikhil. The weight of him seemed to anchor her.

They couldn't stay like this forever though. Willing herself to make another attempt, she turned away and ducked her head a little, managing to slip out this time.

'You're a little eel,' he growled. But he let her escape, albeit reluctantly.

She sat up and slipped her nightshirt on, shivering a little. February was a pleasant month, but this particular hour was still harsh. A good hot coffee would sort that out, though. She put on her slippers and went into the kitchen.

She wasn't looking forward to the moment when Nikhil would leave the house. She always felt an uncomfortable twinge when the door shut behind him. But it was necessary. Tisha didn't know about the two of them, which meant he could only come over after she had fallen asleep for the night. And then he had to be home well before she woke up. It wasn't an ideal arrangement but it was the only way for now. Anyhow, she told herself, it was good he was always out of the house before Jamuna arrived.

She poured out two cups of steaming coffee, its smell almost as comforting as the fact that she had him for another hour. This 'ungodly hour', as he had put it, was actually the best time of the day for them – sitting together at the dining table over a cup of strong coffee, while it was still dark and quiet outside. It felt like they could be the only two people in the world.

—

'You know, you look gorgeous in the mornings.'

Natasha looked down at herself doubtfully. She knew Nikhil never bothered with false compliments. Right now, she was at the table wrapped in an old shawl, a monkey cap covering her short hair. Her feet were tucked beneath her and the shawl enveloped most of her, except the hand balancing the cup on her knee.

He caught the look on her face, took a sip of coffee and added, 'As far as night watchmen go, of course.'

That was more like him. She rolled her eyes and he grinned and stretched lazily. He never felt as cold as she did, and was wearing just a light blue T-shirt – one of the few he had left over here. She watched him and thought, with a strange mixture of pride and envy, that he looked good most of the time, even now with his brown hair all tousled.

He continued, teasing, 'How many people in the office would still be intimidated by you if they could see you now? Even Deepesh wouldn't break into a sweat. You better be careful I don't take a snap of you like this and put it on the notice board.'

She smiled. 'Yes. That would definitely damage the bitch-boss image I've worked so hard to cultivate.'

He frowned. 'Don't call yourself that.'

'Why not? I know they call me stuff like that. And I don't have a problem with it.' She sipped her coffee again. 'Gets the job done. That's all I'm interested in.'

'Hmm.' Nikhil nodded slowly. He looked unconvinced.

In a few short weeks, they had got to know each other really well. It didn't feel like they had started seeing each other only recently. It meant a lot to Natasha that he understood there were things she wasn't ready to talk about. She had told him the first time that they had been together the circumstances of her father's death – the basic details. That she had been young, very attached to him, much closer than she had ever been to her mom. That it had been an accident, and a big shock. And that's where she had stopped. He had listened quietly, content with whatever she had chosen to tell him – he didn't even question her about her mother. And that was something she was grateful for since it was the one question she never felt prepared to answer.

He reached out and stroked her cheek lightly. She blushed. It was the kind of gesture she had never allowed anyone else. There was a certain familiarity about him – she realized it had been there from the time she first laid eyes on him. It was a little weird. Not that she believed in any of that 'soulmate' crap, but she had to admit there had been some kind of connect with him from the start. And she found herself feeling immensely glad that they had come this far.

'What are you thinking about?' he asked gently.

'Nothing,' she said lightly. She didn't want to admit she was thinking about how she had behaved the first night. She thought her initial reaction was best forgotten.

Their lovemaking had felt like the most natural thing in the world. Natasha had had her fair share of lovers over the years and it wasn't as if it had been the wildest, most passionate with Nikhil. But it was as if the two of them were meant to be, instinctively knowing what to do as they explored each other's bodies. There had been none of the usual first-time awkwardness, bumping of noses. It was as if they fit together.

The panic attack that had hit her that night had definitely been unprecedented. He had blinked awake well before dawn and had found her fully dressed and pacing the room. He had watched sleepily for a couple of moments before asking, 'Hey. What are you doing?'

She had gasped, startled. She had been contemplating how to wake him and talk to him and was planning her little speech. He sat up, rubbing his eyes, asking, 'What time is it?'

'Look, Nikhil.' She circled around to his side of the bed and sat down at the foot, deliberately keeping a little distance between them. 'What happened here ... You don't have to ... It's not as if...' He frowned and waited for her to finish and she did, in a rush. 'I mean, look, we can just forget the whole thing if you want.'

He blinked for a moment and then his frown cleared and was replaced by a grin. 'Well, that's easy. I don't want that.' He looked challengingly at her. 'Do you?'

She hesitated, biting her lower lip. All the implications. He was her colleague, and she had never had an affair with one before. What if word got around? How would it affect their reputations? And what about his daughter? How would she react? And besides, he was older and she had no idea about his expectations, and...

She'd opened her mouth to say that she actually thought it would be far better to stop right now before things went too far, but said, 'I don't want that either. But...' She bit her lip and looked at the floor, unsure.

'Hey.' He'd moved in one smooth motion to sit closer to her and reached out to cup her chin, gently turning her face towards him. 'I know, Natasha ... I know. But have you heard of living in the moment and seeing where it goes?'

'Heard of all that,' she admitted. 'Bloody alien concept to me.'

'I can imagine.' He laughed lightly and let go of her chin.

She found that she had been holding her breath – his touch did strange things to her. 'Come here and let me try and explain it to you.' Despite her misgivings, she allowed him to draw her in. As he began to kiss her softly on the neck, she breathed, 'Okay.'

—

'So, busy day ahead? Meetings lined up?'

'No,' she said, going over a mental checklist. 'Fairly easy day, just that one stupid review with Rishabh on his pet project.'

Nikhil chuckled at her expression. He'd already told Natasha that she got a weird look around her jaw when she spoke about Rishabh, since it was usually through clenched teeth. She tried to relax her face.

Thankfully, nothing seemed to have changed in the office. Since they had been lunch partners for a while, no one seemed to notice anything different. Their paths didn't cross all that often at work. She noticed that Rishabh had begun to invite Nikhil a lot less into their functional reviews, stating that the innovations business had a strong enough pipeline to work on, thanks to the boost given to them by the earlier meetings. She had tried not to laugh out loud as Renu gave him an admiring look. She knew that Nikhil had only agreed to come into the initial meetings out of politeness and had been, like her and a few others, bored by the long-winded fancy-worded monologue that Rishabh called a team meeting.

Natasha had to admit that, of late, her powers of concentration at work were actually better than before. She was sleeping better and the dreams were less frequent – or maybe just less intense. She had cut down on smoking, not that Nikhil said anything to her – she didn't want to tempt him, given that he had recently quit. The nights he came over, she skipped her evening smoke on the balcony. She felt more energetic than before – stronger somehow. Whatever this was and however long it lasted, she was determined to enjoy the time they had together.

'How are things with Tish?'

'Good!' said Nikhil, but it seemed like an automatic reaction. Since they never pressed each other for details, she waited.

'Her piano classes are going really well,' he said after a while. 'Apparently she's way ahead of the rest of her class and her music teacher has written to me about getting her solo lessons.' He laughed a little incredulously. 'Said she's gifted. Isn't that cool?'

'I still haven't heard you play,' Natasha reminded him quietly. 'And I'd love to.'

'Well, that you'll have to come over for. I told you I'm not sneaking my drum set here at odd hours of the night. The guards may think I'm smuggling in something.'

Natasha frowned. 'Have they been saying something at the gate? I told them—'

'No, no,' Nikhil interrupted. 'They've been fine. They don't react at all. Not after you came down and yelled at them that one night.'

Natasha tossed her head. 'It's none of their business. They had no right to stop you, they should have just called me on the intercom.' She muttered, half to herself, 'Judgemental pricks. They think they can just…'

'So, um … Tisha.' Nikhil rubbed his forehead. 'She's fine, mostly. Maybe she's just growing up or something. It's just that she kids around with me a lot less these days. I mean, earlier when I came home from work, she would run up to me, trying to tell me twenty different things at the same time. Now, she barely looks up from her book to say hi and gives me these monosyllabic answers when I ask her how her day went.'

'Still reading Pippi?'

'That and everything else. I seriously think she's read more books than I have already. Crazy.' Nikhil shook his head, but Natasha knew he was proud of Tisha for this. 'I just wasn't prepared for her to grow up so soon – it's like living with a teenager.'

'So what do her teachers say?'

'Her class teacher said she's fine at school, although she does tend to go quiet. She's got this one circle of friends who're a little on the notorious side – they're a bit spoilt, apparently.

I just hope they're not a bad influence on her or something.'

'Well, I don't know much about kids,' Natasha said cautiously, 'but she certainly didn't strike me as anything close to *spoilt*. In fact, she's kind of cool. And quirky.'

'Yeah.' Nikhil smiled. 'I suppose … It can't be easy for her all the time, especially now that she's growing up and the other kids ask her about her mom. Do you know?' He turned to Natasha. 'Yesterday, she came and asked me what divorce is. And after I tried to explain it to her, she just said, "Oh, cool. I'll go and tell that boy from third F that he's wrong, you and Mom are not divorced, it's just that she's dead!"'

Natasha was horrified, but Nikhil was chuckling. She still felt unsure about how to react when Nikhil spoke about his wife, but the moment passed.

'You should come home,' he ventured. 'I'll play my drums, and you can get to know Tisha better. And vice-versa.'

Natasha set her coffee cup on the table and lowered her feet to the floor. 'Remember what you said about letting things *flow*?'

He nodded slowly, looking resigned. She got up from the table and bent to give him a quick kiss on the cheek. 'It's time. Now go home,' she instructed. 'And I'll see you at work in a few hours. Okay?'

'Fine, fine,' he grumbled good-naturedly.

He got up and stretched one more time, remarking, 'I don't know if you've noticed, but you can be a little bossy sometimes.'

'Really?' she said wryly. 'Next time you're over, I'll *show* you who's boss.'

He raised an eyebrow and gazed at her appraisingly. Now he looked even more reluctant to leave.

TWO

MUSICAL HIGHS & LOWS

'Didi ... *Koi aaye hai...*'

Jamuna's voice floated in from the hallway and Natasha set down her hairbrush. Who could it be at this time of the morning? She walked out of her room and stopped in her tracks when she saw him.

'Vicky?' she said disbelievingly. 'What are you doing here?'

Her former fitness instructor grinned. He was dressed in jeans and a well-fitting T-shirt. It was neon-green and she felt a mild, irrational envy of him for being able to carry off that colour.

'Hey, Natasha ma'am! It's so good to see you.' He stepped forward to give her an impulsive hug. She was taken aback but he seemed so excited, she found herself laughing as he rocked her back and forth. He always brought so much extra energy with him. Also, extra *people*, she realized, when she saw a young, slightly heavyset woman in a pale-pink salwar kameez hovering in the doorway. Vicky released Natasha and beckoned to her, 'Oye! Come in.' He turned to Natasha. 'I want you to meet someone, Natasha ma'am ... this is Riya.'

Natasha smoothed her hair and stuck out her hand. 'Natasha.' This seemed to take Riya by surprise for a moment before she grabbed her hand and pumped it up and down, saying, 'Hello, Natashaji, I've heard so much about you from Vicky.'

Natasha looked over at Vicky, who beamed and said, 'Natasha ma'am, Riya is my wife!'

Natasha was shocked. 'What? You got married…' She didn't finish her sentence. Just a few weeks ago, he had been saying he wasn't ready for marriage and now he had suddenly produced a Riya. Her hand finally released, Natasha looked at her closely, noticing the glowing skin, large brown eyes and pretty, pink mouth. She seemed pleasant and a becoming blush had taken over her cheeks as Vicky announced their relationship.

'I know what you're thinking,' said Vicky in a rush. 'Why weren't you invited, right?' Natasha opened her mouth to protest but he went on, 'It all happened very suddenly. We've been family friends since we were children, but we met more recently at a function in my hometown, and it was as if I was seeing her for the first time ever. And just a couple of weeks ago, I told my parents to talk to uncle-aunty and then, before we knew it, things were happening because her brother had to fly back to America on the fourth, and it just so happened that it was the most auspicious time of the year, so we had a quick ceremony then and there! Ma says she will never forgive me for denying her a big fat Indian wedding, but I think Papa's quite happy when he calculates the savings.' He gazed at his blushing wife fondly. 'Isn't life strange? I thought I'd never want to get married, but meeting Ri-Ri made me feel like I'd been waiting for her all my life!' He smiled at Natasha. 'And I have you to thank for it, Natasha ma'am.'

'Me?' Natasha said warily. 'What…'

'If you hadn't shaken me up that day,' Vicky said almost reverently, taking Natasha's hands in his, 'if you hadn't really got me thinking about who I was and where I was going with my life, I'm telling you, Natasha ma'am, I wouldn't even have been open to the idea of finding someone. Your words were playing on my mind constantly … That's why, when I met Ri-Ri, it just clicked … all because of *you*.'

Natasha had to stop herself from smiling at the Ri-Ri, so she covered it up by laughing. 'Oh, don't be silly. Why don't you guys come in and sit down?'

'No, no! You're probably getting ready for work,' said Vicky. 'I just came by to talk to your club secretary about starting early-morning sessions now that I'm back. The timing would suit me better than the evening hours.' He looked at Riya again. 'I think Ri-Ri would want me back home in the evenings, right?'

Ri-Ri looked too shy to respond and, in fact, a little appalled that Vicky would even ask her this in public. Natasha came to her rescue and said, 'Well, that sounds like a great plan, Vicky. As it happens, my yoga's been on hold too, so the morning hours would be great.'

'Wonderful. It'll be wonderful to have you in the class.' Vicky slapped Natasha on the back so hard she almost lost her balance. 'Hey, you've become weaker without the workout, eh?' he commented.

Natasha was about to say she was fine, but it didn't matter because Vicky didn't really give her a chance to speak before he turned to Riya, saying, 'Natasha ma'am is very fit. The only lady in my class who can do thirty push-ups.'

The admiring look Riya was giving Natasha made her squirm. Riya said, 'Vicky has said you are like an older sister to him ... You are such an inspiration. Do you mind if I also call you Didi?'

Natasha opened her mouth to say that she would really, really hate that, but something made her stop. She looked from Riya to Vicky, noting his guilty expression, which told her he had forgotten to ask Riya to stay clear of older-sister references. She looked at Riya again and smiled. *What the heck.*

'Why not?' She smiled at Riya, aware of the look of relief on Vicky's face.

She now had a Ri-Ri calling her Didi. Life was getting weirder.

On her way out of the building, Natasha glanced at her watch. She was running just a little late, but there were no important meetings lined up for the morning. She turned and headed towards Mrs Chopra's house. The door was open, and Natasha walked right in. 'Mrs C?'

'Here,' called Mrs Chopra from the kitchen.

'Why's your door open?'

'Oh, I thought you'd be dropping by,' said the old lady as she came out of the kitchen. Natasha couldn't help but think that Mrs C was aging before her very eyes.

'Still.' Natasha adjusted her bag over her shoulder. 'I don't think you should leave your door open like that.'

'Actually,' Mrs C said, holding out a key, 'I got an extra key made for you.' Natasha stared at it. Mrs Chopra added, a little gruffly, 'Just in case I lose mine.'

Natasha hesitated, but only for a moment. 'Okay, sure.' She took the key to put into her purse. It felt like a big responsibility, but she knew it made sense to have the key in case of an emergency. 'So, er, Preeti's coming in regularly in the afternoons after school, right? You're all set with her?'

'Yes, she's all right. Has more sense than that mother of hers.' Mrs Chopra indicated Natasha's flat upstairs. 'Do you know she is *still* dropping the water on to my balcony every morning? What kind of a person cannot understand something so simple?'

'Okay, but Preeti?' Natasha pressed impatiently. 'She's all right?'

'Yes,' Mrs C admitted. 'Although I'm telling you, I really don't need anyone. Still, she is a bright girl. I've told her to make sure to bring me her school books. I can help with her English, Hindi and basic mathematics. The kind of things they teach in these government schools, it's hardly an education...'

'That's great!' Natasha cried. 'I'm sure that will be a huge help for her.'

Mrs Chopra looked pleased. 'We'll see how she does.' Natasha had a feeling this was working out well; Mrs Chopra would be far more accepting of help if she felt that she was being useful herself.

'So why are you hanging around?' Mrs Chopra demanded. 'Get to work now.'

Natasha laughed. 'Okay, Mrs C. See you later.' Her heels clicked in the hall as she headed out, feeling lighter than usual and yes, downright *happy*.

Natasha's good mood lasted all morning and even the thought of the review meeting on the call centre project with Rishabh couldn't dampen it. She was running a little behind schedule and had messaged Nikhil that she would probably have to skip lunch today. She felt a twinge of regret; she wasn't sure if he was going to be able to come over tonight. But she put her feelings aside as she ran a quick glance over the meeting's agenda.

She saw Rishabh was approaching and quickly stood up. 'Hi, Rishabh. Shall we start? I'll call Deepesh…'

'Actually, I just met him and told him that we'll be skipping today's meeting.'

'Oh?' Natasha was both relieved and surprised. 'How come?'

'I've been wanting to do some blue-sky thinking and I figured that maybe this particular project is taking up more of our time than I had initially anticipated.' Rishabh's tone was breezy. 'Given that the new financial year is coming up, I thought we'll start our annual planning process and put this project on hold for the rest of this quarter. If we agree that it fits into our annual plans and strategy, and we can allocate budgets and personnel to it, we'll fit it in during Q1. What say?'

Natasha struggled not to judge him for the 'blue-sky thinking' bit as she nodded. She didn't know what had caused him to change his mind, but it was best to quickly accept it before he did an about-turn again. 'Yes, Rishabh. I think that would be best.' She bit back the 'I told you so, moron' which was at the tip of her tongue.

'So anyway,' he said, 'since we're not having that meeting now … you want to get lunch?'

'You bet.' Natasha snapped her laptop shut. 'I'd cancelled, but I'll be able to go and grab something and get back before my 2.30 call. Thanks, Rishabh!' She continued to pretend that she had misunderstood the invitation implicit in his question and gave him a friendly little wave as she walked off towards the lift. She dialled Nikhil's number to say that she was going to be free for lunch after all. Ignoring the feeling that Rishabh was watching her, she quickened her pace.

—

'So what are you doing later tonight?' she asked Nikhil over lunch. 'Homework as usual?'

'Yes – but this week it's going to be piano homework!' he said. 'Tish has a recital at the school on Saturday. There's some sort of music festival they're putting up…' He sat up straight. 'Hey! You want to come with us?'

'What?' Natasha was taken aback but quickly recovered. 'I don't think so.'

He looked crestfallen and she cringed inwardly. She hadn't meant to be so blunt. But a kiddy recital at a school?

'Natasha,' he said carefully, after another moment, 'it would mean a lot to me if you came – Tisha has been practising really hard for this thing, and she's really good. And she'd love to see you there, too.' Natasha had her doubts about this, but he pressed, 'Seriously. She's been asking me when she'll get to see that pretty, weird lady again.'

She ignored the teasing. 'Nikhil, I'm really sorry, but it's just not my scene.' She added, 'And besides, you only asked me as an afterthought. It's not as if you'd been planning for me to come. So just go ahead and have a nice time, okay?'

He still looked disappointed but said mildly, 'Well, I know I didn't ask you till you brought it up, but that's because I assumed you'd say no.' He shook his head. 'And that's exactly what happened.' He sighed. 'I understand. Let's just forget the whole thing.'

Those words triggered the memory of their first time together. 'We can just forget the whole thing' – that's what she'd said. But then, they had had a wonderful time together. She had certainly let go of some inhibitions to get this far. Couldn't she give up a few more, if it meant that much to him?

'Well, if you'd like some company, I wouldn't mind coming,' she said haltingly. 'As long you're sure it won't be strange for Tisha.' The next part came out in a rush. 'I guess I do want to hear her play.' She was surprised by how true this was.

Nikhil grinned broadly and reached out to squeeze her hand, then went back to his food with renewed enthusiasm. His reaction made her feel that it might actually be worth it to do a little experimenting of this nature – after all, Tisha was an integral part of him – how long could they keep her from knowing about Natasha being in his life too?

So she pushed away the little voice inside her head that was beginning to insistently suggest that this might be biting off more than she could chew and she busied herself with asking the much easier, logistical question, 'Um, so what time is the thingy on Saturday?'

'Dress? Jeans? *What?*'

For the first time in ages, Natasha found herself feeling nervous as she tried to decide what to wear. She knew how to dress for office and she definitely knew how to dress for a party. But she had absolutely no clue as to how to dress for a piano recital.

What if she wore jeans and it turned out too casual? But a dress might just look too dressy. Was it formal, casual or semiformal? It wasn't a workday, so most of the parents wouldn't be coming straight from work in their work clothes. That would have been the simplest thing to do. But no, the school-people had to go and hold it on a Saturday, just to confuse her and make things more difficult.

She didn't want to make things awkward for Tisha. What if people mistook her for Tisha's mother? How would Nikhil handle that one? 'No, this isn't her mom, just this random colleague from work that I'm seeing but don't tell Tish that, okay? We'll break it to her gently once we know where it's really going.' This was not going to work, she decided. She would call Nikhil and tell him that she wasn't up to it and that they should go ahead without her. This was Tish's big day and her being there might end up spoiling it.

As if on cue, her phone beeped with a message from Nikhil: 'Tish is super excited you're coming. We'll pick you up at 4.'

She bit her lip. This was just like Nikhil. Did he have some kind of radar that told him exactly what she was thinking? Now he was claiming that Tish was all excited and Natasha would feel guilty about backing out. It would seem as if she was unwilling to make time for something that was important to both father and daughter.

Okay. She typed out the word and then flung the phone on the bed. 'Okay,' she growled and turned back to face her cupboard with a menacing scowl. 'Let's *do* this.'

'Hey,' Nikhil called as she walked out of her building. 'Nice dress.'

Natasha had chosen a sober but elegant body-hugging

black-and-grey-striped dress – it was hardly fancy, but Nikhil looked impressed. She grinned at him and then walked over to the other side of the car. She poked her head in and said to the little figure in the back seat, 'Hi, Tisha! Now *that's* a killer dress.' She looked approvingly at the sleeveless dark-blue frilly dress that Tisha was wearing. Her curly hair had been tamed into a ponytail and she flashed Natasha a shy grin in response.

Natasha got into the front seat and put on her seatbelt, aware that Nikhil was still looking at her. 'You know, you girls are making me feel underdressed.'

'Yeah, yeah, you look fine,' Natasha assured him. In his crisp, blue shirt and corduroy pants, he did. 'Besides,' she pointed out as he started the car, 'I did *ask* you.'

Nikhil gave her a quick warning look and then a guilty smile. When in desperation she had messaged him 'What are you wearing?' she had received a cheeky 'Hold on, babe. Now's not the time. We'll do this later, though' with a winking smiley.

Tisha's voice rang out from the back. 'Ask him what?'

Nikhil coughed and Natasha looked back at Tisha and asked a little too brightly, 'So you ready for your performance?'

Tisha nodded and looked out of the window. Natasha thought she seemed subdued. This was that same kid who couldn't stop talking nineteen to the dozen? Maybe she was nervous. But Nikhil had mentioned how great it was that Tisha wasn't ever nervous before a performance – she didn't seem to know the meaning of the word, he'd said.

Nikhil glanced at the rear-view mirror. 'Tish? So which one have you decided you'll be starting with? Remember, you can't keep changing your mind – they'll announce it and you'll have to play in the same order...'

'*Kindergarten Blues*,' whispered Tisha, '*April Shower. Sour Lemons.*'

'Wow, you're playing *three* songs?' Natasha exclaimed.

'They're all pretty short pieces,' said Nikhil. 'That last one's a little tough, but I'm sure she'll sail through. Right, Tish?'

Tisha didn't answer. She was sitting directly behind her, so Natasha could see her little face in the side mirror – she was still gazing out at nothing in particular. Natasha glanced over at Nikhil. He looked worried as he tried to catch Tisha's eye in the rear-view mirror. Whether Tisha was nervous or not, he definitely was. She could only hope that Tisha's mood had nothing to do with Natasha being there.

The rest of the car ride was silent.

An hour later though, Natasha was beginning to enjoy herself.

There hadn't been any of the awkwardness she'd expected before they'd taken their seats. Most of the adults there were strangers to each other and had exchanged only a few pleasantries before proceeding to focus on their children. Natasha and Nikhil had good seats in the fourth row, even though Natasha had claimed the aisle seat as if she needed a clear escape route.

A lot of the kids who were performing were really talented. Kids of all ages were playing instruments, from the guitar to the piano to, impressively, the cello. There was also one slightly unfortunate attempt involving a violin. That one had made Natasha grit her teeth, the raucous cacophony of the instrument apparently not bothering the perpetrator herself – a skinny girl with glasses, about ten years old, with a serious disposition and possibly tone deafness. The applause was wild when she finished, but Natasha knew it was more relief than appreciation.

Nikhil was fidgeting, craning his neck for Tisha and murmuring, 'Next, maybe? Next? What, they've put her last? That's okay though. She'll be fine.' He was talking more to himself than to Natasha, so she just found his hand and squeezed it. The teacher then announced, 'And now we have Tisha on the piano. Let's give her a big hand.'

Nikhil clapped hard, as did Natasha. He looked tense, as if he wasn't breathing at all. Tisha looked very small as she walked across the stage to the piano. When she sat down, only her legs and the top of her head were visible. And then she started to play.

She played the opening strains softly and then got louder and more confident. Natasha realized Tisha was way ahead of the other kids. Natasha realized Tisha was good, in fact better than some of the older kids who'd played piano before her. This piece didn't sound like it was easy, but her playing was flawless and the whole hall was still. Natasha noticed a few surprised faces, but then she was lost in the music herself as Tisha took it up to a crescendo and finished with a flourish. The audience applauded and she turned a page on her music book and went on to play another piece and then the third, each better than the previous one.

When Tisha finished and stood up, the applause was even louder than the one Violin Girl had received. She had a polite little smile on her face but looked like she was searching for something as she looked out into the audience. Natasha realized she was probably looking for Nikhil and she nudged him. He seemed rooted to his seat in amazement and relief, but raised his hand to attract Tisha's attention. When she spotted him and gave him an excited wave, her smile was bright.

'Bow,' he mouthed, 'bow.' But Tisha didn't see that. Her eyes had already wandered over to a group of girls who were sitting together in the audience, on the other side of the aisle. Natasha's sharp eyes noticed the change in her expression. It was only a moment, but she caught it, just before Tisha finally seemed to remember to take a low bow. She then speedily exited the stage.

Natasha looked over at the girls more carefully. They looked about the same age as Tisha – four or five of them, rather carefully dressed for seven-year-olds. They weren't performing as far as she could remember, and they had all chosen to sit together. Natasha gathered that the well-dressed, stiff-looking adults in the row behind them were the parents. The girls had their heads together and were whispering about something. They looked at Tisha's retreating back and Natasha was surprised to see the spiteful anger on one or two pretty little faces.

She turned back to Nikhil, who looked happy. He grinned at her and she knew he was really pleased she was with him right now. For a second, she forgot about everything else and found herself glad to be with him too. Happy about being at a school's musical recital, she mused, shaking her head at herself. Yes, she was definitely changing in unexpected ways, and she had to admit it didn't feel half-bad.

Tisha was even quieter on the ride home than on the way there.

'You were great, Tish,' Natasha remarked, and then remembered she had already told her that when they had picked her up from her class.

'Thank you,' came the quiet and dignified response.

'I have an idea,' Nikhil announced grandly. 'How about we get some of your favorite food – pizza!' He then glanced over at Natasha teasingly. 'It's Natasha's favourite too.' She made a face and then laughed.

'I'm tired, Dad,' said Tisha shortly. 'I just want to go home.'

Nikhil looked worried. Natasha gathered that pizza had never been refused before. 'Well, okay,' he recovered. 'So we can order in from Domino's, can't we?'

Tisha considered this and then said firmly, 'No. Pizza Hut, then.'

Nikhil broke into a smile. 'Natasha, you'll come home and celebrate with us, right?'

Natasha wasn't sure how to answer; she still didn't know how Tisha felt about her presence. She struggled for a moment and then said, 'You know what, you guys go ahead. I'm tired too – I think I'd just like to get home, if that's okay?'

Nikhil glanced at her quizzically but Natasha couldn't possibly tell him right now that she just wanted to give him and Tisha some space. He nodded and said, 'Okay. We'll drop you on the way. It was very nice of you to come. Right, Tisha?'

A small 'Right' came from the back, and Natasha had to smile at that. Nikhil addressed Tisha, 'You really did play wonderfully today, sweetie. And I think you had everything perfect – you really nailed the dynamics!'

No word from Tisha. Natasha saw, in the side mirror, that she was once again gazing out of the window with a serious expression. She didn't know what Nikhil had been referring to, musically speaking, but she had a sneaking suspicion that there were some other type of dynamics that *he* wasn't quite getting.

THREE

REST AND PEACE

'So, it looks like we're on track this quarter. Good job, guys.'

Natasha looked at her team members and a gratified murmur went around the room. She also heard a few gruff thanks from the speakerphone and added, 'Especially Mumbai. Great work, Anirban.'

'Thanks, Natasha.' His voice was warm and confident. He even managed to sound older. She grinned and said, 'Bye.' The conference call was over and everyone got up to leave.

Outside, Natasha ran into Rishabh and he remarked, 'Sales review?'

'Yes,' Natasha said briskly. 'You'll be happy to know that all regions are actually above their target run-rate for this quarter. The trainings have really worked. I think April will be a good time to introduce the certification programme too. We can build it into the AOP, and—'

'That's a great idea,' Rishabh interrupted and Natasha fought to keep the frown off her face. Rishabh was in love with his own voice, so she couldn't expect better from him.

He continued smoothly, 'Why don't we use the time on our Mumbai trip to discuss it? You said you would be setting it up?'

She had been hoping he would forget about that. 'Actually, Rishabh,' she said, 'now that the Mumbai branch has actually picked up pretty well and the team seems to be shaping up under Anirban's leadership, there's no real crisis there. I can go ahead and handle this month's visit with them and perhaps you could do Bangalore?'

Rishabh's mouth tightened for a moment. When he spoke, his tone was condescending. 'Natasha.' He shook his head. 'This is exactly the sort of thing that I am supposed to coach you on. It's not as if we should show our strength and commitment only if the team's morale is down. It's equally important to be with them to celebrate the turnarounds and the highs. Now's the time to ride the wave of success with them and let them know we appreciate their efforts ... This is our opportunity to—'

'Okay, fine,' Natasha snapped just to shut him up. She couldn't take one more puff of air from this windbag. 'Coach her' indeed. 'Next week. How's Thursday? Or Friday?'

'Sounds good.' Rishabh gave her a highly satisfied smirk that she wanted to wipe off his face.

She gave him a nod and then turned and walked to her desk. She wanted to get out early. Nikhil had said he would be coming over because Tisha was supposed to be at another sleepover. Natasha found herself feeling very kindly towards the westernization of the country. She hoped Tisha would get invited to more and more sleepovers.

Natasha was in her car when she got a call from Nikhil. 'Hey,' she said, sticking the key into the ignition. 'Just got in the car. Thought I'd leave early and get ready for our date. What do you feel like eating?'

'Natasha.' He sounded uncomfortable. 'I'm really sorry about this. Tish called – she sounded like she's a little under the weather. She was sniffling and saying she doesn't feel like going to the sleepover. So I told her not to worry, I'll be home and we'll figure out what to do.'

'Well, that's okay,' said Natasha quickly. 'You should definitely be with her.'

'Oh.' He paused. 'I was hoping you would come over and the three of us could just, you know, hang out. We'd still get time together, and I really think you might enjoy getting to know her some more.'

'Well, yes,' Natasha said carefully, her mind racing. 'But, Nikhil, she really sounds like she needs you tonight, and may not be in the mood to socialize. We don't want her to feel like she can't get quality time with you, right?'

After a few moments of silence, he sighed. 'Okay. I guess you're right. I'm sorry, I was so looking forward to seeing you at a relatively decent hour today. If she's really unwell, I might not be able to come over later either.'

'It's okay, Nikhil,' Natasha said, trying to hide her disappointment. 'We'll have other times.'

'Okay. So I'll see you maybe tomorrow? And you'll come home next week and hang out?'

'Sure.' Natasha bit her lip. She hated to be insincere.

'Great. Bye.' He hung up.

She started the car and drove home, slower than usual. Now why had she agreed to go home with him as early as next week? Things were moving at their own pace and she didn't want to rush into anything. She still wasn't sure how it was all going to work out. She knew she could possibly make a good girlfriend, but god knows she wasn't stepmom material. Or worse, what if she was? She chuckled as she imagined herself as an evil queen going, 'Mirror, mirror on the wall.' She stopped smiling – it wasn't funny.

She just didn't have a clue about how to deal with kids. She genuinely liked Tisha and even though they had met only a couple of times, Nikhil talked about her a lot. While she had initially thought of him as a slightly obsessive parent, she realized how much pleasure and meaning he derived from being a good father. He was definitely the most involved dad she knew, and that was good for Tisha. The last thing she wanted was to be the stranger invading their home.

She thought back to the concert and Tisha's stricken face as she looked at the other girls in the audience. What was going through her head? She hoped Nikhil would pick up on it and help her work things out. Maybe she should have said something to him. It might have looked like she was interfering though. After all, what the hell did she know about little girls? She sighed. Maybe they both needed to talk about taking things a little slower. They had said they would let it flow, but how long could they ignore the fact that there was a certain little person who was going to be affected?

She decided she was glad to have time alone today. She didn't enjoy the pangs of disappointment she had felt when Nikhil told her he couldn't come over. Was she dependent on him now? That wouldn't do.

After she had parked her car, she walked over to her building and turned to Mrs Chopra's place. She rang the bell, deciding she wouldn't hang around for long; she'd just check in on her and be off.

It was after several moments that Natasha heard the slow shuffling. *Uh-oh. What now?*

When Mrs Chopra finally opened the door, she greeted Natasha with a gruff 'You' and shuffled back indoors.

'Yes. Me.' Natasha walked in and shut the door. 'Preeti's left? It isn't even 7 yet.' She frowned. 'I hope she's staying for the full five hours we agreed on?'

'I told her to go.' Mrs Chopra sounded crankier than usual and she sat down on her sofa, looking tired and ill. 'I couldn't take her chattering any more. It was giving me a headache.'

Natasha stared at her. Preeti was so quiet and painfully shy that it was rare to hear a peep out of her. 'Chattering?' she repeated. 'Preeti?'

'Yes,' Mrs Chopra affirmed. 'Talks too much.'

'Okay.' Natasha sat down and looked at Mrs Chopra. 'So what was she talking about?'

Mrs Chopra hesitated. 'Well, you know. She said she saw a van come in today ... Dogcatchers. They were rounding up the strays in the colony. Apparently there was an incident with one of the dogs snarling at a resident and they used it as proof that they are all vicious, and there was this big agitation and they are getting them removed. She said they caught two right in front of her – took away about eight or ten.'

Natasha frowned. 'I thought there was some law against relocating strays? What's going to happen to them?'

'Who knows?' Mrs Chopra said dismissively. 'What can anyone do about it anyway? That's what I told the girl. Kept on about it. I told her if she was going to start crying, I would fire her.'

Natasha froze. 'Did Preeti say Kalu was caught too?'

'I didn't ask her, of course. She probably doesn't even recognize him,' Mrs Chopra said in a tone that implied it was the silliest question she had ever heard. She looked pale, Natasha noticed.

'Are you all right?' Natasha felt anxious. Perhaps Preeti could start staying over some nights, at least when Mrs Chopra was ill, like she seemed now. That way, she could call Natasha if needed.

'Of course,' Mrs Chopra snapped. 'I'm just tired … That silly girl ... doesn't know when to be quiet … I am going to sleep now.' She looked up at Natasha. 'Shut the door properly on your way out. Make sure it locks.'

There was a brief silence and then Natasha muttered, 'Okay.' This was the first time in ages that Mrs Chopra was being so abrupt with her. She knew it was because the old lady was worried about Kalu. She stood up. 'If you need anything, just call.'

Mrs Chopra acknowledged this with a grunt. Natasha walked away, leaving her on the sofa. She glanced back once at the door and saw that the old lady had one hand pressed against her forehead. She closed the door behind her softly but firmly and waited until she heard the lock click.

So much for turning in early.

She checked the time on her phone yet again. What was the point of trying to sleep early? This was stupid. The late nights and early mornings with Nikhil had her averaging only about five or six hours of sleep a night. Maybe her body clock was just out of whack. She remembered reading somewhere that every hour before midnight was equal to two hours after midnight in terms of quality of sleep. Well, it was already 12 a.m.

She couldn't shake the fear that this thing with Nikhil might be a bad idea, even though she couldn't deny the attraction or the fact that the two of them were so good together. But it *wasn't* just the two of them. Stupid of her to go and fall for a man with a child.

She tried to get Tisha's upset face out of her head. At least she was sure it had nothing to do with her and that it was none of her business. She took her pillow and rammed it over her head, turning on to her side and squeezing her eyes shut.

She was feeling disoriented. She was walking through a place that looked vaguely familiar – it was the house she had seen in those dreams, in which there was always that little curly-haired girl. It had been a while since she had seen her.

What was she up to now? Natasha felt a mild curiosity even as she groaned inwardly, 'Here we go again.' She resigned herself to following the little girl around as she ran from room to room. The house was full today – who were all these people and what was all the commotion about?

Then she arrived at one room at the end of the house, pushing her way past white saris and kurta-pajamas and all the loud wailing suddenly faded away. Natasha held her breath as the little girl took a couple of steps towards the figure lying on the ground, covered with a white sheet. She knew she was curious about who was under there and she was pulling at the sheet now. Stop her, someone, Natasha screamed, but no sound emerged from her throat. The sheet slowly slipped down to reveal a grey head.

Mrs Chopra lay dead.

Natasha sprang upright in panic. Just a dream, just a dream, she told herself. Her heart was still pounding. She looked out of the window – it was early morning – she probably still had a few more hours to sleep. She tried to calm herself and lay back down. It was no use – she suddenly felt like the sheet was stifling her and threw it off.

She got out of bed and fumbled for the switch on the lamp. She found her robe and slipped into it, shaking a little. She didn't believe in signs, but Mrs Chopra had been very sick. She had to go and see if she was all right. She put on her slippers and practically ran out of the house, just about managing to remember to grab the keys to Mrs Chopra's flat and her own, hanging on a hook by the door side-by-side.

Natasha stood shivering outside the Chopra's door. What time was it? Oh god, what was wrong with her, she had come without her phone. This was so stupid. What if she had to call for help? She contemplated doubling back upstairs to get it but decided that if it were an emergency, there wouldn't be a second to lose.

She knocked softly. And then louder. She rang the bell. No answer. She waited several long moments and then decided she couldn't wait any longer. She put the key in the lock and turned it. The door opened easily – yes, Mrs Chopra hadn't bolted it last night, Natasha remembered.

She walked over to Mrs Chopra's bedroom, feeling as if she were floating. It was still dark outside. The bedroom door was open and she held her breath as she looked in. A pale sliver of light from the window lit up the head of the bed. Mrs Chopra's face was grey. Natasha stepped in to get a closer look – she was certain by now that Mrs Chopra wasn't breathing. Her face looked exactly as it had in Natasha's dream; it was finally peaceful.

Natasha felt something wrench inside her. Now that she was here and had confirmed what she had already known, she realized she didn't have a clue about what to do next. As it turned out, it didn't matter. Mrs Chopra snapped open her eyes and saw her, and immediately let out a blood-curdling yell. Natasha shrieked too, equally shocked at this apparent return from the dead.

Getting a hold of herself, Natasha hissed, 'Shh … Mrs C. It's me … it's *me*!'

Mrs Chopra abruptly stopped screaming and glared at Natasha. With some effort, she propped herself up on her elbows and Natasha spoke quickly, mortified, 'I … was just worried about you, so I came to check if you were all right … and then you didn't answer the door…'

Mrs Chopra looked over at the wall and looked back disbelievingly at Natasha. Natasha looked up at the wall too and saw the clock. It was 3 a.m. 'Sorry,' she mumbled.

Mrs Chopra was still staring at her. 'What is wrong with you, Natasha?'

Natasha murmured, 'Nothing. I … couldn't sleep. Guess I had some sort of dream.'

Mrs Chopra snorted. 'Well, I suppose I appreciate you thinking you're looking out for me, but I am capable of taking care of myself.' She rubbed her eyes. 'Besides – my time is coming and I am ready to face it. I'm not afraid.'

'Oh, don't talk like that.' Natasha felt guilty that not two minutes ago, she had been of the firm opinion that Mrs Chopra was past tense.

Mrs C waved her protest aside. 'A fact is a fact. I've also told you this, Natasha – we come alone and we go alone. I have accepted that and I'm much stronger for it.'

She looked keenly at Natasha. 'Perhaps if you understand that, you will be able to get some sleep at nights.' She added gruffly, 'And let your old neighbours get some too.'

'I'll shut the door on my way out,' Natasha said sheepishly before she turned and fled. She heard the door click shut behind her and stood there for a moment, leaning against it, suddenly weak. She closed her eyes tight, shaken by the feeling that was getting too familiar. *Oh god, I'm so going to be Mrs Chopra when I grow up, I mean grow old.*

It took her a few moments to fortify herself. She made her way back to her apartment unsteadily, every step making her feel as though her feet were made of lead.

FOUR

SCHOOLGIRL BLUES

'What is it?'

'Nothing.' Natasha stared straight ahead through the car windshield.

'We're here,' Nikhil reminded her. 'Want to get out of the car at some point?'

She coughed a little. They'd been in the car for a few moments, she was aware of that. She just felt reluctant to move. Nikhil leaned back in his seat. 'Wow. It's not the first time you're coming home. I thought you'd be nervous about meeting my *parents*, but...'

'What?' Natasha spun her head towards him, her voice higher pitched than usual. 'Your parents are home?'

'No, no, they aren't...' Nikhil reached out and gave her shoulders a squeeze. 'Calm down, will you? I was saying I thought you'd be nervous about meeting my parents, but you're way too nervous about even hanging out with Tisha.'

'I'm not nervous,' Natasha muttered. Come on, she told herself, this is ridiculous. She's only a little girl. *Who means everything to this man, who means way too much to me.* 'Let's go,' she said briskly. 'What are you waiting for anyway?' She got out and slammed the door shut.

She wasn't sure why she had agreed to this, but Nikhil was the gently persistent sort. He liked to move things forward slowly but surely. He had reminded her that she'd said they would hang out at his place 'next week', latching on to her careless statement just as she'd predicted he would. She had delayed it this far but he knew she was planning to travel to Mumbai on Thursday and Friday, and had been so dogged about making this happen that she had finally given in.

The incident with Mrs Chopra may have had something to do with it. She had to admit: it gave her a chill to think about ending up like her – an old woman with no friends, no family, not even a dog - just a house to her name and a bunch of old memories. She shuddered and quickly passed through the gate Nikhil held open for her.

He rang the doorbell and smiled reassuringly. She smiled back, trying to look nonchalant. This was going to work out fine. The maid opened the door and bobbed her head politely in a namaste. Natasha nodded and went through, Nikhil close behind her.

Tisha was at the piano, playing what sounded like a complicated little piece. She was frowning with concentration at the music and apparently hadn't heard, or been bothered by, the ringing of the doorbell. Natasha glanced at Nikhil's face and saw that he was enraptured. He caught her looking and grinned sheepishly. Tisha finished playing with a flourish and turned around, swinging her legs as she gave a shy little smile. 'Hello, Dad. Hello, Natasha.'

'Hey, Tish.' Natasha smiled back.

'I guess it's not going to be "Natasha Aunty" after all.' Nikhil tousled Tisha's curly hair.

'Thank god for that,' Natasha muttered as she sat down on the sofa.

'What will you have?' Nikhil asked. 'Cup of tea? Coffee? Or would you prefer a glass of wine?'

Natasha froze and gestured with her head towards Tisha. Was this really an appropriate offer to make in front of her? Nikhil looked confused at her stricken face for a second and then rolled his eyes. 'It's okay, Natasha. Tisha knows about wine – and how it's not for little kids.'

'I'm going to have a sip of it on my sixteenth birthday,' Tisha said complacently. 'And Dad says if I'm good, I can have it whenever I want after I turn thirty.'

Nikhil looked guilty and tried to cover it up by prompting Natasha. 'So? What do you feel like having?'

She felt like having a good stiff peg of whiskey but said, 'Well, a glass of wine would be lovely.' She waved away his next question pre-emptively. 'Red, white, whatever, just bring it on!'

Nikhil grinned and went into the kitchen, where she assumed he stashed his bar goodies. Tisha gazed wide-eyed at Natasha. 'My dad said we're going to watch a movie. Which movie?'

Natasha hadn't known of this part of the plan. 'I don't know.' She called over her shoulder, 'Nikhil, you got a movie planned?' This was a good idea, she told herself – it meant less talking. Less talking meant fewer chances of screwing up.

'Yeah,' his voice floated in. 'I thought it would be fun. You girls can pick something from the collection.'

Natasha frowned a little. *You girls?* There was an age gap of nearly thirty years between them. Tisha bounced over to the

TV cabinet and opened the door. A large number of DVDs were stacked up – Natasha could see they were mostly children's flicks, animated ones.

'What would you like to see, Natasha?' Tisha pulled out a bunch excitedly. 'We've got *The Lion King*!'

Natasha's mind raced. *The Lion King*. The king died in that one, right in front of his son's eyes, and Simba ended up blaming himself and running away from home. 'Nah,' she said. 'What else you got?'

'*Finding Nemo*!'

Hmm. Fish's wife dies in front of his eyes, leaving him to raise their only surviving kid as a single parent. She made a face. 'What else?'

'The older movies … *Snow White*?' Tisha looked up hopefully.

'No!' Natasha almost shouted.

'What's going on?' Nikhil walked in with two glasses of red wine.

'Natasha doesn't like any of the movies,' Tisha informed her father sedately.

Nikhil looked questioningly at Natasha and handed her a glass of wine. 'I see.' He sat down next to her. 'Why is that?'

'No, I mean, I'm okay with them all.' Natasha felt distinctly uncomfortable. She said out of the side of her mouth to Nikhil, 'Just not completely convinced about the suitability of the content with regard to the mental state they might induce in those below a certain age, particularly when placed in the context of past events in their own lives.'

'Huh?' Nikhil frowned. But he had clearly got the gist because a moment later, his response was murmured out of the side of his mouth, 'Kindly consider the fact that one's own experience has demonstrated that over-protection of any kind usually leads to the opposite of the desired effect as far as the development of one's progeny goes. Besides,' he added in his normal voice, 'we've already seen all these movies.'

Of course. Natasha's cheeks turned pink. What was she trying to do anyway?

'Cheers,' said Nikhil softly and she clinked her glass against his. She wished she could just rest her head against his shoulder for a minute like she did when they were at her place. But right now they had to keep their distance. She deliberately lingered with her glass against his and then took a fortifying sip.

'Choose anything you feel like, Tish.' Nikhil settled back on the sofa, getting comfortable.

Tish brightened and went through the DVDs again. She settled on *Monsters, Inc.* and Natasha felt relieved.

The movie was turning out to be fun – it was one Natasha hadn't seen before. She usually caught these things on TV months after they released, but had somehow missed this one. To her surprise, she found that it had been an hour already and she was actually enjoying herself. Thank god for movies, she thought, feeling more kindly towards Disney than she ever had before.

Nikhil's phone rang. He clucked in annoyance and then frowned as he saw who it was. 'Aman.' He sat up. 'It must be the AXL final negotiation – they could end up developing three of our new products!' He glanced at Natasha. 'I'll have to take this.'

'Of course.' Natasha couldn't help smiling at the undercurrent of excitement in his voice. She was familiar with the feeling of being this close to cracking a partnership, even though here BizTech was the customer for a change. Nikhil got up and went into the other room. 'Hey, Aman,' Natasha heard him say before the door shut.

Tisha called out, 'I'm pausing it, Dad,' and pressed the pause button on the remote. She was sitting on the far end of the sofa. Nikhil had been sitting between them. As Tisha busied herself with the remote, Natasha felt like she should say something.

'How's school going, Tisha?' That sounded all adult and sensible. Good.

'Fine,' came the short reply. It was also unenthusiastic – she noticed that Tisha's face had darkened. She searched for something else to say.

'And the piano lessons?'

'They're okay,' said Tisha. Her face seemed to close up even further. Natasha couldn't figure out this kid's mood pattern. And then she murmured, 'I'm going to tell Dad I don't want lessons any more.'

'Why?' Natasha couldn't help sounding surprised. 'You're so good at it. You've got so much talent…'

'Yes,' said Tisha, 'but I don't like it any more. I think I want to be in dance.'

Natasha thought about it for a second. 'Are your friends in dance?'

'Yes,' Tisha admitted. 'All of them.'

'Okay. And what dance is this?'

'I don't know.' Tisha shrugged. 'Just some dance. But it's cooler than piano.'

'I see,' said Natasha seriously. 'You really think so, huh?'

'Yes,' said Tisha. 'Piano is…' – she seemed to be searching for a word – 'for dorks.'

'What's a dork, Tisha?'

'A dork is ... someone not cool. Someone like me.' Her lower lip quivered once.

Natasha didn't know quite what to say. 'You're not a dork at all,' she began. 'You're the coolest kid I know.'

'How many kids do you know?' Tisha turned her large eyes towards her.

'Not many,' Natasha admitted. 'But I will tell you one thing. If my friends said that something I loved wasn't cool and it made me a dork – I'd think really hard about whether they were my friends at all.'

Tisha stared at the remote in her hands, but her ears were perked up and Natasha knew she was listening.

'You know' – Natasha didn't know what made her go on – 'when I was a little kid, about your age – maybe a year or two older – I had this group of friends. They thought I was too serious about my studies – and they made fun of me for it, and soon I began to feel really bad about it.'

'So what did you do about it?' Tisha's voice was challenging.

'Well.' Natasha frowned as she thought back to what was now a rusty old memory, untouched for years. 'I guess ... one day when it got really bad, I went home and talked to my parents and they said...'

'I knew it! You just ran to your parents?' Tisha cried and she jumped off the sofa. Natasha was surprised to see that she was quivering in anger. 'That sounds like something a real dork would do!'

'Tisha!' Natasha jumped at Nikhil's voice. Neither of them had noticed he was back in the room. 'Why are you using that tone with Natasha?'

But Tisha's eyes were full of tears and she turned away from Natasha, who was open-mouthed with surprise. She ran past Nikhil in the hallway, her bare feet pat-patting against the wooden flooring. The sound of the door slamming shut made Natasha wince. She pressed her lips tight, looking at Nikhil and feeling helpless and guilty.

'I'll go in and talk to her. Don't worry, okay?' said Nikhil reassuringly. He disappeared down the hall to her room.

Natasha sat alone on the big sofa in the big drawing room, suddenly feeling very small.

She couldn't stay here any more.

Without thinking, she picked up her bag and all but ran out the door, heels clicking. The maid said something to her as she passed her in the kitchen, but Natasha didn't bother to stop and listen.

Uber. Yes. She fumbled with her phone as she walked to the colony gate. In just a few minutes, she'd be sure to find a taxi to take her home where she would be alone – no Nikhil, no Tisha, no complicated situations or talk of feelings. Yes, she'd be perfectly alone. Just the way she liked it.

FIVE

MUMBAI

'B*haiya, thoda jaldi chalenge*, please?'

Natasha managed to keep from sounding snappy, trying to work some respect into her tone on account of the driver's age. Why would they send her someone who was about eighty years old? Especially when she was in a hurry to catch a flight. She'd chosen the earliest one of the day, just to avoid having to fly with Bloody Rishabh.

The balding old man peered through thick glasses into the rear-view mirror. '*Haanji, madamji, kyun nahin.*' He nodded and took the car into fourth gear. He then cranked up the volume of the bhajans on the music system and sang along, '*Radhey Krishna, Radhey Krishna.*'

This was more than she could take. 'Please, music *band hi kar dijiye.*' She hadn't slept well the previous night, or any night last week – the stupid dreams were back. She'd tossed and turned fitfully and when morning came, she had no recollection of the actual flow of the dream but knew that little curly-haired intruder had been the main feature. And now she had a full day ahead. She looked into the rear-view mirror, noting the dark circles under her eyes. She would need a lot of black coffee to survive this Mumbai trip.

The driver switched off the music reluctantly, murmuring 'Radhey Krishna, Radhey Krishna' as they sped along at a steady fifty kilometres per hour. Natasha gritted her teeth. They were on the highway, and this guy was driving as if it were a village lane. She made a mental note to tell the admin department to change their taxi service.

Her phone buzzed and she fumbled for it in her purse. Who on earth would be calling so early? It was Nikhil. He had remembered she would be up at this unearthly hour, heading for her flight. She felt a little guilty about not returning his calls for two days, so after a moment's hesitation, she picked up. 'Hey.'

'Natasha.' He sounded relieved. 'What's up? Headed to the airport?'

'Yes, on my way. How are you? Sorry, I haven't been…'

'It's okay. I thought you might still be upset about that day, the way Tish reacted … You left so suddenly…'

Natasha winced, recalling how she had bolted. 'Look, I'm sorry about that. How's Tish?'

'Good.' He sounded almost surprised, as if he couldn't believe it. 'It turned out some girls have been bullying her … I had no idea. She said that it started a while back, after a sleepover where she had a bedwetting accident. I remember that day – she was upset about it but apparently her so-called friends have been blackmailing her with "their secret" and generally making her miserable.'

Natasha's stomach tightened as she listened. Poor Tisha. Nikhil went on, 'And Tish said she didn't want to talk to me about it because she thought I would be worried. Can you believe it?'

Natasha closed her eyes and rested her tired head against the window. Yes, Nikhil, she wanted to say, I do believe it because you are clearly oversensitive about parenting and derive your sense of self-worth from a seven-year-old. But she said nothing.

'Natasha? Are you there?'

'Yes, I'm here,' she said. 'Look, I'll be reaching the airport soon, okay? So…' Her voice trailed off.

'Natasha' – he sounded worried now – 'what's wrong?'

'Nothing's wrong,' she snapped. 'Why does everything have to be psycho-analysed, Nikhil? Can't I just have a really busy day I need to focus on?'

There was a short silence.

'Okay,' he said carefully. 'You go ahead then.' He paused again and when he spoke, he sounded uncertain. 'See you when you get back?'

'See you.' She knew she sounded noncommittal but she took the escape route his words provided, and before he could say anything else, she hung up. She flung the phone into her bag, hands trembling. A deep breath turned into a cough. To try and get things back to normal, she told the driver icily, 'Bhaiya, if you can't get your cab to go any faster than this, why don't you just climb in the back and let me drive?'

The old man looked affronted by this suggestion and pressed on the accelerator. Natasha leaned her head back, trying to think straight. It was all she could do to keep from yelling at the cabbie for the steady stream of 'Radhey Krishna, Radhey Krishna' that was getting louder and louder as they sped along the highway at the speed of sixty-five kilometres per hour.

'So we've got a fairly healthy pipeline as we get into the new financial year, too,' Anirban concluded. He looked at Natasha and then at Rishabh for their reaction.

Natasha spoke first. 'Well, I think that's a great job, Anirban. Holistic and showcasing long-term thinking too. I particularly like the idea of the eight-quarter rolling plan, rather than focusing only on the upcoming year. In fact, I think we'll adopt it at a national level for the quarterly reviews.' She smiled at Anirban encouragingly and he grinned. He was still a little boy in some ways, she realized, as she saw the colour creeping into his fair cheeks. Her smile widened.

'Well, that's wonderful,' Rishabh declared. 'Natasha has summed it all up nicely. I just want to add that if you keep this kind of performance up, you know that you will get all due support and more from the corporate team – I will personally ensure that.' Natasha struggled to keep her disapproval from showing; it was all supposed to be one team, not a corporate one and a branch one, and support was to be given to all branches irrespective of performance. Rishabh went on, 'And of course, there will be various other types of rewards waiting for you too. We'll talk about it at appraisal time.'

He looked around the room and his gaze settled on Anirban. Natasha wanted to grab a chair and throw it at his head. Bloody Rishabh. Some people were smiling nervously, but Anirban looked unruffled as he replied, 'We're all motivated just by the thought of being the best branch in the country, Rishabh. But thank you.' He then looked over at Natasha. 'And thanks, boss.'

Natasha couldn't help but feel gratified at his response – and by the way he called her boss even though he addressed Rishabh by his name. She was surprised to feel the colour rising in her own cheeks now. She said in her usual brisk tone,

'Okay, guys. Thanks a lot for a great review. Keep up the good work.' And with that, the meeting broke up.

Anirban crossed the conference room to her. 'Will you be having dinner with the team?'

'Anirban, I'd really love to but I can't tell you how tired I am today. I'd really rather get to the hotel and get some sleep.'

'Totally understand.' He grinned. 'Let me check on your car.'

Rishabh interrupted, 'Natasha will ride back with me. We're both staying at the Taj. My driver is here.'

Natasha suddenly wished she could change her mind and accept Anirban's invitation to have dinner with the team. It would be better than riding back with this presumptuous fool. But on the other hand, she was tired and looking forward to just crawling into bed. 'Okay,' she conceded. 'Thanks.'

The ride back to the hotel didn't involve much conversation, thankfully. Rishabh seemed busy with his Blackberry, and in the middle of writing an email, he got a call from his wife, which seemed to annoy him given the brusque way in which he spoke to her, murmuring in a low voice that he had already told her his plans about returning the next day. Natasha ignored him, staring out of the window at the large advertisement hoardings that distinguished the busy Mumbai roads from Delhi ones.

They reached the hotel and as Natasha was unbuckling her seatbelt, Rishabh turned to her. 'Dinner? You want to get some in the restaurant or get a drink in the bar first?'

Natasha froze for a second. 'Actually, Rishabh, I think I might skip dinner altogether and go straight to bed.'

'Oh, come on,' he said smoothly. 'We still haven't had a chance to catch up – that was one of the ideas of travelling together, remember?'

One of *your* ideas, Natasha thought. Besides, they had just shared a thirty-minute ride and he had been busy playing with his stupid phone. She didn't have the energy to argue, though, and said, 'Fine. Let's meet at the restaurant in fifteen minutes.'

—

'I like the way you've handled this branch's leadership issue,' Rishabh said to Natasha as she sat across the table from him. 'Anirban seems to have things in control now.'

'Yes,' agreed Natasha, looking around the dimly lit room for a waiter. Could they just place their order and get this evening over with? 'He's doing well. Deepesh has spent time coaching and guiding him, of course, but he's picked up mostly on his own.'

'You're just being modest.'

Natasha stared. 'Now *that's* something I've never been accused of.'

He laughed and leaned in. 'Seriously, Natasha. Why is it that you don't ever let your guard down with anyone?'

Primarily because I don't trust snakes like you. She looked around and clucked her tongue. 'Where is that waiter?'

As if on cue, a tall skinny fellow appeared with two glasses and a bottle of champagne on a tray. Natasha frowned and told him, 'Wait, we didn't order this.'

The fellow hovered uncertainly and Rishabh indicated to him to go ahead and serve. 'I did.' He smiled at her. 'I thought we should celebrate how well this branch is doing. Thanks to you.'

Easy there, tiger, Natasha wanted to say. Why had he suddenly turned into Natasha's number one fan? And if they were celebrating the branch's success, shouldn't they have been doing it with the branch? She opened her mouth to protest that she really didn't want any champagne, but then closed it tight. If he wanted to run up the company's travel bill on frivolous things like this, it was his business.

She picked up the glass and eyed it. The liquid inside was a clear golden, light and bubbly. She looked at Rishabh, who was eyeing her encouragingly. He held his glass out to her. 'To a successful year ahead.' She nodded and clinked her glass against his lightly and then proceeded to sip. It wasn't bad and seemed to make her heavy head feel lighter.

He was watching her expression. 'Good?'

'Umm-hmm. Although I might have preferred a Bloody Rishabh.'

'What?' He stared.

'Bloody Mary. Mary,' she blurted.

She took another sip quickly, hoping he would let it pass. She was just so used to thinking of him as Bloody Rishabh that it had slipped out. She was so exhausted.

'Natasha.' Rishabh shifted his chair a little closer. 'I want *us* to make a new beginning, too. We may not always agree on every issue, but that's not a necessity for any two people working together, right?'

'Right,' she said carefully. That much she agreed with.

He leaned back and surveyed her. 'I know one of the things I'm supposed to do is help groom you to get into my position. And I want you to know that I'm a 100 per cent committed to that.' He flashed her a shark-like grin. 'But to be honest, I haven't got the sense that you're open to the idea.'

'Well.' Natasha sipped again and decided to be straightforward. 'I'm not, actually.'

Rishabh clearly wasn't prepared for this. 'And why is that?'

She tried to formulate a politically correct yet honest response. 'I think it's just that I already know what I'm doing.'

'But surely you're not saying that you're doing everything perfectly, Natasha?'

'I'm focused on the results, Rishabh. And the results have been good. Haven't they?'

'Yes, they have,' Rishabh said. 'But on the relationships and people front, you know you've got a few things to learn.'

'Agreed.' Natasha couldn't stop herself from adding, 'It's just that I don't agree with *your* way of getting around relationship and people issues.'

'And you perceive *my* way as being?'

'Charming them. Flirting. Showing them a financial carrot.' Natasha surprised herself with her bluntness. 'Or in my case, when all else fails – pulling rank and saying it's your business.'

Rishabh stared at her. 'Oh dear. This is about that one day, isn't it?'

'Yes,' Natasha said. 'But also the days before and after it.' She shook her head. It was beginning to buzz and she quickly fortified herself with a long swig of champagne. She stared at the table and sighed. 'Rishabh, can't we just agree that we won't agree on most things, and get on with life?'

She looked up and saw him gazing thoughtfully at her. 'Absolutely. But isn't there another possibility, Natasha?'

'What?' She looked around for the waiter again, but the fellow seemed to have disappeared. Did they serve food in here or not? What was the idea of leaving the place so deserted when there were paying customers waiting to place an order?

Rishabh leaned forward and whispered softly, 'Natasha. You can't deny this ... attraction between the two of us. It happens sometimes between powerful people. It shows up when you try to use constant lunches with someone else to make me feel jealous. It showed up in the way my name came up on your tongue just now. And it can be the cause of a lot of friction. We just have to recognize it and decide what we want to do about it.'

Whoa. Natasha couldn't believe her ears. *Using lunch with Nikhil to make him feel jealous?* After she'd made it amply clear that she was one person who was completely immune to his charms, he still thought she was attracted to him. Or maybe it was *because* she was immune that he had convinced himself that she was just trying hard to resist him. What an egomaniac. She was tempted to tell him she had said 'Bloody Rishabh' because she thought of him as a bloody idiot.

'Rishabh.' She swallowed, and then went on as evenly as she could manage, 'I assure you there is nothing of the sort.' He could be the best-looking man on earth and she would still be repelled by him for his cocky self-assuredness and pure fatheaded idiocy.

'Really?' he asked softly. 'So this doesn't do anything to you?'

This couldn't be happening. No, he couldn't have just put his hand on her thigh. She was too shocked to react, which was something he mistook for encouragement because he actually flipped up the end of her skirt and touched the inside of her left thigh. The contact of his palm against her skin brought her back to life and she slapped his hand away. Her chair screeched back when she sprang to her feet, trembling with rage. She stared at him wild-eyed as he looked up at her, his expression a perfect blend of bafflement and innocence. She wanted to throw her drink in his face, but her body seemed to be frozen. *How dare he*? She realized now that she had always known this about him, but had never thought she would fall victim to it. No, she wasn't a victim to *anything*. She was a vice president in the company, almost the same level as him. What was he thinking?

'Hey,' Rishabh murmured, eyes darting around the room to see if they were still alone. 'Calm down, will you? Have a seat and we can talk about it…'

Natasha gave him a look filled with hate. She said through gritted teeth: 'There's nothing you could say that would interest me. And I certainly have nothing to say to you.'

She noticed a couple of waiters had materialized from the bar area and were now headed towards them, looking curious and concerned. She hated scenes and couldn't be a part of one. She whipped around on her heel and stormed out of the restaurant, not looking back.

SIX

FALLING

'Madam? Madam?'

Natasha looked up to see Muthu standing there with her cappuccino on a tray. She gave him a blank look and realized her laptop and papers left no room on the table.

'Sorry,' she murmured and cleared a spot for the cup, which he placed gingerly on the table. Somewhat invigorated by the smell of coffee, she managed a small smile for Muthu. He smiled back and walked away.

She was glad to be back at the café – she had been spending a lot of her time working from here. Even the occasional presence of unruly teenagers didn't bother her any more. After all, she didn't own the place. It still felt better than the office. No one bothered her here, no chance of seeing Nikhil around and most of all, no interaction with that Bloody Bastard Rishabh.

It had been a week since their trip to Mumbai, and Natasha still felt the same disgust when she remembered his clammy touch against her thigh. He had acted as though it had been the most natural thing for him to do, as if he had some sort of right over her by virtue of being the hot-shot boss. She was still furious but couldn't decide what to do about it. She had felt disoriented over the last few days. The dreams were worse than ever, and she found herself lying awake for hours, staring at the ceiling, feeling something that she was not used to – a feeling she hadn't experienced in years: self-doubt.

She hadn't done anything to encourage him, that much she knew. There had been no flirting, no mixed signals on her part – and even if there had been, there was nothing that justified this. She had made her disdain for him clear from the start, and only a megalomaniac like him could have mistaken it for her playing hard-to-get.

So why couldn't she figure out the right course of action now?

Natasha knew very well that had it been anyone else in her position, she herself would have seen it all in black and white. No questions about it – go ahead and report the jerk, she'd have said. Have him kicked out of the company. File a sexual harassment case. Make sure the slime ball's family finds out. The works. But now that it had happened to her, she felt overwhelmed. And there were so many other things going on, what with the confusion about Nikhil; and then, the lack of sleep and the cough, both of which made her feel physically tired. Why was her body giving up on her? And now, it seemed her mind was too.

Sexual harassment was something she assumed usually happened to younger women – those just starting out in their jobs, trainees. Not a woman at her level. And a personality like hers – 'Hitler' for goodness' sake; the toughest in the leadership team. Natasha hated the thought of being seen as a victim of *anything*. If something had to be done, the right moment had been when it was happening. Why hadn't she created more of a ruckus, slapped him across the face or made a formal complaint that very night? Why had she just run away from the situation? Now, with every passing day, it seemed like there was no excuse for her silence. It was just indecisiveness – another problem Natasha had never faced before.

Her coffee was getting cold. She picked up the cup, which felt heavier than usual. What was going on with her? She couldn't help but feel sorry for Rishabh's wife. Did she have any inkling of the fact that she was married to a womanizing creep? And his children, would they grow up like him? Didn't he think about his family at all? From the practised way in which he had executed his little stunt, she knew it wasn't the first time he had placed his hand on a woman's leg under a restaurant table. And given his surprise at her reaction, she also guessed it wasn't often that such a gesture was rejected. Maybe women were enthralled by his charm or overawed by his position, or both. Or just too weak to complain. Was she going to be one of them?

She took a sip of her cappuccino but barely tasted it. What if she did raise a complaint and his wife got to know about it? How would she react? Would their marriage end? What would happen to their kids? She knew this chain of thought involved a misplaced sense of guilt – but that didn't stop her from going down that road.

Why had she changed so much over the last few months? Was it something to do with Nikhil? Ever since she had started seeing him, things had been different with her. She didn't feel as strong as she used to – she felt strangely *exposed*. The times they'd spent together with his daughter, the sensitivity that he displayed to everyone around him, his subtle but persistent digging into her mind and her feelings brought out a side of her that she hadn't known even existed. And increasingly, she was convinced that it was her weaker side and one that she had no room for.

Her phone was buzzing and she ignored it. She knew it was Nikhil. He had been calling and messaging her, but she just couldn't bring herself to speak to him. She didn't want to tell him about what had happened with Rishabh – it was her problem. She needed to be by herself for a while to clear her head and make her own decisions. She waited for the ringing to stop and when it didn't, she pressed the red button to cut his call. Maybe he would assume she was out at a client meeting. She knew she was lying to herself, but she couldn't deal with him just yet.

A message popped up on her phone. She assumed it would be another concerned one from Nikhil, asking what was up with her. Her blood boiled when she saw who it was. Rishabh had the guts to Whatsapp her:

> Natasha. It's been long enough now. Will you please stop avoiding me? Where are you?

She stared at the phone. It was the first time he had reached out to her since that day. She saw he was typing something else. Her lips tightened as she waited.

> I wanted to apologize for what happened the other day. It was just a misunderstanding. Can we please forget the whole thing?

Natasha had not intended to reply, but this was too much. She breathed in sharply and then tapped out:

> No misunderstanding.
> You knew exactly what you were doing and there is no excuse for it.
> Just leave me alone.

He was already typing before she sent him the last line. It took him a few seconds, and then she read:

> I need to know that this will go no further than the two of us. Please understand that these things happen. It would be to the serious detriment of the organization if it were to get out. We would both lose credibility.

Both lose *credibility*? She scowled at the phone. If Rishabh were in front of her right now, she would break his neck. She couldn't believe the next words he wrote.

> I'm worried about you, Natasha. You must understand that. It's different for a woman. You do realize that people would blame you. That's the price of being a single woman. It's unfortunate, but true.

The bastard. The asshole. The—

> And keep in mind, these things follow you from organization to organization. You wouldn't want to risk your career on account of one little incident, right? Once you get tagged a trouble-maker it's impossible to shake

it off. I'm just sharing my experience with you, Natasha. Believe me. Let's just talk about how we want to handle this. Okay?

She felt her face getting hot as she assimilated the meaning of his words. There was a threat in there. This guy was definitely a pro. He had done this countless times before. He wasn't really worried, even though he knew he had tried it with the wrong person this time. He was cleverly turning it into something that she would be expected to feel apologetic for if it were made public. Unbelievable. The white-hot rage welling up inside made her feel like her chest was about to burst.

'Natasha?'

This voice was familiar, even though the entire heart-skipping-a-beat thing still wasn't. She looked up to see Nikhil standing right next to her. She was not prepared for a conversation with him. She reminded herself that he knew nothing about what was going on with her. She composed her features into a nonchalant expression. 'Hi, Nikhil.'

He sat down next to her, his handsome face creased into a frown. 'All right. What's going on, Natasha? Why have you been avoiding me?'

It wasn't just him she was avoiding – it was everyone. But she knew that answer wouldn't satisfy him. 'Just been busy,' she murmured, avoiding eye contact with him.

'Yes. I see.' He indicated the papers and her laptop. 'Is this your new office?'

'Kind of,' she said, shrugging. 'I get some peace around here.'

After a brief silence, Natasha placed her phone on the table. She had been clutching it so hard, her knuckles had turned white. Nikhil stared at her. Finally he spoke. 'Will you please *talk* to me?'

'There's nothing to talk about, Nikhil.'

'Why aren't you telling me what's bothering you?'

'Why are you assuming something is bothering me?' Natasha snapped, feeling exposed. 'Can't a person just be—?'

'Yeah well, you're always busy, Natasha, but this is not you – the way you've been acting, ever since the day with Tisha…'

'I'm not *acting* like anything, Nikhil.' Natasha coughed. She closed her eyes, feeling sick. 'This is just me being *me*. I don't know what you were expecting. It's clear that you don't really know me.'

Nikhil murmured softly, 'Why are you sabotaging this, Natasha? Was it too good to be true?'

Natasha glared. 'Maybe. Or maybe *you* thought I was someone else. Maybe I'm just good as a girlfriend for a while; but I'm not equipped to be with someone long-term – and certainly not to be someone's mommy! We said we would just see where this would lead. Well, this is where we are. Maybe it wasn't *meant* to go anywhere at all.'

'Do you really mean that?' Nikhil demanded. 'Are you saying that we had nothing?'

Natasha sighed. 'We had something. I'm not denying that. But maybe the one thing we never had was a future. And that seems clearer than ever right now. Why can't you accept that?'

'I can – but I don't. Because I do know you and I know you care, and that you want to be with me – with us,' Nikhil said through gritted teeth. 'I know you better than you know yourself.'

Natasha clenched her jaw. 'Don't *ever* claim to know me better than I know myself, Nikhil. You don't have that right.'

Nikhil looked stunned. Natasha's phone buzzed again, and he glanced at it instinctively. She continued to stare at his face. He had to accept this wasn't going to work. It was all too complicated. His expression froze. He glanced up at her again. 'Okay. I guess I don't have the right after all.' In one abrupt motion, he got up and left. The café door swung back and forth behind him, and it took Natasha some effort to quit gazing after him.

She looked at the message from Rishabh that Nikhil had just read:

> Please remember I'm a married man. I wouldn't want this to get out either.

Natasha barely knew what she was doing as she drove home. She felt sick. Every time she coughed, her chest and stomach hurt. She had a strong suspicion about what was causing her physical deterioration, but wanted to delay finding out. There was too much for her to deal with. She suddenly realized she was already in her parking spot and staring out of the windshield. How long had she been here? It would take a while for her to get back to normal.

The timing. The bloody timing of Bloody Rishabh's bloody message. She had wanted Nikhil to understand that she couldn't take the pressure of a relationship with him, but she certainly hadn't wanted him to think it had anything to do with Rishabh. There could have been nothing further from the truth and it must have hurt him to think she had something going on with that monster. She squeezed her eyes shut and groaned. Oh well, she thought, perhaps it would actually end up making things a little easier for Nikhil. Let him believe she really was a bitch. She dragged herself out of her car and into the building. Mrs Chopra was pacing up and down slowly in the hallway.

'Natasha,' the old lady called, 'I was waiting for you.'

One look at her and Natasha's heart sank further. She had actually started using a walking stick, and right now she stood stooping over it. Natasha smiled wanly. 'I've just been busy, Mrs C.'

'Well, come in for a while, a cup of coffee will do you good.'

'Please, don't trouble yourself…'

'Oh, that Preeti of yours is here. She has started staying the nights.' Mrs Chopra added defensively, 'Be good to keep her away from that no-good drunk father of hers.'

Natasha couldn't help but feel relieved at this news. 'Oh, that's really good. I'm glad.' She refrained from saying anything further and followed Mrs Chopra through her open door.

'Preeti, *do* cup coffee *banao*.' Mrs Chopra seemed to use a kinder tone with Preeti than with anyone else. Tired, Natasha made her way to the sofa and sank into it.

'So why do you look like you're going to die?' Mrs Chopra enquired in her usual crisp manner. Coming from her, the irony was not lost on Natasha.

'I haven't been all that well.'

'So take better care of yourself, why don't you? What happened to all your fancy dieting and exercise?'

Natasha sighed. 'Out of the window for the moment.' She bit her lip, thinking about the champagne she had sipped with Rishabh just a week ago. It felt so wrong now, on so many levels.

Perhaps it was the perceptive way Mrs Chopra was gazing at her or the fact that she was really the only person in the world Natasha could talk to right now, but she found herself confessing hesitantly, 'Mrs C, things … aren't going very well.'

'That much I guessed,' Mrs Chopra said. 'What happened?'

'Oh, it's just…' Natasha found herself struggling to explain. 'It's a lot of things … Things at work. Things with … a relationship I have.' *Had*, she reminded herself. 'My … physical state just now. I…' She found she couldn't get herself to say it. 'It's everything, actually.' She took a deep breath and let it out slowly. 'It's quite hopeless.' She was surprised to feel tears pricking her eyelids. She blinked them back.

To her mortification, Mrs Chopra cackled. Natasha felt a burning mix of shame and resentment – here she was, opening up like a fool to this old woman and she was being mocked.

'Oh, Natasha. Things aren't hopeless. *You're* acting *helpless*. That's the only thing that's wrong.' She leaned forward. 'Everything in life is a decision. If you're feeling the way you are, it's because you simply haven't made the right decisions yet. Surely you know this. You're a woman of real action.' She leaned back and said proudly, 'Like me.'

Natasha stared. 'What do you mean? What are you suggesting I do?'

Mrs Chopra laughed even louder. Natasha couldn't help but feel glad Mrs C was coming back to life, even though her mirth was at Natasha's expense. 'How can I presume to tell you what to do? You've told me nothing about what the problem is' – she raised a hand when Natasha started to speak – 'but I don't have to know. All I can tell you is – you already know what you're supposed to do. You just haven't decided to do it yet. Because your decisions – like mine – always come from here.' She tapped the side of her head. 'Where the ego lives.' She paused for a moment. 'But sometimes the answers lie elsewhere.'

Natasha stared at her for a long moment. Time seemed to stop and she could almost hear things click into place. After a while she said, 'Mrs C, by any chance, are you a *Star Wars* fan? Do you know who Yoda is?'

'*Star Wars*? Yoda?' Mrs Chopra frowned. 'No. I only know Osho, no Yoda. Who is…?'

'Never mind,' Natasha muttered. She turned her head towards the kitchen. 'Preeti, coffee *thoda jaldi*, please! I have to go somewhere.'

SEVEN

THE JOURNEY

'Are you sure you don't want me to come?'

Priya looked a little worried as she scanned Natasha's face. They stood together, just outside New Delhi railway station. Natasha smiled at her old friend. 'You've done enough, driving me here so early in the morning. You know you didn't have to.'

'I wanted to,' Priya said briskly. 'And you know I'm glad you're doing this, right? It's just that you look so weak – and in your condition…'

'I'm fine, Priya,' said Natasha. She felt again the shame that kept coming over her in waves since her call to Priya yesterday. She had treated her so badly over the last few months. And yet, at the first hint that Natasha needed support, Priya had come through without batting an eyelid.

'Look, thanks for everything. I'm so sorr—'

'I've already told you, it's okay,' Priya interrupted. 'We'll catch up when you're back – when?'

Natasha took a long shuddering breath. 'I don't know … Don't know how long. We might not even last a day together.'

'You will,' said Priya. 'Call when you reach?'

'Okay.' Natasha bent, picked up her duffel bag and swung it over her shoulder. She gave Priya a quick, slightly awkward hug and walked away towards the platform. Priya gazed after her. Natasha had her short hair pulled into a tiny ponytail. She was dressed in jeans, a light pink jacket and sneakers. She didn't look like the corporate powerhouse she had become in recent years, but just a pale, older version of the reticent young girl Priya had known. She turned once and waved before disappearing into the crowd. Priya murmured to herself, 'Good luck, Nattu.'

—

Natasha gazed out of the window at the vast green fields that the train was rushing past. It had been such a long time since she had done this – all her work travel in recent years had been by air and usually to other big metropolitan cities. The train's smell, gentle rocking and din felt familiar though. There had been so many trips like this in her childhood and they had always filled her with a delicious sense of anticipation. Priya had offered to drive her all the way, but Natasha knew this was something she had to do alone.

Apart from a few more pukka houses and the tangles of ugly black wiring clustered above the villages, the scenery didn't look very different from all those years ago. Was it really fourteen years ago that she had been up to the cottage last? Yes. That had been her last trip up here after her MBA, when she had come to talk to her mother about her new job – and the fact that she was moving to Mumbai.

It was for her mother's sake that Natasha had opted to do her MBA from FMS – because it was in Delhi and was a non-residential course – even though she had an offer from the number one school. She remembered how upset she had been on that last journey from Delhi to Kalka – what was the point of it all? She had gone ahead and made the sacrifice but her mom had barely been around for the last couple of years. She'd taken to spending more and more time up in the hills, getting the cottage renovated.

The cottage had been their summer getaway till Natasha was about ten – but they had stopped going there after her father died. Which had suited Natasha just fine; the memories were too much for her. So why had her mother chosen to go back there?

She had managed at one point during that last visit to get her mother to sit down amidst all the renovation work, local labourers milling about them as they broke down a wall and repaired patches in the ceiling. She had told her mother, who sat stiffly and unwillingly throughout, that it was time for her to pursue her career opportunities seriously and that it was a great job and she had arranged for both of them to stay together in a company flat. Her mother had listened quietly and then informed her that she should go ahead and that her own plan was to finish getting the cottage ready and move into it.

'*Move* here?' Natasha had said, unable to believe her ears. 'Why?'

'Because I consider it my home.'

'This isn't your home … It's a … holiday getaway, Ma,' Natasha had cried. 'This is a stupid idea. How can you even think of it? There are no facilities, no one else around, there's going to be nothing for you to do…'

'I'll find something,' her mother had said bluntly and Natasha had stared at her, uncomprehending. She hadn't even managed to get a rise out of her, despite the deliberate use of the word 'stupid' to describe her plan.

Natasha's voice had dropped to a whisper. 'After everything that's happened … you're really thinking of *living* here? I thought you were renovating to sell this damn place – or rent it out, maybe. But...'

'Natasha,' her mother said in a tired voice, 'it wasn't the cottage's fault. And my mind is made up. I don't want to sell it, I want to live here. And you are most welcome to start your new life in Mumbai but—'

Natasha hadn't waited to hear the rest of the sentence. With a cry of frustration, she had got up and stormed into the guestroom and started to pack immediately. I hate this place, she thought while cramming her things wildly into the suitcase. *And if you think I'm coming back here again, you're wrong, Mom.*

Natasha was pulled back into the present by a loud 'Chai-coffee, madam?' She looked up to see a server in a blue uniform with a tray.

'Chai, please.' She didn't know what made her opt for tea this time. Strange craving. Oh yes, of course, made sense. She watched as he deftly poured the steaming beverage into a paper cup and handed it to her, moving on to the row behind her, droning, 'Chai-coffee, madam?'

There was a middle-aged couple sitting in the same row as Natasha. The woman, right next to her, was wearing a plain salwar suit with a shawl wrapped around her shoulders, and the man, wearing thick glasses, was in grey pants and an old black sweater. Though they had only exchanged tentative smiles, the woman now held out a pack of Marie biscuits to her.

Natasha shook her head but couldn't help smiling. This

was something that never happened on a plane. Long live the camaraderie that arose on the great Indian train journey. She looked out of the window again and found herself pondering over the question that had no answer, even though it had been a while since she last allowed herself to think about it: what would life have been like if they had decided to take the train up to the cottage that day?

She supposed it was a good thing that she had no memories of the actual accident – she was pretty sure she would have had a much tougher time learning how to drive or even travel in a car if she had remembered more.

All she remembered was feeling excited about the thought of going up to the cottage again. It had been her absolute favourite place in the whole world. The slightly musty, full of treasures, brown cottage-home that her parents had built on a piece of land they had acquired soon after they married. There wasn't any television there, but there were rocky ledges to climb and perch on, a breathtaking view of a green mountain lake, clouds that settled right in the garden. And if you waited long enough at the gate, there was a good chance a villager would walk by with a herd of sheep, perky little brown and white things bleating plaintively. It was the most exciting thing in the world – you certainly never got to see that in Delhi and she was proud they had a summer home like this one.

She remembered her mother crossly telling her to stop kicking the front seat of their Maruti Esteem before she turned to Natasha's father and said, 'Should I drive now?'

He had gazed at her fondly and returned, 'No, darling, I'm fine. Maybe since Nattu can't keep still, she'll scoot over to kick Mom's seat for a bit?'

Natasha remembered how he had caught her eye in the rear-view mirror, and that his eyes had twinkled. She had grinned at him and acquiesced, shifting to the left to settle into the seat behind her mom. She was glad that he had listened to her and shaved his moustache a few days ago – she had always insisted that it was too prickly and would run away from his kisses. Mom hadn't been approving of the new 'overly modern' look at all, but Natasha thought her dad was the most handsome man in the world – even though she privately agreed with her mom that the moustache was a better look for him.

She had been staring out of the car window for a few minutes at the jagged rocks on the left as they drove up the hill. She never saw it coming. All she heard was her mother's panicked voice shouting, 'Rakesh, look out!'

And then she'd banged her head against the car door and everything had turned black.

Natasha closed her eyes tight. The feeling of sickness was crawling up her throat – she knew it had nothing to do with train-travel; she had never been train-sick. She felt dizzy and weak, and opened her eyes slowly, cautiously, to see if the spinning had stopped. Her tea was still sitting on the tray-table in front of her. She picked it up and brought it to her lips; it was lukewarm, but bearable. It would be all right, she told herself. Everything would be fine.

It had been years since she let herself think through the sequence of events leading up to the accident and all that had followed. She had woken up in the hospital. Her mother had been with her and the smile she had given Natasha hid her pain. Mom had a bandage on her own forehead – no other bruises, at least, not the visible kind. Little Natasha hadn't even asked where Papa was. She was afraid to ask and instinctively knew the answer.

They hadn't talked about it. Snippets of conversation between the adults in the family as they rallied around to commiserate with her mother had helped her piece it all together. Her father could have chosen to swing the car to the right when that truck came at them on the wrong side of the lane as they turned the corner. Some people thought that he went the other way because if he had misjudged the swing to the right, the car could have gone down the cliff. But Natasha's mother was firm in her belief – although Natasha had heard her say it out loud only once to her own parents – that he had instinctively known there wasn't enough time to avoid a collision, and had made the split-second decision to swing the other way to keep the left side of the car from the impact of the truck. It had just meant that he got the worst of it.

Natasha had tried to be there for her mother. She had been as responsible as she could have been. The ceremonies had been ordeals in themselves – her mother sat through stoically as the centre of attention and sympathy. Natasha instinctively knew that she hated it. She had hated it all too. What was with all these people coming up to grip her mother's hand, crying loudly as if it were *their* loss? Every single time for the weeks and months that followed, when it had looked like they might actually move on, some distant relative turned up, wailing and weeping. Natasha never saw her mother cry. She would just sit there next to the weeping relative and murmur about god's will. Which was as funny as it was fake, because Mom had never been religious. Natasha knew her mother only did those pujas during Diwali because her papa's side of the family liked it – as had Papa himself.

No one bothered to commiserate with Natasha. They had looked at her with pity but seemed to think she was just a little girl who would grow up without any recollection of all this. The real sympathy had been reserved for her mother. It hadn't bothered Natasha – what had troubled her was the way her mother acted, like it was her own, private loss. Left to deal with the pain on her own, Natasha had thrown herself into her textbooks and had topped every class since. She was on the roll of honour at school, and one of the best all-rounders, captain of the volleyball team and head girl. She had been sharp with people, but they respected her because it was clear that she was hardest on herself. She was committed and managed to do well at everything she tried. She learnt at an early age that she could make people feel afraid of her, and had revelled in that power ever since.

Her mother had gone back to her job as a senior member of the finance department in the big company that she worked at – it was unusual in those days for a woman to have such a senior post but her mother was made of the same tough material she had passed on to Natasha. The two of them had busy lives, living in the same house and meeting every evening. But they had an unspoken pact not to discuss the past or to dwell on their feelings, and it had seemed to work.

So why had her mother spoilt everything by uprooting herself with the hare-brained decision about the cottage? She should have moved to Mumbai with her. Of course, Natasha had never offered again. That separation had marked the beginning of the end of their relationship, with Natasha steadfastly refusing to come back to the cottage. Their phone calls were punctuated by too many silences and Natasha felt increasingly resentful. After all, there was no support for her during the early years of her struggle as a single young girl living in Mumbai, managing a home and a job by herself. Her mother was too busy with her self-indulgent early retirement to the hills.

Well, there was no way she was going to be there for Natasha as a grown-up if she wasn't there for her when Natasha was a little girl. The gap between them widened over the years and there was an uneasiness when they did interact that suggested that it was better if the two of them didn't speak to each other again. She had stopped calling her mother, didn't return her calls, and eventually her mother stopped calling too. For the longest time, Natasha had told herself it was better that way.

Natasha felt a pang of uncertainty. Considering how long it had been, she had no idea how her mother would react to her landing up like this. Priya, who was their one remaining link, had already called her mother and told her to expect Natasha. She had given her a new mobile number too, and Natasha had saved it under the name 'Mom New'. This was all going to be very strange. The only thing she took comfort in was that there was unlikely to be any sort of scene. Like Natasha, her mother hated drama. Although, Natasha thought, even having the door quietly but firmly shut in her face would not be a pleasant experience. Still. There was something inside her – as well as outside her, in the form of Mrs C – that made her feel this was something she was meant to do. And so she would.

She rubbed her temples, trying to control the spinning.

How long before they reached Kalka? She glanced at her watch. Another two hours to go. Dear lord. She thought she might have to rush to the toilet and throw up. The aunty sitting next to her was giving her another concerned and tentative smile. In the true Indian tradition of not taking no for an answer, the woman held out the pack of Marie biscuits again, this time with a motherly smile.

Well, sweet and dry was good when you felt sick. Natasha acquiesced, pulling out a thin Marie biscuit and dipped it in her tea.

'Thank you,' she said to the aunty, who looked immensely satisfied as Natasha bit into the biscuit. Strangely, the half-dry, half-soggy thing was delicious.

EIGHT

MOTHER

'Hello.'

The greeting was all Natasha could manage now that her mom was in front of her. The eloquent speech she had been mentally rehearsing for hours had flown out of the window. She stood there, adjusting the strap of her duffel bag, feeling uncomfortable under her mother's cool gaze. She hadn't aged much these last few years. Her straight hair had grown even longer and was streaked with grey, but she stood tall and slim and strong as ever. The same old impenetrable fort, its drawbridge up.

'You should have told me which train you were coming by. I would have picked you up,' her mother finally said.

That sounded about right. A reprimand, albeit a mild one. Natasha shrugged. 'Can I come in?'

Her mom stepped aside and Natasha walked into the cottage, taking it all in. It looked different now – lived-in. There wasn't much light but it felt warm and cosy, the living room done up with a lot of antique-looking wooden furniture and pretty silk cushions on the sofa. It was definitely Mom's touch, although it clashed with her austere appearance in that plain blue kaftan. The only thing Natasha found familiar about the cottage was the dark wooden flooring creaking under her feet. She found it reassuring and took a little walk around the room, dropping her duffel bag on to the sofa.

'You must be tired,' Mom said stiffly. She called out, 'Amma?'

Natasha froze. 'Amma's here?' The last she knew, their old maid, Amma, had refused to move out of Delhi. She had been with the family for generations, bringing up Natasha's mother before Natasha herself, and she had not approved of the split when Natasha decided to move to Mumbai and her mom to the hills. Amma had told Natasha about wanting to stay with 'her own family, even though some people didn't know what sticking together as a family meant'. Clearly, something had changed in the intervening years.

Amma materialized from the back of the house – probably in her seventies now, she was grey-haired and her shoulders stooped, but the energy and speed with which she approached Natasha completely belied her age. '*Nattu-beti aa gayi*!'

She wrapped her arms around Natasha, coming up to shoulder level. Natasha was delighted and shocked in equal measure and looked over at her mother as if to say: 'You never told me.'

Her mother just gave her a wry smile, one that implied: 'When did I have the chance?'

Amma looked up at Natasha, tears streaming down her face as she remarked to her mother, 'She's so beautiful even … and even with this short-short hair … I can't believe it.'

Natasha allowed herself to be enveloped in another tight embrace, a disbelieving grin on her face. She was home.

—

'Is your room comfortable?' her mother enquired when Natasha materialized at her study door. 'You'll be staying long, I hope?'

Natasha cringed inwardly at how formal her mother sounded. But could she really blame her? It had been two years since they had even spoken – she had stopped calling without giving her any real reason and Mom had tried only a couple of times before giving up – as she always did, so easily, when it came to Natasha.

'The room is fine, Ma.' It took some effort to call her that. She felt exhausted even though she had taken a two-hour nap and a bath with lukewarm water from the rusty old geyser. It was already afternoon – a sunny one at that – but the air in here was always cool.

Natasha's hair was still wet and she shivered as she pulled up a chair next to her mother. There was a large pile of papers on the desk in front of her and Mom peered through her glasses at the sheet in her hand. After a moment or so, Natasha said, 'What are you working on, Mom?'

'Corrections,' came the short reply.

Natasha almost laughed out loud. She had actually gone ahead and done it: retired from the fancy-shmancy corporate finance job at the peak of her career and moved to the hills and become a schoolteacher. It sounded like something out of a movie. Ridiculous, but then, she looked peaceful and content.

Natasha could sense the difference between the Mom she had known and the lady who sat before her now. She was still quiet and aloof but there was no air of unspoken resentment. Apparently, not even against the daughter who hadn't spoken to her in two years.

'Mom,' Natasha ventured. Her mom looked up. 'I'm only here for a couple of days,' Natasha said. 'And I've come to talk to you. So can we? Talk, I mean.'

Her mother's expression suggested it was the last thing she wanted to do, but she sighed and put away her papers. Then she took off her reading glasses, which left behind little dark impressions on either side of her nose. Mom squared her shoulders. Fire away, her attitude suggested.

Natasha cleared her throat. 'Mom.'

As a subconscious delaying tactic, she found herself summoning up the cough, which had become a part of her life. To her surprise, it wouldn't come. Her throat seemed clearer now than it had been in months. Must be the air here. Okay, no more stalling, she told herself. 'Mom,' she repeated, 'I bet you're wondering what I'm doing here.'

Her mother's expression didn't change apart from the right eyebrow rising slightly. Man, she really wasn't going to help this one along, Natasha thought.

'And I also bet you're wondering how come I stopped speaking to you … returning your calls. You know.'

Her mother's lips became a thinner line. Natasha hurried on, 'Well, anyway, I just thought it makes sense for us to … not be mad at each other any more.'

'For your information, Natasha,' her mom said, 'I am not "mad" at you, as you put it. I simply assumed that you wanted to be left alone to live your life. After all, you've been taking care of yourself for so many years and you have a career to pursue. My assumption was that you simply reached a point where you wanted to break ties with the past and move on. I don't take things personally any more.'

Natasha felt her cheeks getting hot. Why was her mother being so clinical? Her detachment had always driven Natasha crazy, and clearly it still had that effect on her.

'What do you mean?' she said. 'It doesn't *bother* you that we have not spoken in two years?'

'I have been occasionally in touch with your friend Priya, who always assured me you were fine. Apart from the last few months, when she said you had not been speaking to her either.'

'Fine,' Natasha muttered, seething. 'Yes, I've been just fine. And I guess I've been right in my assumption that you're fine too. You look fine.'

'I am fine,' her mother affirmed.

'Well, then, I guess, everything is fine!' Natasha snapped.

They stared at each other for a few minutes in stony silence.

Amma, clearly eavesdropping from the kitchen, cackled. Her voice came floating out into the pin-drop silence between them. 'Like mother, like daughter. Stubborn, both of them. Foolish girls.'

'What, Amma?' they both called in sharp identical voices.

'Nothing, nothing.' Amma continued to mutter but kept her voice low.

'So, anyway,' Natasha continued, trying to focus despite her growing frustration, 'I realized I've been carrying some … feelings … about the … you know, past.' She swallowed and continued with some effort, 'And I need to have this discussion with you.'

To her mother's credit, she didn't actually say the words

'Must you?' though the reluctance was clear in the wary and taut expression on her face.

Natasha went on in a rush, 'See, I thought that when Papa died, you sort of blamed me, maybe subconsciously, because I was sitting on the side that he was trying to keep the impact from. And also, you didn't really talk to me about it afterwards and it always seemed like you were avoiding the topic because it was too painful for *you* – as if it didn't matter what I needed. I just followed your lead and didn't talk about it either … but I felt really angry.' She took a long shuddering breath and concluded, 'I am a really angry person. And I *do* take things personally. Almost everything.'

Her mother stared. Just when Natasha felt she might burst a vein with the tension of waiting for a response, Mom reached out and put her hand on Natasha's. It felt cool but Natasha was too shocked by the gesture to pull her hand away. Her mother said, 'I know, Natasha. I'm sorry.'

Now it was Natasha's turn to stare. That was it? An 'I'm sorry' as if she'd inadvertently stepped on Natasha's toe? Natasha opened her mouth to protest, but her mother continued: 'I'm sorry that I wasn't available to talk about it with you. I was too focused on my own pain to be a good mother, although I tried to keep the house and your education going.' She paused for a moment and looked away thoughtfully, then looked back. 'But that part about blaming you is utter nonsense. I always believed he did what he did to save both of us. And I would have to be a real monster to think like that, anyway, even subconsciously.' Natasha opened her mouth, but her mother went on. 'But it's something that a young, confused girl assumed and never had a chance to clarify. My fault, again. I failed you.'

Natasha puffed out her cheeks, exhaling slowly. She knew her mom was uncomfortable with this kind of thing, and it wasn't really up Natasha's alley either. She shook her head. 'You didn't fail me, Mom. It's just … You never wanted to talk about anything that really mattered.' She paused. 'And by the way, that's exactly how I am too … I'm…' She couldn't complete the sentence because she suddenly felt all choked up as she thought about Nikhil and how right he had been. *Always sabotaging the relationships that mean the most to me.*

She opened her eyes and gazed at her mom. 'How come you insisted on moving here? It was because of the cottage that we were driving up and had the accident. Don't you get hurt by the memory of it every day? Wouldn't you want to just forget about the whole thing? Why are you clinging to the past?'

This time there was a long silence. Her mother gazed at nothing in particular and reached up to smooth her already straight hair. The sun's slanting rays caught her hair through the window. Natasha watched the black and silvery strands gleaming. The hair that she had always wished she had inherited instead of the wavy mop she got from Dad. Finally, her mother spoke.

'Natasha,' she began and then hesitated for a moment. 'Do you know something? I was married to your dad for thirteen years. And this year will be the twenty-fifth since he died.' She turned to Natasha and looked her in the eye. I've been widowed almost twice as long as I've been married.

The words echoed in Natasha's ears. She'd never thought about it that way. Something inside her chest tightened.

'And yet,' her mother continued with increasing confidence, 'I wouldn't give up those thirteen years for anything in the world. So if this is the way life had to turn out for me, I've accepted it.' She gestured around the room. 'We built this cottage together, your father and I. We had some wonderful times here together, both before and after you were born. It's the one place I feel is mine. Ours. And I don't mind being reminded of him every day. I feel more in touch with him here than anywhere else in the world. And I've never explained my decision to anyone. Till now.' She looked at Natasha searchingly. 'My ego, I suppose. It made me lose touch with something far more important that he and I created together.'

Natasha was not prepared for the tears pricking at her eyelids. It wasn't in their blood to cry. They had so much in common despite the distance that had crept in between them over the years. She never explained anything either. She blinked the tears back and stared at the table in front of them. Finally she managed to say, 'I also thought you got all the sympathy for it, and no one really thought about how it affected me...'

'Natasha, I did think about it. I thought about it a lot. It's simply that I made a very wrong assumption – I thought that because it was easier for me to not discuss it, it would also be easier for you.' She looked at Natasha's face. 'I know, it's not that I asked.' After a moment's silence, she went on, 'But I didn't need or want any of that sympathy myself. I would look at those people who came up claiming to feel my loss and weeping on my shoulder, and all I could think was: "You know, I feel sorry for *you*. You didn't know him like I did." He was a wonderful man.'

Natasha found herself struggling to articulate what she was feeling. Finally she blurted out, 'I don't think I remember anything about him.'

Her mom looked at her searchingly. 'You were ten. Surely you have some memories of times with him?'

'I think I've blocked them out.' Natasha exhaled. It felt like she was confessing her darkest secret. 'I figured it was better not to think about him at all. I think I managed to suppress them all pretty well. But now I've lost them all.'

Another pause.

'I'm sure they're in there somewhere, Natasha,' her mom said in a kinder tone than she had used so far. She patted Natasha's hand again. 'They'll come back. You'll remember. Maybe you just have to be open.'

Being open – the one thing Natasha had trouble doing; it was what stopped her from really knowing anyone else either. This reminded her of Mrs Chopra and she grasped at the opportunity to change the subject.

'So, uh, I made a new friend this year – this weird old lady in my building – Mrs Chopra. Acts real tough but is an old softie inside. She's secretly half-adopted this sweet stray dog, Kalu—'

She cut herself off – she was unused to volunteering unsolicited information, especially to Mom. Her mother said, 'Well, I look forward to meeting the odd couple.'

Meeting them? Her mom was saying she would come and visit? Well, of course. Why not? A smile slowly spread across Natasha's face. She felt a wave of exhaustion wash over her. 'Thanks, Mom.' She got up slowly and the dizziness got more violent. She gripped the table to steady herself. 'I think I need to lie down.'

'Use my bedroom,' said her mother, getting up too, her tone as brisk as ever. She was clearly in her comfort zone when talking about practical matters. 'Your blanket is still being aired, it was a little musty because that room hasn't been used much. In your state, you should really take extra care of yourself.'

She led the way out of the study, and indicated the room

towards the back of the house. Natasha followed slowly and a little unsteadily. *In her state?* Did Mom know? Nah, it wasn't as if she was psychic or something. Priya had promised not to say anything about it to her. Maybe she just meant Natasha was tired.

Naturally, her mom would use the bedroom in the furthest, most isolated corner of the house. It was strange how this place still felt so familiar despite how long it had been. So much about her had changed and yet a part of her felt as if it was stuck in time, like the cottage itself.

She turned into the room and paused at the door. Even though the memories were fuzzy and this room had been completely bare but for the figure under the sheet, she remembered when she had been here last. She thought it would creep her out, but instead she felt drawn in. For the first time, she understood the reason her mother had chosen to have the ceremony here, even though Delhi would have been so much more practical.

This was now her mother's room – and it was warm, cluttered, cosy and full of life and colour. She had books lined up tightly on the wall-shelves and a hundred other trinkets and paraphernalia on the table. And right on the side table, near the head of the bed, were two framed pictures.

One was of a handsome man with a moustache and curly brown hair. He was laughing – presumably at something someone had said off-camera – frozen in time in that happy moment. The other was of a little girl playing with a ball. She had curly hair and looked about eight years old. Natasha's heart skipped a beat when she looked at the little girl's face.

She knew she wouldn't be having those dreams any more.

NINE

THE RETURN

'You? When did you get back?' Mrs Chopra demanded as she stood at her door, looking piercingly at Natasha.

'Yesterday, in the afternoon.' Natasha had to laugh at Mrs Chopra's greeting. She could never expect a simple 'hello, how are you' from the old lady. But it seemed Mrs C was in better shape, back to her usual self. Natasha was about to remark on how well she looked when suddenly something behind Mrs C caught her attention.

'Is that Kalu?' she cried. Mrs Chopra looked a little embarrassed but opened the door wider, letting Natasha in. The dog came bounding up to her, tongue hanging out of the side of his goofy grin. Natasha was glad she had decided to drop in before getting ready for work because he was ruining her track pants. It was a relief that he hadn't been impounded. He looked cleaner and healthier than before and – wait, he had a collar around his neck.

'What's this?' she asked Mrs Chopra. 'You've officially taken him in?'

'Well.' Mrs Chopra turned and headed into the drawing

room. 'I thought it might be a good idea. He's too stupid to be out on the streets alone. Can't take care of himself. And he at least looks menacing, so it might fool some people into thinking that I've got a guard dog.' Her voice fell to a mumble. 'So yes, I've spoken to the colony office, and got him vaccinated so he can stay here with me.'

Natasha stared at her for a second and then looked down at the dog, who was now happily sniffing at her slippers. 'Well, that's great,' she said. 'What about the whole robbing-him-of-his-freedom bit?'

Mrs Chopra looked irritated. 'Are you a lawyer or something? Can't people change their minds? We've already had him sterilized. Preeti is taking him for walks every day and he's fine on the leash. Gives the girl – who *you* insisted should hang about here – something useful to do. I went out with them for a while yesterday to the park and watched.' She glared challengingly at Natasha. 'He doesn't look too unhappy here. Does he?'

Natasha pretended to examine Kalu seriously. She concluded, with an effort at keeping her face straight, 'No. He looks pretty happy.' *And so do you, Mrs C.*

Mrs Chopra looked mollified. After a few moments, she said, 'Well, stop prattling on about the mutt. How was your trip?'

'It was…' Natasha paused and then concluded, 'Pretty good, actually.' She could hear the surprise in her own voice. It had turned out better than she expected. She grinned. 'Mom says she looks forward to meeting you when she comes to visit.'

'Good,' said Mrs C tartly. 'I'll have a thing or two to tell her about her incorrigible daughter who plays practical jokes involving potbellied yoga teachers on her unsuspecting old neighbour.'

Natasha's cheeks burned. Mrs C had never brought that up before. She really needed to call Ramakant sir and apologize, or maybe send him flowers or something. Or laddoos. She gave Mrs C a guilty smile and cleared her throat. 'So anyway, I just came by to tell you that I'm home now. So if you need anything...'

Mrs Chopra dismissed her offer with a wave, irritated again. Natasha allowed the grin to stretch across her face. The old lady was looking years younger. With the mutt and Preeti around, Mrs C would be just fine. Natasha gave Kalu a pat and a gentle nudge, getting him to roll over off her feet. She then turned and went upstairs to get ready. And to finally do what needed to be done.

Natasha stood on her balcony, gazing at the pills in her hand. There were two of them – long, flat, sunset-yellow things. They looked almost like multivitamins. She marvelled at how something with such deadly potency could look so innocuous. She picked up her glass of water and stared at them again. They had been prescribed to her by Dr Aradhna, her mother's gynaecologist and a family friend. She had been the one to deliver Natasha, but it had been years since they'd last met. Natasha had taken her new address from Mom and gone to see her first thing, when she got back to Delhi. She had been welcoming and not at all judgemental about the whole thing.

Natasha suspected that her mother had called ahead because she seemed prepared and calm and didn't ask any questions other than the necessary ones. Mom hadn't asked why Natasha needed to see her, but Natasha knew she would have guessed.

She was supposed to take both the pills together and then, after a few hours, the bleeding would start. She hovered uncertainly for another moment and then took a deep breath before quickly popping the first. She took a sip of water to gulp it down. It wasn't as if she had a choice.

It was the thought of the word 'choice' that made her change her mind in a split second. Instead of swallowing the pill, the bitter taste of which she could already feel in her mouth, she found herself spitting out the entire mouthful over the balcony railing, spraying the water in a spontaneous and completely uncouth splatter. She stood there, shocked at herself, and was snapped back to reality only by the sound of the enraged scream from the balcony below.

'Jamuna! You and your bloody plants! Can't you be careful? Again, while I'm doing my puja.' Mrs Chopra ranted on and Natasha felt mortified only for a second before laughing and calling out, 'Sorry, sorry, Mrs C. It was me this time,' but the old lady wouldn't stop shouting long enough to hear her. Natasha gave up.

But she *did* have a choice – she could at least talk to Nikhil. Oblivious now to the raucous yelling from below, Natasha took aim at the top of the tallest, thick-leaved tree across the road right in front of her balcony, just beyond the colony's boundary wall. She flung the second pill there with all her might, watching it fly in a graceful arc through the air, falling just short of the very top of the tree and disappearing between its leafy branches – but not before glinting once in the light of the morning sun.

'Natasha! Morning!'

Natasha turned and saw Deepesh waving from the crowd that emerged from another lift that had stopped a second after her own. She slowed down a little to let him catch up and they walked together through the corridor. The office was buzzing with the morning action – people chattering, the smell of coffee and the general air of starting something new and worthwhile. Natasha breathed in deeply. It felt good to be back.

'So, holiday, huh?' Deepesh seemed curious. 'How come?'

'What do you mean "how come"?' Natasha said breezily, knowing full well what he meant.

'Uh, well, you know.' Deepesh smiled nervously, his bald spot shining. 'You haven't actually taken a holiday in … um, ever as far as I … I was just hoping everything is … okay with you.'

It wasn't like Deepesh to question her like this. Natasha glanced at his face. He was concerned about her? They'd only ever talked about work and numbers and the team and performance, but she realized there was more solidarity here.

'Had to go visit my mom.' It sounded natural, and Natasha liked how easy it was to talk about it now. *Visiting her mom* – it was such a normal thing to do. 'She's fine. It had been a while, that's all.'

'Okay, okay, good.' Deepesh looked relieved. They reached her desk and she put her laptop down. 'Well, it's great to have you back,' Deepesh said, looking almost shy. 'There's a lot to talk about – I thought you'd like to know. Looks like closing is on track. South is a little behind, but Anirban is making up with the west – they're also working on cracking a couple of big new accounts in ITeS, and we're hoping you'll make a trip…'

Natasha's phone buzzed and she glanced down at it. 'Sorry, Deepesh. But we'll catch up on this in an hour for sure. I have to take this call.'

He smiled easily and nodded before walking away. Natasha figured it would be a good idea to find an empty conference room to take this call. She pressed the green button to answer and murmured, 'Hey, Priya.'

There was a lot to talk about with her too.

As Natasha emerged from the washroom later that afternoon, she had a spring in her step. It was a day of surprises. There had been shock, an unexpected twinge of disappointment which had quickly been transmuted into immense relief. She was glad she'd decided not to take the pill, even though it wasn't like her to change her mind. She'd always believed that strong people stuck to the decision they'd made. She didn't feel weaker for it though – she felt stronger than ever.

'Natasha.' She stopped in her tracks but found she was prepared for even *his* voice. She turned around and raised an eyebrow at him.

'Back from your little holiday, then? I'm so glad. It gave you some time to think, I suppose?' Rishabh said with the shark-like grin that emphasized the warning implicit in his words. 'I was a little surprised to hear from Aman that you had decided to take leave. How sudden. I thought you would inform me, as your direct boss, but then I thought that maybe you just—'

'Rishabh,' Natasha said in a loud and clear voice. He looked around nervously to see if anyone in the hall was listening, but it was empty. She went on slowly and deliberately,

'You do know you picked the wrong person this time, right?'

He looked a little perturbed though she could see him struggling to keep a nonchalant expression. 'I thought we talked about this, Natasha – I was hoping you'd see sense and we could agree to let it go. How about we discuss it some more in my office?'

'Said the spider to the fly,' Natasha murmured.

'Excuse me?'

'No,' said Natasha firmly. 'I won't. Just so you know, *we're* not going to be talking about it, Rishabh. In fact, we're not going to be talking at all. And as for being my boss – you know your days are numbered, so let's drop that bullshit, shall we?'

'Natasha.' He lowered his voice, a threatening note creeping in. 'I'm warning you—'

'We're done, Rishabh. I've just sent out the email about your gross misconduct to HR, copy to Aman. And' – she returned his sharkish grin – 'thank you so much for your insistence with Renu that we become a progressive twenty-first-century organization. Last month, we had the inaugural meeting of the Sexual Harassment Committee. Guess the first case it's taking up?'

She wiggled her fingers at him in a little wave and allowed just her middle finger to remain up for a second at the end of it. She knew it hadn't been classy, but as she turned on her heel and walked away from him, she decided that the look on Rishabh's face had been well worth it.

'So what's going to happen now?' Nikhil said, a frown creasing his forehead. He looked handsome even when he was worried,

Natasha thought. She hadn't realized just how much she had missed him.

They were sitting across the table at the café and Natasha thought about how different things had been the last time they were here. She had thought it would be difficult, but the attentive and non-judgemental way in which he had listened had made it easy for her to open up and tell him the whole story.

'I don't know, exactly.' She sighed. 'I know there will be an investigation. At the end of the day it's going to be his word against mine. And he's pretty convincing, as you know.'

'He's a bastard,' Nikhil muttered. 'I wish I could deal with him myself.' His hand was clenched, knuckles white. He noticed her looking at it and unclenched it, apparently with some effort. He managed to give her a smile. 'But unfortunately, this isn't college and we can't handle it the way we used to. This is the civilized world of the great Indian office.'

'It happens everywhere, Nikhil.' She sighed and leaned back. 'Not that it makes it any better.' She paused. 'You used to beat up people in college?'

'I had anger issues as a young man,' Nikhil confessed. 'I'm much better now. I've worked on it.'

'Yes. It seems to have worked,' she said wonderingly, trying to imagine him as an angry young man. Must have been hot in a different way.

She took a sip of her cappuccino. 'What surprised me is that it actually took me this long to decide to take it up. Me! No wonder so many younger women just suffer in silence – they think it's their fault somehow or that their reputations would suffer.' She shook her head. 'Well, I'm going to make sure things change, at least in our organization. We've got so many women here in junior and mid-management.' She admitted,

'The lowest percentage is in my function. I think I've been sexist in my selections. Talk about hypocrisy.'

He reached across the table and took her hand in his. 'Hey, there's not a trace of hypocrisy in you.' He smiled again and from the way the dimple finally showed up, she knew it was genuine. 'There's a whole lot of other crap, of course, but not hypocrisy.'

'Wow, thanks,' she muttered. 'Well, I'm going to make up for it with some mentoring.' Maybe she'd even pick those two young girls she had frightened in the restroom for calling her Hitler. That would be quite a challenge. For them too, of course. The thoughts ran through her head even as she found herself getting distracted by his dimple and she knew her cheeks had pinked at his touch. It was in full public view but she found herself hoping he would keep holding on to her hand.

He let go.

She cleared her throat. 'Okay, Nikhil. Now, there's something else too. I don't know if you're ready to hear it.'

'Go on. I really don't think anything else could surprise me today.' He took a sip of his latte. 'Shoot.'

'I know I acted weird, running away from you and Tish and all that … but it's just that I didn't think the whole thing would make sense. You know, you guys are so close to each other and I couldn't see her ever accepting me as a mom – or for that matter, *me* accepting me as a mom…'

He nodded slowly, his face serious. 'I know, Natasha. But I also know another thing – Tish said last night that she told me what was going on because "if it was what Natasha would have done, it couldn't be the dorky thing to do".' His face broke into a smile. 'She thinks you're cool.'

This made Natasha smile despite herself. That evening hadn't been such a disaster after all. Her smile faded.

'But…' Natasha hesitated. 'What you don't know is that about the same time as all this stuff with Rishabh was going on … I kind of … took a home pregnancy test.' She looked up at him. 'And it turned out positive.'

'What?' he whispered.

His coffee cup trembled slightly and he placed it on the table. 'Are you serious?'

'Hang on, hang on,' she said. 'Yes, it did turn out positive and I was … I was going to take…' He looked shocked and she went on quickly, 'But I didn't.'

His face showed that he had just been put through a whole range of emotions. She hurried to finish, 'And then today, in the office, I got my period. So it turns out it was a false positive all along. I was feeling sick all this while but I guess it was because of other things – I just … sorted out things with my mom, and I've been feeling so much better.' The growing realization hit her again. Even that stupid, persistent cough appeared to have vanished. It had all been psychosomatic. She looked at Nikhil's face tentatively.

'So…' He tried to grasp the situation. 'Finally, we are … not pregnant?'

'We never were. I thought it might have been a condom failure.'

He leaned back. 'So, where does that leave us now?'

She looked at his face closely. 'Are you actually … disappointed that it turned out to be a false alarm?'

He hesitated and then admitted, 'Well … only a tiny little bit.' He added, 'I thought for a second there that you'd *have* to marry me.' He grinned sheepishly. 'But then, I know you better than that. You'd probably just do it alone if you wanted to.'

Natasha stared at him. She was a heavily flawed person and he saw all of that – but he looked through it and was able to focus on the good things about her. And for some reason he appeared to continue to want to be with her through all of the turbulence. He was one of a kind.

'You know what?' she said slowly.

'What?'

'I was really relieved to get my period, of course,' she confessed, 'but there was this other weird feeling too.' She couldn't bring herself to say any more about it, so she changed the subject. 'Anyway, the fact is – I couldn't go through with the pill thing without talking to you first and it made me realize that I could change my mind about stuff and...'

'And...?' he finally prompted.

'What I'm saying,' Natasha hissed, irritated at having to spell it out, 'is that I think I kind of ... am ready to be with you ... I mean, I'm open to giving it a shot. With you, *and* with Tish. I've been thinking about her and how upset she got last time and how I just ran away. I don't want to run any more, I think I can talk to her. I was kind of like her when I was growing up. That's something.' She looked up at him, a hint of uncertainty in her eyes. 'Right?'

His face broke into a slowly widening smile. 'It is something,' he said carefully. 'I'm not sure exactly what ... but it is definitely something. Just like you.' He drew his chair closer and gave Natasha a warm hug. She breathed in the scent of his familiar aftershave, and heard him whisper into her hair, 'Weirdo.'

She allowed him to hold her like that even though she was

aware of Muthu and Ludhiana Boy watching them from the back of the café. Complete public display of affection, this. And it felt right.

Mrs C was wrong after all, she thought as she relaxed into his embrace, reaching up and wrapping her arms around his neck. *And so was I.*

We *think* we come alone and go alone.

Truth is: we're probably never alone.

ABOUT THE AUTHOR

Yashodhara Lal is the bestselling author of eight humorous fiction books, including two for children. She is a graduate from IIM Bangalore, and after almost two decades in the corporate world, now runs Allsomeness, her coaching and therapy practice, dedicated to helping people live their fullest lives. She is also a TedX speaker, fitness instructor, music enthusiast and long-time student of yoga.

Yashodhara is married to Vijay who has been the subject of two of her books – '*Just Married, Please Excuse*' and '*How I Became a Farmer's Wife*' (soon to be a major motion picture). Her three children, who star in her books for kids, are innovatively nick-named Peanut, Pickle & Papad.

Yashodhara lives with her family in Goa. Know more at yashodharalal.com and follow her on Instagram and Facebook on @Yashodhara Lal

Just Married, Please Excuse

Caution: Marriage Ahead … Yashodhara, a quick-tempered gal from the big city, is hitched to Vijay, a laidback desi boy from a small town – in one word, trouble! The young couple must learn to adjust to married life and to each other – whether it is Yashodhara's 'tamper tentrums' or Vijay's foot-in-mouth syndrome – with a little help from their idiosyncratic staff Zarreena and Vinod, their nutty friend Vivi and, of course, their respective families. With the unexpected arrival of baby Anoushka a.k.a Peanut, the battles escalate, fuelled by their vastly divergent views on raising a child. Will their many differences – so endearing at the start of their romance – actually turn out to mean that they are just incompatible? Will they ever manage to agree on anything? Or have they just bitten off more than they can chew? A fresh and honest take on marriage and parenthood, this is a story of self-discovery that will have you laughing out loud – and sympathizing wholeheartedly with its quirky and likeable cast of characters.

Sorting Out Sid

A hilarious and insightful perspective on modern-day living and relationships – from within a man's head! Siddharth Agarwal, a.k.a. Sid, looks all set in life – after all, he has been married for a good long ten years, has a bunch of close friends. And, he is slated to become the youngest VP in his company at the young age of 36. Of course, he is in denial about the fact that his life is slowly falling apart, with his marriage on the rocks, parents who treat him as if he is still twelve years old, and his overly-interfering and back-stabbing best friends. Then, there's the manipulative HR vixen and the obnoxious boss in that office which sells … wait for it … toilet cleaners. When lovely, pocket-sized, spunky single mom Neha materializes into his life, it appears that there's some hope. Or is it just the calm before the storm? Who said it would be easy sorting out Sid?

There's Something About You

This is not your typical boy-meets-girl story. Okay, they do meet, but there are some complications. Trish is twenty-eight. She's unemployed, overweight, single and snarky. She knows all that. And if one more person – just one more person – tries to fix her, she might explode. Sahil is thirty-five. He has superpowers. Well, kind of. He seems to think so, anyway. He's also hot (in a geeky kind of way, but still). And he plays the guitar, helps the underprivileged and talks about his feelings. Aren't guys like that supposed to exist only in fantasies? When Trish and Sahil meet, magic happens. Real magic, you know, like fireworks, electricity, that sort of thing. But here's the problem. Trish doesn't want anyone in her life. She has enough to deal with – dependent parents, flaky neighbours, bitchy editors, the works. And yet, Sahil is determined to be in her life. From the bestselling author of *Just Married, Please Excuse* and *Sorting Out Sid*, here is another zinger of a book.

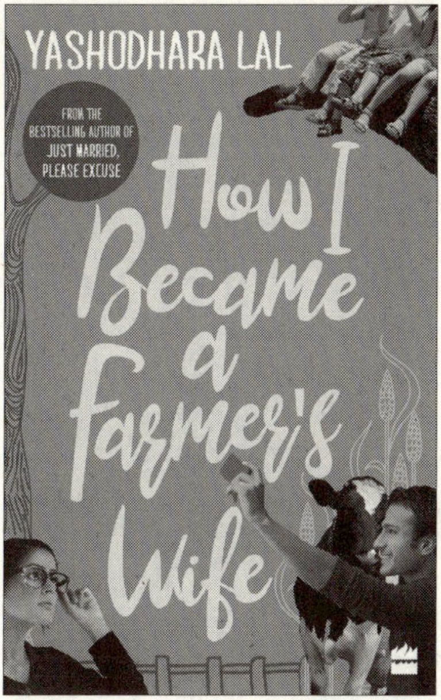

How I Became a Farmer's Wife

Mild-mannered Vijay is the perfect good Indian husband – responsible and predictable. Well, at least he was, until he decided to turn Farmer! Vijay's unsuspecting wife Yashodhara is caught off guard when, tired of the rigours of city life, he actually rents land and starts dairy farming! As if Yash didn't have enough going on already, what with her high-octane job, three children and multiple careers. As Vijay dives deeper into his quirky hobby, the family is plucked out of their comfortable life in the steel-and-chrome high-rises of Gurgaon, and thrown headfirst into a startlingly unfamiliar world – complete with cows and crops, multiple dogs and eccentric farmhands, a shrewd landlady and the occasional rogue snake. Will these earnest but insulated city-dwellers be able to battle the various difficulties that come with living a farmer's life? A laugh-out-loud romp that'll leave you wanting more!

Those Days in Delhi

Delhi in the Nineties. And this time, it's going to be Gudia's summer. So what if she's the quintessential awkward middle child? So what if it seems like everything – from the hair sprouting on her legs to teachers making her life miserable – is conspiring against her? She's taking matters into her own hands, and there's no way that she's going to fail. After all, there are three things Gudia is obsessed with – Basketball, the Boy with the American accent…and Winning. But in her desire to win this campaign of middle-school one-upmanship and conceal her plummeting grades, Gudia might just lose all that's important to her – including herself. Best-selling author Yashodhara Lal is back with this funny, bittersweet and entirely relatable story about growing up; of that summer of innocence, when the world was simpler, and even our problems seemed sweeter.